The Sentinels

Award winning author Peter Carter lives in the Cotswolds.

Michael Jones wrote in *Books for Keeps*

'To keep one's eye on heaven and one's feet on the muddy earth and not overbalance is a gift, a rare one, but some possess it.'

These words apply not just to one of Peter Carter's characters (*Madatan*) but to the author himself. His books are the antithesis of commercially crafted 'teenage readers' which confine rather than challenge the reader's imagination. They can be demanding in terms of historical context, emotional power and linguistic level, yet they have a sufficiently wide appeal to be translated into several languages.

At a time when, even in the book world, there are those who would insult or enslave the moral imagination of young readers, just for profit, we need the time fictions of sentinels like Peter Carter.

D1385731

PETER CARTER

The Sentinels

Richard Drew Publishing
Glasgow

First published 1980
by Oxford University Press

This edition first published 1987 by

Richard Drew Publishing Limited
6 Clairmont Gardens, Glasgow G3 7LW
Scotland

British Library Cataloguing in Publication Data

Carter, Peter, *1929*—
  The sentinels. — (Swallow).
  I. Title II. Series
  823'.914[F] PR6053.A739

  ISBN 0-86267-195-7

Set in Chinchilla by John Swain & Son, Glasgow
Printed and bound in Great Britain by
Cox & Wyman Ltd., of Reading

In memory of the millions of Africans taken into slavery, and the thousands of seamen of the Royal Navy who died to free them.

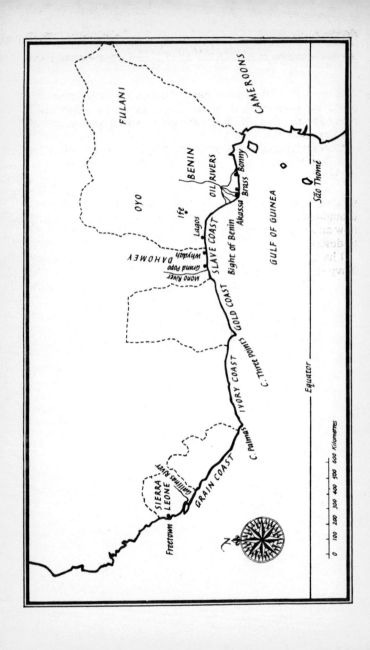

Author's Note

This is a work of fiction but many of the incidents described are based on records of the time. Students of the period will recognize in the trial of Kimber and his men the notorious case of the slave-ship *Felicidade*.

Captain Denman and Governor Doherty were real people, as was Mrs Norman. Pedro Blanco and Da Souza were slave-dealers at the Gallinas river and Whydah.

Lyapo is a Yoruba speaker from the region known in the nineteenth century as Old Oyo. It is unlikely that he would have thought of himself as either a Yoruba or an Oyo but, as Yoruba is now an accepted term for his social group, I have used that term to describe him here.

I have simplified some naval terms. In this period the Royal Navy sailed under the red ensign.

February, 1979

A Yoruba called Lyapo was drinking at the Pool of the Leopards when he heard a rustle in the reeds behind him. He turned and saw two Dahomey men staring down at him.

'Aiyee,' thought Lyapo, 'I am a dead man now.'

One of the Dahomey men gestured and Lyapo stood up. He was taller and stronger than the Dahomeys but they had clubs and short, heavy swords, as well as spears.

Lyapo touched the fetish bag on his arm. Why had he come into the forest today? Why had he ignored the signs which had told him to turn back; the little green snake which had looked at him from under a stone, the parrot's wing on the path, the spider's web across his trap?

In the forest a sun-bird called, a sharp, shrill whistle. Something splashed heavily in the pool. The men, the Dahomeys and Lyapo, stood looking at each other, poised, as if waiting for a signal. Yes, as if even the terrible Dahomeys needed some stimulus before attacking.

Lyapo breathed hard. He thought of jumping into the pool and swimming away but from the corner of his eye he saw a long, blunt shape gliding through the green scum and he abandoned that idea. Instead he leaped at the smallest of the Dahomeys. He knocked him aside, but as he ran a foot caught his ankle. He stumbled and fell. A club thudded across his back. He yelped with pain but the cry was stifled as a noose was slipped around his throat and tightened. He lunged and twisted, choking on the noose, but within seconds his hands had been expertly trussed behind his back and a wooden gag rammed into his mouth. Then he was jerked to his feet.

The Dahomey men laughed and grinned. They slapped each other on the back and one of them sang a little song. Twitching with fear, Lyapo watched them. He knew very well how they felt. They were behaving as he and his friends did if they caught an animal, a deer or a leopard, a fine sleek prize of the forest, and bore it off in triumph.

The Dahomeys poked and prodded Lyapo, feeling his arms and his legs, and then, still laughing, made off into the forest, pulling Lyapo behind them, as one might lead a goat to slaughter.

Four thousand miles away; a January dusk falling on sodden Northampton fields, January rain falling on sodden Northampton cows. John Spencer, fifteen years old and orphaned just six weeks, locked in stiff mourning-clothes, peered through a streaming window but kept a sharp ear cocked to the muffled voices in the next room.

There, standing before a small fire which was visibly dying of starvation, Hector Radley, tea-merchant of Wapping, London, looked down on Honoria Spencer, spinster, and aunt of John.

'And so,' Mr Radley said, 'I really think that, all in all, my plan for the boy is best. What do you think?'

Miss Spencer was uncertain. 'The Navy . . . is it not a very hard life? Such rough men . . . mutinies . . . Captain Bligh. . . .' She was somewhat vague about the Royal Navy.

Mr Radley tut-tutted. 'Captain Bligh indeed! Ma'am we are in the year eighteen forty. The Navy is quite different, as the world is quite different.'

Miss Spencer shook her head. 'I'm sure I don't know. Poor Betty always thought that John would make a fine parson.'

Mr Radley waved an impatient hand. 'Come now, what is the use in talking of parsons? The boy has a mere twenty pounds to his name. He has no more chance of becoming a parson than I have of becoming a duke. I tell you, he is lucky to have the chance of going to sea. If I did not know someone in Wapping who owes me a favour, and who knows a sea-captain who owes *him* a favour, then he would not even have this opportunity.'

Miss Spencer sighed. 'Where did you say this ship was sailing to?'

Mr Radley, who had told her twice already, snapped his fingers. 'To Africa, ma'am. To Africa.'

'But is that not very unhealthy? Do not numbers of white men die there?'

'Ma'am,' said Mr Radley, 'numbers of white men die in *England* every day. Mark you, I do not say that the place is a health resort. It is not Brighton or Bath and, to be honest, I would not care to send one of my own boys there. But what are we to do? The lad must be placed somewhere. Besides, I am told that those who do die are dissipated men, gin-swiggers and . . . ah . . .

men of bad habits. No, I am persuaded that a strong boy like John will do all right on a well-found Queen's ship under the eye of a good captain. And I am most particularly assured that Captain Murray is a worthy man, a most worthy, religious man. He is a pillar of Exeter Hall where the anti-slavery societies meet and, being a Whig, he has influence at the Admiralty.'

'He is a Whig?' Miss Spencer, a devoted Tory, looked timidly at Mr Radley.

'Yes, ma'am, a Whig,' said Mr Radley, who was one himself. 'A supporter of the governing party. The party of Reform, Free Trade, and enlightened religion. It is a most useful thing for a sea-captain to be.' Mr Radley fished out his watch and peered at it. 'Time is passing. Shall we call the boy in?'

'Yes,' Miss Spencer sighed. 'Call him in.'

John was summoned, left his window seat, and stood re-spectfully before Mr Radley.

'Now, John,' Mr Radley said. 'Your aunt and I have been discussing your future, and you do have a future, you know. You must not think that because your father and mother are now dead the world has come to an end. No. It is in the nature of things that parents die before their children and that the children must carry on living. Your mother had to do so when her parents died, I had to do it when my parents died, and now you must do so, too. Do you understand?'

John understood very well. In fact it had never occurred to him *not* to continue living.

'But the question now,' Mr Radley went on, 'is *how* you are to live. Your aunt here is very willing to give you a home, but what will that lead to? What is to happen when *she* dies? And she will die, eventually. Is that not so, ma'am?'

Miss Spencer agreed, somewhat reluctantly, that she would die one day, although it was clear the prospect had little appeal for her.

'Well then,' Mr Radley turned to John. 'The point now is to find you a trade or profession. I would have liked to take you into my own business, but I tell you frankly that I have four sons already engaged in it and it simply will not bear another young man. No, that will not answer. But by great good fortune I have a certain interest with a captain in the Navy. He will be good enough to take you into his ship as a gentleman volunteer. He will introduce you into the sea-going profession and as soon as maybe rate you a midshipman, which is a species of officer. Do you follow me?'

'Yes, sir,' John followed him.

Mr Radley looked thoughtfully at John. He was a just man and, although John meant little to him, being merely the son of a cousin, he was anxious to do right by the boy.

'Do you approve?' he asked.

John hesitated. 'Is it what my mother wished?'

'No it is not,' Mr Radley said. 'She wished for you to be a parson, but I must tell you there is not money enough for that.'

John was vastly relieved. He had absolutely no wish to spend his days in a pulpit, whereas the Navy — he had a vision of men in blue and gold, cannons banging, pirates! He lifted his chin and said, firmly, 'If you think it right, sir, I shall be very pleased to go with this captain.'

'Excellent, excellent.' Mr Radley was as pleased as John. He patted him on the shoulder. 'The Navy is a most honourable profession and if you attend to your duties I am sure you will be an ornament to it.'

He smiled and John smiled back. 'And where will I be sailing to, sir?'

'Why, you will be off to Africa, to the Guinea Coast, for Captain Murray will be on the West African Squadron, the anti-slave patrol. Think of that! You will be freeing God's creatures, doing His will, and,' Mr Radley lowered his voice and looked thoughtfully at his hands, 'and, John, for every slave freed, the Government pays five pounds a head. Think of that, five pounds sterling.'

But as he lay in bed that night it was not of pounds sterling that John was thinking but of elephants and giraffes, monkeys and lions, and of the wicked crocodile, smiling as it chopped its pointed teeth and slid into the waters of the Oil Rivers among the yellow, dripping mangroves which dipped their ambiguous roots into the half-world of land and sea.

A month later, though, as he stood at the top of a flight of weed-grown steps in Portsmouth harbour, John did not have the great, green crocodile in mind. Instead he was merely wishing that his uncle would hurry up with his farewell so that he could board his ship and get out of the uncommonly cold and piercing wind.

From the bottom of the steps a hoarse voice asked if the 'Capting' was ready, then.

'One moment,' Mr Radley cried. He turned to John. 'Well. . . .'

4

'Yes, sir?' John blew on his frozen fingers.

Mr Radley looked down on the bright face, then glanced across the harbour. On the grey waters a score of ships bobbed slowly up and down, their rigging tapping out a melancholy tune. Three drunken seamen lurched out of a tavern and shambled down the street bawling incoherently. He felt a deep twinge of conscience.

'John,' he said. 'It is not too late. If you should not wish to go on this voyage . . . if you have changed your mind. . . .'

John stamped his feet. 'Oh no, sir.'

'You are quite sure?'

'Quite sure.'

Mr Radley sighed with relief. 'Then I wish you every success. Write to me and your Aunt Spencer. And, here —' He pressed a parcel in John's hand. 'You will find ten guineas in there which you must give to the Captain. It is merely for any luxuries you might care for. There is also a book, a present from my sons. *Pickwick Papers*, I believe.'

From the bottom of the steps came a strange, snorting noise, as if from a stranded marine monster. John took the hint and scrambled down the steps into the ferry-boat.

'Goodbye, sir,' he cried.

'Goodbye, goodbye.' Mr Radley waved his hand. 'The boat is paid for. God bless you. Goodbye.'

The boat slipped away and Mr Radley called once more, a long, wavering cry, echoing flatly across the chill waters. 'Say your prayers.'

A gull floated across the bows of the ferry and fixed John with a cold, yellow eye. The boatman lifted his head from the oars.

'The *Sentinel* you'm wanting, ain't it?'

John pulled the collar of his coat around his ears. 'Yes.' He pointed to the biggest ship in sight, a towering vessel whose triple tier of guns loomed menacingly over the harbour. 'Is that it?'

The boatman laughed. 'That? She'm the *Agamemnon*, first-rate ship of the line. If she was to bump into youm little tub she might mistake youm for a porpoise.' He spat. 'No, youm be in the outer harbour.'

He backed on his oars, giving way as a steam-tug, hissing and sizzling like a frying-pan, crossed his bows.

'Where'm she be off to then, youm *Sentinel*?'

John squared his shoulders and sat upright. 'To Africa,' he said proudly. 'On the Slave Patrol.'

The boatman shipped his oars and let the tide carry the boat down the harbour, past ship after ship after ship, frigates, sloops, brigs, first-rates, second-rates, third-rates, in line after line, the imperial might of Britain spelled out in the cannon which gaped blackly at John as he was carried past them. And then, in the remotest creek, by the mud flats of Whale Island, as the pale sun dropped from sight, the boatman jerked his thumb at a stubby ship.

'That's yourm,' he said. 'That's the *Sentinel*. Bound for the Slave Coast, is she? Well, God help you, sonny.'

Across the dark Atlantic, the sun gilded the weathercocks of Baltimore. In the docks the shipyard's hammers began to thud and, quietly, and without fuss, a ship, black from stem to stern, glided into the waters of Chesapeake Bay.

Two caulkers hammering oakum into the planks of a whaler spared the ship a glance as she drifted past them.

'She's off to Havana,' one said. 'Into the sugar trade.'

He laughed and his mate laughed with him.

'Her sides cut for twelve guns and him on board —' he pointed to a man striding the deck, a tall man with yellow hair. 'Well, brother, she may be going to Havana, but that's only her first port of call.'

'And what might be her second?'

'Why,' the man spat on his hands and swung his hammer. 'They've called her *Phantom*, haven't they? And I guess that's a good enough name because her next stop is at the gates of hell.'

6

Lyapo's captors were stragglers from a Dahomey warband which had struck east, slave-hunting. For a day or so they wandered aimlessly through the countryside looking for more slaves but all they found were ruined, smoking villages. On the second day they hid in a clump of bush as a band of Fulani swept past them — Muslim cavalry from the north, preaching Islam and catching slaves.

When the Dahomeys saw the Fulanis they were frightened and they hurried Lyapo to a village on a river, where they sold him to a Mandingo trader. He laid out his wares: blue-haft cloth, from Manchester, fake grigory beads, brass kettles made in Birmingham, poisonous Dutch gin, flawed iron from Marseilles, and a rusty Dane gun. They took the gun and handed over Lyapo.

The Mandingo was a tall, thin man, with a squint and a twisted smile. He dressed in a spotless indigo gown and always carried a musket. His servants chained Lyapo to a baulk of wood and threw him a piece of salt fish. The Mandingo sat on a little stool and watched him eat.

'You from Oyo?' he asked, pointing to the tribal marks on Lyapo's face. 'I know those cuts. I've bought a lot of you people over the years. That's how I come to speak your language.'

He motioned to the servant, who brought Lyapo a bowl of water.

'Tell me,' he said. 'Why are you Oyo people fighting each other all the time? What's happened to you? Once upon a time Oyo was very strong. Nobody even dared to try to capture one of you. Now look. It's silly. You fight each other and that makes it easy for those Dahomeys and Fulanis to come in and capture you.'

He shook his head as if saddened by the follies of the Yoruba, then brightened. 'Still, it's good for me, eh? Plenty of slaves, plenty of business. Of course, it's not so good for you.'

Lyapo finished the water. 'Let me go,' he said. 'I can pay you.'

'That's interesting,' the Mandingo said. 'What can you give me?'

'Anything you want,' Lyapo said. 'In my village I've got ivory, and gold.'

'Gold? Ivory?' The Mandingo smiled his lop-sided smile. 'That's good. I'd certainly let you go for that. Where is your village?'

'Over there.' Lyapo waved his hand vaguely. 'A few days walk.'

The smile left the Mandingo's face. 'Eat your fish,' he said coldly. He walked to the gate of the compound. 'You be good,' he said. 'If not —' he raised his musket and squinted down the barrel. 'Boom!'

The Mandingo kept Lyapo in a yard. In one corner was a shelter of grass thatch. Next to it was a small clay hut like a dog-kennel. During the day Lyapo sat in the shelter. At night he crawled into the hut. The walls of the yard were high and he could see nothing but the sky. He could hear noises; dogs barking, goats bleating, men shouting. There were no women's voices, or children's. It wasn't that sort of village.

For a week Lyapo lay in a stupor, in a profound state of shock, like a man suffering from a terrible accident. He lay in his shelter, watching the long-legged spiders run about the thatch, hardly able to comprehend what had happened to himself. He knew about slaves, of course. There were two or three in his own village. One of them was an important man, responsible for the weights and measures. But that he himself could become one . . . it was a concept he could hardly grasp.

Occasionally thoughts as vague and formless as rain-clouds drifted across his mind. Why was he here, chained to a log? Were the men of his village looking for him? What was his wife thinking?

Once he had a dream. A little green snake reproached him for going into the woods.

Lyapo was angry. 'I didn't know that the Dahomey men would capture me,' he said.

'You should have known,' the snake said. 'I told you. The parrot told you. The spider told you. But you didn't listen.'

'I didn't know,' Lyapo moaned.

'Yes you did. Yes you did,' the snake hissed. 'Now the Fulani and the Dahomey will come into the land of Oyo. They will break your pots and burn your villages. The monkeys will live in your huts. The Fulani will cut down the sacred trees and destroy the shrines. The Yoruba fetish will be like dust in the wind. The Yoruba will be scattered and sold into bondage, and you will be no more.'

The snake laughed and glided away under an iroko tree as Lyapo awoke, in tears.

The Mandingo was not cruel to Lyapo. His servants brought

him rice and fish and even palm wine. But one day they came and gagged him.

'Some Yorubas in the village,' the Mandingo said. 'That's why I'm gagging you. They've got the same marks on their faces as you have. You shout out and if they hear you they might start thinking you should be let go free, you being from the same tribe.'

The next morning the Mandingo removed the gag. 'The Yoruba have gone,' he said. 'But listen. I'll tell you something funny, cheer you up. I bought a man from them. You'll laugh.'

He clapped his hands and his servants dragged a man into the compound. It was one of the Dahomey men who had captured Lyapo. Half his face was blown away.

'Look at him,' the Mandingo said. 'That Dane gun I sold him blew up in his face. You've got to be careful with those guns, they're always blowing up. It's best to hold them away from you when you fire. Of course it's hard to hit anything if you shoot like that. Anyway, he wasn't careful. See, all his jaw is smashed and he's only got one eye left, that's why I got him so cheaply. Maybe he'll die. It's a gamble, really. But it's funny. He came out catching slaves, now he's one himself.'

But Lyapo wasn't listening. He growled deep in his throat and began to crawl across the yard to the Dahomey, dragging the baulk of wood with him. Without malice the Mandingo put his foot on Lyapo's neck and sent him sprawling.

'You stay away from him,' he said, 'or I'll nail you to the door by your ears.'

The Mandingo bought more slaves. A boy who spoke a strange, barbarous tongue and who cried day and night, a remote, haunted woman who never spoke, and an old man who never stopped talking.

The old man was from Ife. He was a dyer of cloth. Did Lyapo know that town? It was a big town. The Fulani had come at dawn and set fire to the town. They had guns and horses. They had killed many people, many, many, many. They had killed his wife but he had been captured with his sons. The Fulani had played *ayo* for him and his sons. The winner had taken his sons, the loser had taken him. These were terrible times, terrible. Once the King of Oyo had protected his people. What had happened? And who were the Fulani? Where did they come from? No, he had never heard of Lyapo's village and he didn't care if he never heard of it again. All he was interested in were his sons.

On and on the old man mumbled. The child cried in his corner.

The Dahomey moaned. Only Lyapo and the woman were silent. There was nothing to do but wait, to sit in the compound and watch the vultures wheeling in the blue sky.

The woman stopped eating. The servants brought the Mandingo, who had her whipped until she ate some rice.

'I've got to do it,' the Mandingo said, apologetically. 'If she doesn't eat she's going to die, then I lose my money.' He looked around the yard. 'I've not done very well anyway, this trip.' The crooked smile crossed his lips. 'Still, it's all as Allah wills, the Most High and Merciful.'

A few days later the captives were brought out of the yard and chained together.

'We've got to move,' the Mandingo said. 'The rainy season is coming, no more slaves coming in and if we don't get started we'll never get where we're going.'

'Where is that?' Lyapo asked.

'Just keep moving,' the Mandingo said.

It began to rain as the captives were herded down the village street to the river. There were other Mandingos there, each with his musket, his servants, and his slaves. On the river bank was a line of canoes. The Mandingo waved his slaves forward. Clumsily and painfully they slithered through the mud and climbed into the Mandingo's canoe. Boxes and bundles followed them, the Mandingo's servants, boatmen, and the Mandingo himself.

The Mandingo sat in the stern under a huge umbrella and gave a sharp command. As the canoe slid into the water the Mandingos on the bank laughed and shouted. Some fired their muskets in a cloud of black smoke. Three or four canoes, moving fast, came down river and swept across the bows of the Mandingo's craft, the men in them whooping and whistling. In front of Lyapo the old man gave a despairing cry. 'My son,' he shouted. 'My son is in that canoe.'

A sickly dawn light on the mouth of the English Channel, and a bitter north wind. HMS *Sentinel*, ice on her masts, bucking and heaving as the long Atlantic rollers met the tide pouring down from the North Sea. The last of England falling away behind her stern.

A league away the frigate *Dauntless*, thirty-two guns, came out of a snow squall. A puff of smoke billowed from her side and a few dots of colour, as bright as confetti, gleamed in her rigging.

Samuel Potts, midshipman, twenty-one years old, braced himself against the bulwark and clapped a telescope to his eye. '*Dauntless* signalling, sir.'

Edgar Brooke, First Lieutenant of *Sentinel*, nodded. 'Acknowledge and inform the Captain.'

Potts slithered down the companionway which led to the Captain's quarters. He squeezed past the marine sentry and rapped on the door. Without waiting for an answer he poked his head into the cabin.

'*Dauntless* signalling, sir,' he bellowed.

'Very well.' Fully dressed, James Murray, Master and Commander of the ship, swung out of his cot. Potts wriggled backwards up the stairs, skipping aside as Murray made his way on to the quarterdeck.

Brooke touched his cap. 'Permission to change tack, sir.'

'Make it so,' Murray said.

The shivering crew was on deck. Murray stood aside as Brooke set them about their work. A stream of commands, oaths, curses, the grunting of men doing heavy work on a tilting deck, blasphemies as icy water cascaded from the sails on to the men, the groan and creak of timbers and frozen ropes as the yards carrying the sails swung slowly round. The wind, which had been cutting into Murray's right ear, blew down his neck as the ship eased on to her new course.

''Vast there,' Brooke cried through his speaking-trumpet. He faced his Captain. 'Tack changed, sir.'

'Very well.' Murray was satisfied. The work had been done reasonably well; a trifle slowly and clumsily perhaps, but that was to be expected with a crew new to the ship. But the experienced seamen had behaved responsibly, working with a will and pushing the raw hands into their proper places without fuss.

'You may clear the deck,' he said. There was no point in keeping the crew, especially a willing crew, on deck exposed to the freezing weather. He cast a look along the ship. Not a long look for it was not a long ship, being merely a sloop-of-war, barely seventy feet from stem to stern. All was in order, two look-outs in the bows and one unfortunate at the mast-head. Murray wondered whether Brooke would have the sense, and the humanity, to relieve him every half-hour. Looking at Brooke's disdainful face he doubted it. But it would never do to interfere in the petty details of the ship's routine. Besides, it would tell him something about his First Lieutenant.

'Carry on,' he said. He stepped aside, but half-way down the companionway he paused and looked again at the tiny quarterdeck.

'Where is Mr Spencer?' he asked.

'Sick, sir,' Brooke answered.

Murray frowned. 'Sick?'

'Seasick, sir.'

'Too sick to attend to his duties?'

'Yes, sir.'

'And the Bay of Biscay ahead!' said Murray as he disappeared below deck.

John, a damp bundle of misery, was lying in a pool of vomit in a corner of the breadroom. Even when *Sentinel* had been rocking at her mooring in Portsmouth he had felt queasy but here, in the chop and surge of the Channel . . . up went the ship . . . down . . . up . . . down . . . John moaned. Not only was he sick, he was also cold. He had never imagined that a ship could be so cold. The sides of the breadroom ran with moisture, water squirted through mysterious gaps in the timbers, a chill wind blew on his frozen neck. *Sentinel* ran down a long wave and rose, jerkily, on another. John retched, emptily. A thin dribble of slime ran from the corner of his mouth.

Something touched his face. He was vaguely aware of a dim light. 'Mamma,' he whimpered.

Captain Murray stepped away and went through the gunroom into his own cabin. 'Pike,' he called.

'Sir.' The gnome-like figure of his steward appeared from a tiny cubby-hole.

'Is the galley fire alight?' Murray asked.

12

'Yes, sir,' Pike said, acting on his principle of always agreeing with authority.

'Very well. Make me some coffee. Hot coffee. Ask Mr Potts to come and see me at once. And, Pike, in my stores there is a pot of essence of beef-tea. Make a mugful.'

'Beef-tea, sir?' Pike looked as amazed as if the Captain had ordered boiled midshipman. 'Very good, sir. Beef-tea it is — beggin' your parding,' as he writhed away.

A minute later a knock on the door heralded Potts, in streaming tarpaulins, who because of his height and the cabin's lowness was forced to stoop in a simian posture before the captain's table.

Murray drummed his fingers on the table. 'Mr Potts, do you have hopes for promotion?'

Potts, who longed for promotion with more fervour than an Anabaptist, gaped. For a moment he had a wild, amazing, exhilarating thought that perhaps Cawley, the Second Lieutenant, had died and that Murray was about to rate him acting Second in his place.

'Oh yes, sir,' he breathed.

'Then let me tell you, sir —' Murray's voice was as cold as his eyes, and they were as chilly as the grey sea heaving against the cabin window. 'Let me tell you that at this moment there are a score of admirals in the Royal Navy, hundreds of captains, hundreds of them. And there are thousands, thousands of lieutenants, and as for midshipmen, they are too numerous to be possibly counted. And yet there are only some four hundred vessels in commission all told. Are you aware of this?'

Potts was well aware of it. He knew the figures as well as he knew the tables of longitude, in fact rather better. And he knew, too, that because of those figures he was lucky to be on a ship at all, even one going on the worst patrol in the Royal Navy.

'Vurry well.' Murray had a mild Scotch burr which became stronger under the stress of emotion. 'Then you will know that promotion is now given only to men of outstanding ability. Men who are expert seamen and navigators, men who are brave without being reckless and prudent without being timid. But most of all, sir, to men who know that a warship is more than just timber and canvas and guns, but has men on board — men! Do you follow me?'

'Oh yes, sir,' stammered Potts, who had no idea why his Captain was talking to him like this. 'Men . . . more than . . . er . . .

er . . . guns. . . .'

'Then wull ye tell me —' Murray's voice was as sharp as hail. 'Wull ye tell me why Mr Spencer is not in his hammock?'

'Not in his hammock, sir?'

Murray slapped the table. 'The laddie is lying in a pool of his own vomit in the breadroom. Did ye know that?'

'No, sir,' Potts acted on the opposite principle from Pike and always denied any knowledge of anything.

'Then you should, sir!' Murray's voice crackled. 'You are the Senior Midshipman and Mr Spencer is your responsibility. Do not tell me that you thought he was the gunner's charge. He is young. You will see to it at once that Mr Spencer is cleaned, wrapped in a blanket, and placed in his hammock.'

Further sharp words — lightning flashes of authority crackling about Potts's ears, thunderbolts of power crashing about his unfortunate head. Apologies from Potts, apologies and contrition — forgiveness by Murray *this time*. Pike appearing with beef-tea which Mr Spencer was to be ordered — *ordered* — to take. A shaken Potts charging off to John, ramming him into a hammock, forcing beef-tea down him. John, warm and dry, the hammock cutting down the appalling see-sawing of the ship by half, sleeping soundly at last. Potts exasperating every midshipman on board by inquiring after his health and well-being fives times every hour as *Sentinel*, before a brisk nor'-wester, clawed her way around Ushant and into Biscay. The ship's bell ringing out the hours and the half-hours as John, his sea-legs found at last, walked shakily along the deck under the fond and oppressively tender guidance of Potts.

The last rays of the sun catching the topsails of *Sentinel*. In London the gas-lights on, dinner over, the theatres filling, the dosshouses full, the city clocks striking nine. Tamburini singing at the Opera House, performing monkeys at Astley's Music Hall. *Oliver Twist* quite sold out, *The Voyage of the Beagle* selling well. Mr Hill's new Penny Post a great success, a Mr Draper photographing the moon. Steam and science transforming the nation.

In the Palace of Westminster a noble lord, full of port and pheasant, rising to address his fellow peers.

'My Lords, is it not time that this great nation ceased expending its treasure and its blood in a vain attempt to stop the Slave Trade? I yield to no man living in my detestation of this abominable traffic, but is stopping it to be the sole task of

England? Do not tell me that other nations have passed laws against it, they may have, but where are their ships? How many men do they lose? How much do they spend? My Lords, I believe that there are noble lords in this House, I believe that there are honourable members of the Commons, I believe that there are members of the Government who privately agree with me that it is no business of this nation to interfere with the lawful traffic of other countries. I am, in any case, assured that the task of stopping the Slave Trade is impossible — quite impossible. Gallant officers of the Royal Navy have assured me of that. And while vast areas of the world require labour to cultivate them, what right have we to prevent the flow of labour to those parts? Indeed, are we not in danger of flouting the Divine Will by doing so? Cotton in the Americas, sugar in Cuba, the great plantations of Brazil, tobacco — excellent tobacco in Cuba, must these vast and fertile areas remain barren because of a mere shortage of hands to work them? Clearly that is sentimental nonsense. The parts of Africa from which Africans are removed are over-crowded. We do the African a positive service in removing him from those disease-ridden regions and settling him in the wholesome and bountiful quarters of the New World. There, I am told by eye-witnesses, the negro is well cared for, he is well fed and well housed. Baptized into the Christian faith, the salvation of his soul thus assured, he is happy. Yes, he is happy as, his useful day's toil over, he sits outside his cabin surrounded by his wife and children — for he is united in the bond of holy matrimony — an institution unknown in Africa — singing his simple songs while being cared for by a considerate and humane master. I move that this House calls for an end to the anti-slave patrol of the Royal Navy. And let me remind the Whigs of this country and Government who so admire the principles of the free movement of trade. Free Trade in one thing means Free Trade in all.'

The Lord Keston: 'Hear, hear'.

A quarter of a world away, a ship leaving Havana; a clipper painted black, built for speed. Forty hard cases manning her. Water tanks for three hundred souls under her decks, twelve nine-pounder cannon on them. In her hold rum and muskets, fifteen hundred feet of chain, three hundred manacles. Total investment on the ship 40,000 dollars, expected net profit 60,000 dollars. Net return on capital over three months, 150 per cent.

On the quarterdeck, Captain Joseph Kimber, commanding officer, a cigar in his mouth, its glow illuminating his yellow hair in the velvety night. Cracking all sail on *Phantom*, a greyhound with the teeth of a wolfhound. Destination, the Slave Coast.

In Africa somewhere. Lyapo, a Yoruba. Wife and three children. Farmer and part-time trapper. Homeless, wifeless, childless, weeping bitter tears on a great river. Destination unknown.

5

The black rocks of Ushant far astern, the ragged coast of Spain to port; off Corunna, *Sentinel's* bows swinging south, to faraway lands and the sun.

A mile away *Dauntless*, under a cloud of sail, her signal gun barking out its peremptory order. On *Sentinel*, whistles and roars, bare feet hammering on the deck. The Captain swinging from his bed, Potts's large hand dragging John from his hammock and shoving him on deck. Brooke bellowing something vague and menacing through a speaking trumpet. Men running here and there, sails appearing, billowing, disappearing, John pushed, knocked, trampled on, cursed at, ropes writhing, twanging, the ship heeling over until it seemed it would never right itself.

The trumpet pointed at Potts. 'HAWRAWBALLABALLA-BALLA!'

Potts charged into the bows, towing John with him. 'GOWAGOWAGUMBA!' Potts roared and waved his hands. Men jumped into the rigging and did mysterious things with ropes. The ship straightened, the sails filled. Another strange cry from the trumpet. Silence, and a mass of faces turned to Brooke. Casually he touched his hat.

'Evolution completed, sir.'

'Very well, Mr Brooke.' Murray was equally casual. 'I think we might beat to quarters.'

A drum rattled. Like a kaleidoscope being shaken, the crew ran about the deck. The drum stopped. The kaleidoscope was stilled. A new pattern on the deck as every man stood at quarters, the place appointed to him for battle. Every man except John, that is, left stranded in the middle of the deck until a friendly, tattooed arm, reached out and plucked him into the shelter of a gun.

The ordered daily ritual of the ship continued. On the holy quarterdeck the officers assembled with their sextants to measure the height of the sun at noon and so fix the ship's position. Feeling a little lonely, John leaned against the hammocks lashed to the side of the ship to air and dry. Potts passed him.

'Understand all that?' he asked. 'Very important — changing tack — dead-eyes-shrouds-chains —' he reeled off the cryptic sailors' jargon, gave John a friendly rap on the head with tarry knuckles and ambled aft.

John looked at the huge cat's-cradle of ropes and spars above him and tried to remember what Potts had told him. It was all very confusing but still, certain things were beginning to make sense; the front of the ship was the bows, the back was the stern. Port meant left and starboard right. Three masts, *Sentinel* being a ship-sloop: forward, main, mizzen. . . . He felt a sharp poke in the back and found a seaman grinning at him.

'Beggin' your pardon . . . er . . . young gentleman,' the man said. 'Must have a bit of room, if you please.'

John moved down the deck, crowded with the ship's boats, hen-coops full of clucking fowls, the goat-pen, great coils of rope, and the guns; the twelve polished, wicked, twelve-pounder guns.

By the pigsty, where Ginger and Tiger the ship's cats were washing themselves in a contemplative sort of way, he thought of how the seaman had addressed him. He was not an officer, with the title of 'sir', nor a warrant officer, like the gunner or navigator, rating a 'mister'. He was not even a midshipman, who were officers too. Nor was he a seaman or a ship's boy, who were lucky if they were addressed by name. He was a gentleman volunteer, whatever that meant, and the seaman had made the best of it by calling him a young gentleman. But still, he was allowed on the quarterdeck. He sidled unobtrusively behind the marine sentry and watched as the gleaming brass sextants were lowered.

Brooke looked at his measurement. 'Make it noon, sir.'

Murray raised an eyebrow at the midshipmen. 'The same, sir,' Potts cried, echoed with amazing unanimity by the two junior midshipmen, Fearnley and Scott.

'Make it twelve,' Murray said.

A stolid marine rang eight bells in the forenoon watch. The bosun's whistle called the men to dinner. The quarterdeck emptied as a satisfying smell of peas and boiled beef drifted from the galley. Before he left the deck Murray turned to Brooke.

'Young Spencer, he seems to have no battle-station. Put him on six and seven guns.'

In his cabin Murray knelt and bent his head against the ten-pound bow chaser with which he shared his quarters. Noon was the beginning of the naval day and Murray chose to say his morning prayers then. Above him the business of the ship went on but none of the sounds, the scuffle of the marines' boots, Potts's healthy bellow, the easy chatter of Cawley, the Second Lieutenant, who was good-naturedly explaining to John the working of a sextant, none of these sounds disturbed him. Twenty-five years at sea had innured him to any sounds except the ones he wished to hear.

'Oh Lord,' he whispered, 'send down Thy manifold and great mercies on this ship, Her Majesty's sloop-of-war *Sentinel*, on her officers, warrant officers and men, and on John Pocock, sergeant of marines and the men under his command, and on John Spencer, gentleman volunteer. Cleanse our hearts that we might be fit for this great errand of mercy on behalf of our fellow men. . . .'

Four feet away in the ward-room, twelve feet by seven and six feet high, Brooke was eating his dinner with Scott, Fearnley, and the surgeon, Mr Jessup. There was little conversation. Brooke did not approve of midshipmen talking and Jessup, although he held the Queen's commission, he hardly considered an officer, and certainly not a gentleman.

Three feet further on, in the gunroom, ten feet by six and five feet high, the home of the warrant officers, Mr Purvis, the carpenter, stuck a clasp-knife into a piece of cheese, not rotten yet, quite, but trying hard.

'Well,' he said, 'we've got a quiet ship, Henry.'

'Aye.' Taplow, the Purser, who could have dined in the ward-room by right but who had been frozen out by Brooke, who regarded him as even less of a gentleman than Jessup, sucked his teeth. 'It is a quiet ship. A *very* quiet ship.'

And, although John would have been surprised to hear it, *Sentinel* was a quiet ship. And the Sentinels were quiet, too. The bosun and his mates bawled no louder than was necessary and the men went about their work in a subdued, almost solemn manner.

'It's your Blue Lights,' Purvis grunted. 'Wasn't the Owner one of Gambier's lot?'

Both men looked thoughtfully at the table. Gambier had been an admiral, an important admiral — and a religious one, a Blue Lighter as they were called. Murray had been a midshipman with Gambier in the old days and as the admiral had climbed the ladder of promotion, so his favourites had gone up with him. Gambier was dead and gone six years ago but his circle was still powerful at the Admiralty, and in politics, which was why

Murray had command of a ship while hundreds of officers were unemployed on half pay.

'The Number One ain't,' Taplow said.

'No, he ain't,' Purvis said decidedly. 'I don't even know what he's doing on the same ship as the Owner. 'Course, they reckon his uncle's a lord. A big-pot, see.'

'Aye.' Taplow sighed. 'It's not like the old days.'

'You're right there.' Purvis swallowed his cheese. 'It's a different navy to the one I joined. Now it's all *gentlemen*, with excuse me please, and beg your pardons, and spruced up in uniforms. I heard the Owner the other day tell the Number One to *ask* the men to turn out. Christ! I remember Jack Larmour in the *Hind* thirty years ago. When I went on board there he was, a first lieutenant in the Royal Navy with bare feet, a marline-spike in his hand and a gob of tallow as big as a pudding stuck in his hat. I wonder what he would have made of it. *Ask* the men! God Almighty, he would have dropped down dead!'

The two men laughed together creakily, almost affectionately. They had been together on the ship for ten years and, as they controlled the highly saleable stores on the ship, between them they had swindled the Admiralty and the British public out of some thousands of pounds.

'Still,' Purvis went on. 'The world changes and I suppose we must change with it. A woman on the throne, that steamship crossing the Atlantic. All the rest of it,' he added vaguely, oppressed by change. 'Still, there's one or two of the old Navy on board. Old Cobber, there, in the starboard division. They reckon he was in the *Victory* at *you know where.*'

Taplow raised his eyebrows. 'Is that so? Did you hear that, George?' he asked the gunner, who had just come in.

The gunner, Hayes, snorted. 'If every man who says he was in the *Victory* at Trafalgar had been on it she'd have had fifty thousand ratings on board her.'

Taplow grinned. 'We was just talking about changes in the service.'

Hayes squeezed his bulky frame behind the table. 'Well, I'm not saying it was all roses in the days when a man could be flogged to death, *which* I've seen with my own eyes —' tapping them in case of confusion — 'but I don't like a praying ship, neither. Look at this here vessel. Bible readings in the fo'c's'le, the Captain giving out religious tracts and telling the bosun he don't like to hear the Lord's name taken in vain, and half the crew whining psalms down your earhole. Christ Almighty, it's more like a God-damned floating tabernacle than a King's ship.'

'Queen's ship, George,' Purvis said mildly.

'Right, and I begs her pardon, I'm sure,' said Hayes who, having spent forty years serving three kings of England, could still forget he was a subject of Queen Victoria. 'But what I'm saying is, what sort of a man-o'-war is it where you get seamen refusing rum? Tell me that?'

He glared at Taplow, who laughed. 'It's religion, George, and sucking up to the Captain. I never thought that I'd see the day, either. Christ, I remember when I was in the *Dainty*, brig, in 1816. Every man-jack on board from the Captain to the cabin-boy was roaring drunk except me and old Tommy Hodgkin, the sailmaker, and we was half-seas over. The two of us had to handle the ship in a gale on a lee coast. Jesus wept, I thought we was goners that night.'

He chuckled and Purvis laughed with him.

'Aye,' Hayes was sour, not least because, unlike the other two, he did not make money selling government stores, cannon-balls and gunpowder not being in great demand among civilians. 'It's all right laughing, but what I say is, this is supposed to be a ship of force, not an hypocritical revival meeting.'

'It makes for a well-run ship though,' Purvis said.

'*Which* I'm not denying.' Hayes was heated. 'And a gunner don't need telling that rum and gunpowder don't mix. That's all very well for a cruise in quiet waters, but what about when we gets down to the Slave Coast and run up against some blood-sweating slaver in a yankee-built clipper what can run rings round this tub and what has got a dozen long eighteens to knock the snot out of you? What then? I've seen action if you ain't and I'll tell you, God-damned prayers won't keep your men at the guns then. It's rum you need for that. Rum and a rope at the yard-arm waiting for any man what don't stick to his duty. I'll tell you, I thought we was fitting out for a nice quiet patrol on the fisheries or I'd never have stayed on board. I'd have quit the service and stayed home snug with my old woman. And what are we going for? Tell me that?'

'It's to help our black brothers,' Taplow said with a malicious smile.

Hayes glared at him. 'I wouldn't lift my little finger to help my *white* brothers.'

'But they're slaves, George,' Taplow said.

'Bugger the slaves,' Hayes said. 'All I want to do is to get home safe and sound.'

'And amen to that,' said Purvis.

6

All day the Mandingo took his canoe down the river under a grey and oppressive sky. There was no rain, but yellow lightning flashed and flickered over the savannah lands which stretched, it seemed as if for ever, away from either bank. Once a sheet of flame exploded, as a tree a hundred foot tall was struck, its canopy opening in a vast ball of fire. A little later they passed a fishing village. The villagers lined the waterfront, shaking spears and shouting hoarse cries of hatred and defiance.

But the canoe went on, the paddlers swinging tirelessly at their work, the Mandingo sitting motionless under his umbrella, the Dahomey man moaning and muttering, his bloody face slumped against the side of the canoe; Lyapo, the woman, the boy, and the old man, silent in the bows as the miles slid away.

With an hour of daylight left, the canoe pulled into an island.

'We'll spend the night here,' the Mandingo told Lyapo in his dry, affable manner. 'Lots of traders.' He waved his hand at a line of canoes hauled up on the sandy bank. 'We all stick together, see. Then no bad men are going to come in the night and try and steal you.'

The oarsmen built a fire and roasted plantains. 'Eat them,' the Mandingo urged. 'Keep your strength up, you're going to need it.'

The sudden African night fell. The fires glowed in the darkness, flickering on huddled groups of chained men and women and children. Among them the slavers strolled from fire to fire, laughing, joking, gossiping in an easy, relaxed way, like men when the day's work is done.

It was like a village, Lyapo thought, a village in the evening, with families gathered around their fires. Yes, like a village, if you didn't look too closely and see the scars of the whip, or listen too carefully and hear the dull clank of the chains. Lyapo thought of his wife and children and covered his face with his hands and wept.

A dozen canoes left the island the next morning, some of them enormous vessels capable of carrying a hundred people. All the canoes had slaves on board. Lyapo tried to count them, hiding his hands between his knees as he ticked off the numbers. At fifty he stopped counting, 'Awa,' he whispered to himself. 'So many slaves, where can they all be going?'

He twisted his head around, wincing as the chain rubbed his raw neck, and peered down the canoe at the Mandingo, as if hoping for an answer. The Mandingo caught his eye and smiled his lop-sided smile like a man sharing a secret.

Beyond the island the river widened. Lyapo realized that the river they had come down was merely a stream running into a greater river, one so wide that the far bank was merely a smudge on the horizon. On the great river, and under the huge sky, where immense clouds coiled and writhed, their heads purple like enormous fungi, Lyapo felt small and helpless, as insignificant as a fly or an ant. Awa, he murmured, awa, and pressed his knuckles to his mouth.

The sun climbed the sky, its light glaring on the river. In the distance the thunder muttered and growled and the lightning flashed. Near noon the Mandingo dished out cold rice. As Lyapo raised a handful to his mouth the woman jumped overboard.

Lyapo was dragged sidewards across the thwart as the woman hit the water. The canoe tilted, the oarsmen yelled, and the Mandingo roared an order. Lyapo grunted as the chain rasped across his neck. The woman's head bobbed in the water looking already dead, drowned. The chain tightened around Lyapo's neck, choking him. He snatched at the woman, hooking his fingers in her hair and half lifting her from the river.

'Hold her,' the Mandingo bellowed. An oarsman stretched out a muscular arm and grabbed the woman's ankle. The canoe glided into shallow water. As the canoe grounded the woman bumped against the river bed. An oarsman jumped overboard and heaved the woman into the canoe. The Mandingo waded along the side of the canoe and peered at the woman. Without emotion he slapped her face, hard. The woman coughed and spluttered and opened her eyes.

The Mandingo looked at Lyapo. 'She's all right,' he said, his crooked smile flickering under his long nose and cross-eyes. 'You saved her.' He patted Lyapo on the head. 'I'll give you a present for that.'

The present was a handful of kola nuts, bitter and refreshing. Lyapo munched them as the canoe swept down the great river. He offered some to the woman, who lay in front of him, her arms and legs trussed like a goat, but as he put them in her mouth she spat them out and tried to bite his hand.

'I saved your life,' Lyapo said but the woman didn't answer, staring upwards at him with eyes as baleful as the sun.

As on the previous day the Mandingo took his canoe inshore an hour before nightfall.

'Another stop,' he said. 'But we're getting closer all the time.'

'Closer to where?' Lyapo asked, but the Mandingo merely smiled and strolled away.

The huge African stars shone down, fires glowed, the lightning made the stars disappear, insects swarmed in from the river, stinging and biting. Two men walked past Lyapo speaking Yoruba. Lyapo cried out. 'Brothers,' he called, 'brothers.'

The men paused. One laughed and walked on but the other leaned over Lyapo. 'Where's my brother?' he asked.

Lyapo rattled his chain. 'Here,' he said.

The man picked up a brand from the fire and held it up to Lyapo's face. 'Yoruba?' he asked. 'You an Oyo man?'

'Yes,' Lyapo said. 'And you?'

'Oh yes,' the man said. 'I'm from Oyo.'

'Are you a slave?' Lyapo asked.

'No.' The man grinned, his teeth glinting in the firelight. 'No, I'm not a slave.'

Lyapo was confused. 'Then why are you here, with these men, the Mandingos?'

'You're here, aren't you?' the man said.

Lyapo was confused. He was there, yes, of course he was. But he was a captive, a slave, with a chain around his galled neck, not walking freely about the camp, laughing.

'I've got slaves of my own,' the man said.

'Slaves?' Lyapo shook his head, rattling the chain. The old man swore and, from the depth of his pain, the Dahomey groaned, a groan so deep it might have come from the bowels of the earth rather than a human chest.

'I've got six slaves,' the man said. 'Two from Ife and four from Oyo.'

'Oyo!' Lyapo was incredulous. 'An Oyo man with Oyo slaves?' There was as much pain in his voice as there was in the Dahomey's, although for a different reason. 'I don't understand,' he said. 'I don't understand.' That a man should buy and sell members of his own tribe was something he could not grasp. It was as if animals had begun to capture men and sell them. He rubbed his head. 'Brother, I'm an Aseonta. . . .'

The man laughed softly. 'Ah, an Aseonta.' He was amused but affectionately so, like a man reminiscing with a childhood friend about old memories. 'These brotherhoods! I was in one — yes!'

He held out his hand as though Lyapo was about to deny it. 'Yes, I was in a brotherhood. Yes, the Goleah, that was mine. We looked after each other . . . you know.'

Lyapo knew. When he was thirteen he had been inducted into the Aseonta and had taken the oath to protect the fellow members, to worship at the shrine of the fetish, to obey the laws. . . .

The man nodded. 'It's all gone now,' he said. 'Soon there won't be anything left of the Oyo people. Did you have a *bale*?'

Yes, Lyapo's village had a *bale*, a wise old man who knew the laws and the customs of Oyo.

'You had a *janata*, didn't you?'

Lyapo agreed with that as well. They had a *janata*, a strong man who saw that the laws were obeyed. 'Yes,' he said.

The brand was going out. The man blew on it and brought it back to life. 'Much good all that did you, eh?' He held the brand to Lyapo's face. 'Listen, let me tell you something. The old days have gone. Where is the king of Oyo? His pots are broken. The Dahomey, the Fulani, they do what they like now. Listen, I've got men here, slaves, Oyo men — yes, Oyo men, my own people. I'm going to sell them. If I didn't sell them then they would sell me. That's the way it is now. There are no brothers. You've got to learn that. That's why you are being sold and not me.'

'But who will buy me?' Lyapo asked.

The Yoruba shrugged. 'Who am I to say? I am not Olorun to see the future. But I'll tell you what I think. The white men will buy you.'

'White men?' Lyapo wiped his forehead. 'You mean men who are painted white?'

'No, I don't mean that,' the Yoruba said. 'I mean men who are white like ghosts.'

A shape loomed over them, blotting out the stars. Lyapo looked up. The Mandingo was standing over them. Without a word the Yoruba stood up and hurried off into the night.

'Men who are white?' Lyapo asked.

'Don't worry about it,' the Mandingo said and smiled his crooked smile.

7

Lively north-east trade winds singing in *Sentinel*'s rigging, pink and blue jellyfish bobbing away from the bows, whiskered terns screaming in its wake. Blue skies and blue seas, the sun higher, men working bare to the waist.

Latitude thirty-six north; the crew in their best rig lined up facing due east, to Trafalgar. Old Cobber surprising everyone by appearing with a blue jacket and a black silk scarf wrapped around his grizzled head, dressed as indeed he had been thirty-five years ago, on board the *Victory*.

The ensign dipped, Mr Hayes firing the long bow-chaser, half the crew smelling gunpowder for the first time, the smoke clearing to show the all-conquering sun. A growing heat as if far away, a furnace door had been opened.

Sunday; Admiralty orders that there should be read the service of the Church of England, as by law ordained. *Sentinel* in its Sunday best, Sentinels in theirs. Blue and gold, scarlet, chequered shirts, clean bare feet on snowy decks. The Captain's inspection and all well. A white cloth over the binnacle, a Bible on the white cloth. Attentive faces.

In a high, clear voice Murray read the Confession, the Creed, prayers for the Queen and her Ministers, for the Bishops, for the crew and for all mariners; the wind and the pleasant creaking of the ship's timbers adding their own responses.

The sermon. 'Today,' Murray said, 'we heard a lesson from a letter written by Paul the Apostle to the Colossians, a people living far from here, in Turkey, up the Mediterranean — some of you may have sailed those waters. Like us, Paul was a wanderer on the face of the earth, a seafarer, too — ship-wrecked off Malta. Today we heard him say that in Christ there is neither Greek nor Jew, neither circumcised nor uncircumcised, neither freeman nor slave, but that all men are the same in Him.'

Beyond *Dauntless*, beating north on the starboard bow, a sail glinted. A British ship, maybe, homeward bound. Ignoring Greek and Jew, circumcised and uncircumcised, freeman and slave, every eye on board swivelled to the ship. Murray bit his lip with vexation and raised his voice.

'What was the great Apostle saying? He was saying that in the eyes of Almighty God there is no difference in any of His creatures. Rich or poor, black or white, free or slave, we are all His creation. Even the heathen, the sons of Adam are His children and can be turned into the lambs of Christ. God is our Father and all men are His children. Therefore all men are brothers. Even the poor slaves we are sailing to free are our brothers — yes, truly our brothers.'

He paused. Brooke was staring disdainfully forward. The mids were standing upright, glassy-eyed, the warrant officers — Hayes, Taplow, Purvis — were sitting stolidly on their sea-chests, while the men . . . *his* men, those who had followed him from his previous ship, they were leaning forward; pious, beseeching, ingratiating. The others, the unregenerates, gazed blankly at the rigging — their minds, as Murray knew very well, fixed not on the mysterious Colossians but on their dinner, the rum ration, the distant sail, and on the leisure Sunday afternoon brought. But they were all men, Murray thought, all men; the good, the bad, the indifferent, all to be brought to a sense of their sin, then to penitence, and then to Jesus Christ.

'Let us pray,' he said. 'O Heavenly Father, grant that we be pure in heart. On this our voyage let not our hearts be sullied by thoughts of earthly gain —'

There was a slight movement to his right. Cawley was squinting at the sky and Keverne, the ship's navigator, had his mouth pursed, as though whistling an inaudible tune. Murray frowned. Were the men trying to remind him that noon was near? But noon *was* near and in the eyes of the Admiralty, fixing the ship's position was holier than Holy Writ.

'Remember the Sabbath day,' Murray said harshly. 'To keep it holy.'

The drum beating to quarters, every man in his place within seconds. The crew dismissed to dinner, the warrant officers vanishing below deck. The officers assembled on the quarter-deck with their sextants and the mids, to their horror, being sternly ordered to read their findings first.

An hour later the pleasant torpor of Sunday afternoon. On the deck, men enjoying their leisure. By the long boat the Blue Lighters, lambs of Christ, studying 'The Soul's Compass; A Mariner's Guide to the Shoals of UnGodliness and the Reefs of Sin'. In the bows, Dawlish, Yetts, and Smith, able seamen and sons of Adam, off watch and full of greenish salt pork and plum duff, leaned companionably over the side.

'Not a bad old tub, this,' Yetts said. 'Leastways I've been on worse. What do you think, Zeb?'

Dawlish leaned carefully over the rail and spat neatly into the bow wave. 'Well, I'll say this,' he said. 'The Owner keeps the cat *in* the bag, which is where I likes it to be.'

The men laughed and reflected on the pleasure of being on a ship where the Captain disliked flogging and kept the fearful cat-o'-nine-tails in its velvet bag.

'Now it's a queer old thing,' Yetts said, 'but so far as I know there's hardly a man on board what's been down to this here Slave Coast. I wonder why that is?'

'I'll tell you why.' Dawlish folded muscular arms across his chest. 'It's because no one wants to go twice if they can help it. A mate of mine went down there in the *Ardent*, brig, and a right old stink-hole it is, too. They lost three men with the Yellow Jack — that's a stinking fever, that is — and the bosun went blind.'

'Is that right, Zeb?' Yetts asked nervously.

'It is so,' Dawlish said, 'the white man's grave they call it.'

'Then what did you sign on for?' Smith asked.

'Prize money,' Dawlish said without hesitation, 'Just like everyone else. I reckon if we has any luck, me and the missus can start a pub.'

Unrestrained admiration for the commercial acumen of Dawlish and wife.

'How many of them blackies do you think we're agoing to catch, Zeb?' Yetts questioned.

Dawlish grinned amiably. 'Which we ain't agoing for to *catch* 'em, Jack. We're agoing for to let them go.'

'Oh.' Yetts looked worried. 'But we gets paid for them just the same, don't we?'

'Don't worry about that,' Dawlish said. 'It's five quid a head and half shares in any ship we take. It used to be sixty quid. You could make money then.'

'What do you reckon we might make on this voyage?' Smith asked.

'Well now.' Dawlish picked at his teeth. 'Suppose we meets up with a nice big Portuguee vessel with three hundred of them slaves aboard. Three hundred times five, that's fifteen hundred, ain't it? Then half shares in the ship, say another fifteen hundred, so that's three thousand quid.'

Yetts rubbed his hands. 'Three thousand quid. Jesus!'

'Now then, now then,' Dawlish raised a warning finger. 'We goes shares in that. Three-eighths for a captain, one eighth for the lieutenants and mids and the navigator, the standing officers get another eighth, the petty officers and the sergeant of marines gets another eighth, and what's left goes to us.'

Yetts had been listening to the list with growing anxiety. 'But what *is* left, Zeb?'

'Why,' Dawlish was scornful. 'It's a quarter. Divide that among the ratings and we've got . . . well . . . say about twenty-five quid each.'

'You're a marvel, Zeb,' Yetts said with unconcealed admiration. 'If I had your brains I'd . . . well . . . well, I don't know what I'd do, and that's straight.'

Dawlish smiled complacently. ''Course, that's only one ship. My mate in the *Ardent* picked up half a dozen sail. Three hundred quid he drew, on top of pay.'

'Well, I'll tell you what,' said Smith waggishly. 'Next time them Blue Lighters has a prayer meeting I'll be right there with them. O Lord, send us down six great big slavey-ships — without any guns!'

'Might as well make it seven while you're about it,' said the arithmetical Dawlish, to general laughter and applause.

The joke passed along the deck, causing a ripple of amusement among the sinners and disapproving looks from the Blue Lighters who were deep in a discussion of the Nature of True Repentance.

In the three-cornered booth which passed for his cabin, Brooke heard the laughter and lifted his cold face. The laughter died down and he turned again to the letter he was writing to his uncle, Lord Keston.

'. . . As to the Captain, he is one of your canting evangelicals and a Whig, as one might expect, hand-in-glove with the Gambier crowd at the Admiralty and Government appointee, of course. He is full of drivel about the salvation of souls and Exeter Hall clap-trap about the negro being our brother. I must confess I do hate to see an officer on his knees with a pack of rascally, mumbling, hypocritical seamen. It destroys rank, and when that has gone what is left of order in society? There has been no flogging on board, either, for Murray is one of your milk-and-water captains who believes in kindness, as if he were a latterday Nelson. It will lead to trouble, nothing so certain, for the good hands will go slack and the bad ones rotten.'

Brooke drank some claret from his private store and looked again at what he had written. On reflection it seemed a little too sour and it was important that he keep his aristocratic uncle sweet. Certainly Lord Keston had done the minimum possible in getting him a berth on this miserable ship with its miserable errand, but it would not do to appear ungrateful. He took up his pen.

'But as you said to me at Apsley House, one must do these tasks and mix with these people at times. There is a possibility of distinguishing oneself in action, and that will count when the Tories come to power again. I am truly most grateful to you for your kind attentions —'

With weary disgust Brooke threw the pen down. Why was he condemned to write this odious flattery for the sake of a job beneath his talents? He slid the letter into his chest and went on deck.

As he appeared there was a ripple of movement. The helmsman gripped the wheel more tightly, the marine sentry turned into a scarlet ramrod; in the waist of the ship, although it was their free afternoon, men nudged each other, spoke more quietly, and edged furtively toward the bows.

Brooke was pleased by the reaction. Respect, deference, fear, those were the qualities which he believed, quite sincerely, bound society together and what was a ship but society in miniature?

Two miles away, on the port beam, beautiful in the afternoon light, the pennant of its captain fluttering in a long blue ribbon, *Dauntless* dipped and rose, the very picture of a warship. Brooke gazed at it sourly. That was a real ship; thirty-two guns, a dozen officers, one hundred and fifty men. To be first lieutenant on a vessel like that was a real step to promotion — to captaincy and honour, and inevitably to becoming an admiral. Brooke knew the First, Havelock, a bad officer, inefficient, unconscientious, a poor seaman, but first on a crack frigate because he knew the right people. Something like fury swept across him, a baulked, black frustration. He looked about him with a cold eye. By the taffrail a boy was idling, staring vacantly upwards like a cretin. What was his name? Spender, something like that, a captain's pet, brought on board for some mysterious reason.

'You, sir,' he snapped. 'Come here.'

John had been trying to memorize the names of the spars on the masts which carried the sails and was not aware that Brooke was talking to him. As Brooke saw him carry on gazing upwards, his mouth open, his temper snapped.

'You!' he bellowed. 'That boy!'

John started and jumped forward. 'Yes, sir?'

'Just what are you doing?' Brooke hissed.

Faced with the terrifying figure of an enraged first lieutenant, John's mind went a complete blank. He was so frightened he could barely speak. 'Er, nothing, sir,' he stammered.

'Nothing? Nothing? Then go and do nothing at the mast-head.'

'Sir?'

'The mast-head.' Brooke's voice was savage. 'If you can find nothing better to do than idle then do it out of my sight. Get to the mast-head all the way, and stay there until I send for you. Do you hear me?'

'Aye aye, sir.' John, who had no idea why he was being punished, backed away to the mainmast. Not a soul on board thought anything of the incident indeed most of them had been mast-headed themselves in their time, and for lesser crimes than not hearing a first lieutenant.

John looked up at the mast. Two Norwegian pines stepped together, it soared above him, a hundred feet from deck to truck, held firm by the shrouds, the ladder-like rigging which ran up with them, high into the spider's web of sail and rope. John had been up before. The other mids played tag there, swinging about with the ease and confidence of monkeys, and he, finding his way about the ship, had been with them. But he had never been all the way to the top, and he had never gone up alone.

'Are you to be all day?' Brooke roared.

'No, sir,' John whispered. He placed his hands on the shrouds, swallowed, and began to climb.

At thirty feet up he paused. It was surprising how small the deck looked from there. How small the deck and how large the sea. Acutely conscious of Brooke's eyes on him he crept upwards. But other eyes than Brooke's were watching him. Most of the seamen were watching and wondering, with wry amusement, how he would get on when he came to the platform where the lower mast was stepped to the upper one. The reason for the amusement was that there were two ways on to the platform. One was through a little hole, known as the lubber's hole, which was cut into the platform and led on to it without difficulty. The other way was quite a different matter. Running on the outside of the platform was a line of rigging. It was thick and braced as hard as iron. Climbing it was no more difficult than climbing a ladder — except that it ran outwards from the mast at an angle of forty degrees. To get on the platform that way, the sailor's way, meant leaning backwards, like climbing a ladder on the wrong side — sixty feet in the air. Which way a raw hand chose was always a source of sardonic amusement to the crew. John himself had no doubt at all which he was going to take. He went straight for the lubber's hole and poked his head through it. As he did so there was a rasping cry from Brooke.

'You there, take the seaman's way. Do you hear me!'

John heard him, although he wished he hadn't. He took a quick glance through his legs and wished he hadn't done that, either. The cannon looked like toys, the men like dolls. The ship heeled over. Between his feet the deck slid away and the sea sparkled beneath him. Another heel and the deck came back. Another bellow from below and John cautiously snaked a hand outwards, groped for the rigging, found it, groped for another rope, found that, hooked a leg through the shrouds, closed his eyes, and clawed upwards. Then a wave struck the *Sentinel* amidships.

On the deck the shock was barely noticeable. Sixty feet up a slender column of timber, it was. The mast quivered and vibrated and John was plucked from the rigging. He twisted and hung head down, kept from plummeting to the deck only by his leg jammed in the shrouds.

The ship rolled in the hollow of a wave and the mast swung in a huge arc. John gave a despairing squeak as centrifugal force flung him almost vertically from the mast and his leg slid from its hold.

'Mamma!' John screamed. 'Mamma!' But already a vast hand had clamped on to his leg and dragged him on to the platform.

John gulped and looked into the eyes of Martin Rafferty, look-out. 'Now there you are,' Rafferty said. 'Right as rain, so you are. Just you clap on to them ratlines there.'

John grabbed the ropes, and a firm hand seized his ankles. 'Now,' Rafferty said, 'cool and easy does it. Don't you go looking down and old Dawlish there will let you down like a little cherub, so he will.'

Supported by Dawlish John half slid, half climbed down the shrouds and, his heart pounding, found himself on the deck, surrounded by a group of affable, concerned seamen.

'Just you go through the lubber's hole for a bit,' Smith said. 'Till you find your way about, like.'

'Thank you, thank you.' John looked up at the mast and took a deep breath. 'Thank you indeed,' he said to Dawlish.

'Why,' Dawlish grinned. ''Tain't nothing at all. Anyway, 'twas Rafferty grabbed you.' He looked at Smith. 'The nipper should never have been ordered outwards. It's —'

His voice stopped abruptly and his smile vanished. John turned and saw the bleak face of Brooke. But Brooke's eyes were on Dawlish.

'Did I hear you speak?' he demanded. 'Did I?'

'Sir?' Dawlish backed away, his hand flicking to his forehead.

'Did I hear you challenge an order? Did I?'

'No sir, never sir.'

Dawlish was grey with fear. Challenging an order was a flogging offence, no matter how kind the captain might be, and challenging an order with others present could be an incitement to mutiny, and that could lead to a rope with one end over the yard-arm, the other end around your neck, and the band playing the Rogue's March. 'I was just helping the young gentleman,' he said.

Brooke hesitated. For some time he had been looking for a serious offence which would force Murray into ordering a flogging. The only way to keep men at their duty was to keep them clasped in an iron hand. But he had no wish to see a valuable seaman like Dawlish hanged, nor was he happy at the thought of his particular order being made public.

'Get for'ard,' he ordered. 'And look to yourself. I have you marked down.'

Dawlish moved away, his back twitching. Brooke turned to John. 'Did I not order you to the mast-head?'

'I nearly fell, sir,' John said.

'Nearly fell? Nearly fell? And because you *nearly* fell are you to spend the rest of the day lounging on the deck with your hands in your pockets like a Piccadilly lounger? Get up the mast as you were ordered to and use the lubber's hole this time, since a lubber is what you are.'

Brooke strode to his cabin past the grave Cawley. John crawled back up the shrouds, half the crew hanging on the rigging around him like a flock of bats. In the bows, Dawlish, Yetts, and Smith stared moodily over the side.

'And we're supposed to be going to make them blackies free,' Dawlish said bitterly. 'Bugger me, it's them what ought to be looking out for us.'

8

The Mandingo kept his slaves on the island for two days. His servants chopped leaves from the cabbage palms and Lyapo and the others built small shelters from them under which they squatted, looking out on the river as the lightning flashed across yellow skies and the canoes of the slavers came and went. Every now and then the Mandingo ordered them from their shelters and they stood, heads bowed, as other men inspected them, the Mandingo talking easily and fluently as he showed off their good points.

The Dahomey man died. His head swelled enormously and turned green and yellow. The Mandingo took off his chains and wrapped a poultice of leaves around his head, but it got no better. Then he wrote a prayer on a scrap of paper and put that on him but the Dahomey died just the same. Lyapo was glad. The endless moaning of the Dahomey had been getting on his nerves and the wound had a foul smell.

On the morning of the third day the Mandingo came and squatted by Lyapo.

'This is where we part company,' he said. 'You go one way, I go another.'

'Go?' Lyapo frowned. 'Go where?'

The Mandingo spat. 'Well, I'm going home. All the way back up the river. Back to the Mandingo country. I shouldn't be this far down anyway but I've had a bad time this year. If I don't get going soon I won't get there at all, what with the rains and the Dahomeys and all. I'll tell you, this is a dangerous business, and I've got wives and children back home. They'll want to see me, and I want to see them. It's not good for a family to be split up too long.'

'And what about me?' Lyapo asked. 'What about my wife and children?'

The Mandingo was silent for a while. He rubbed his long nose and waved the flies from his cross-eyes. 'You've got to forget them,' he said severely.

'Forget them?'

'Yes. Listen. It's a hard world.' The Mandingo fumbled in his gown and brought out a handful of kola nuts. 'Here. Go on, take them.' He forced the nuts into Lyapo's hand. 'Take everything you can get in this world. Listen, I owe you something for saving that woman. That's why I've been good to you.'

'Good to me?' Lyapo gave a little cry, something between a laugh and a groan.

'Oh yes,' the Mandingo was deadly serious. 'You think I've not been good to you? Just you wait.'

'Wait for what?'

'That's what I'm telling you,' the Mandingo said testily. 'Listen, you've got bad times ahead of you.'

Lyapo laughed.

'I know, I know,' said the Mandingo. 'I understand how you feel. But I want to give you some advice. I'm a Muslim. Do you know what that means?'

He leaned forward earnestly as Lyapo shook his head. 'It means I believe in one God — Allah. Just one God. Now you believe in lots of gods, don't you? Every village has got its own gods, right? You think every stick and stone is a god and you spend all your time making sure you don't offend these gods. I know, I've seen them in the villages — idols and sacred trees and stones.' He peered at Lyapo through his cross-eyes. 'But that's no good, all those gods. Listen, there's only one God, Allah the Almighty and Merciful, and Muhammad is his Prophet, Peace be on Him. Why don't you believe in Allah? Become a Muslim. You'll be better off. It stands to reason, one big God is better than a lot of little gods.'

Lyapo gazed dully at the Mandingo. 'Will he let me go free, Allah?'

The Mandingo edged nearer and put his hand on Lyapo's knee. 'I'll tell you something. If you're a Muslim then it's wrong for another Muslim to make you a slave. And all the Muslims you meet, they're supposed to help you.'

Lyapo's eyes lost some of their dullness. 'If I'm a Muslim other Muslims won't make me a slave?'

'That's right,' the Mandingo said. 'At least, good Muslims won't.'

Lyapo looked almost cheerful. 'All right. I'll be one.'

The Mandingo blinked. 'You will?'

'Yes.' Lyapo stretched his shoulders. 'What do I do?'

'Well. . . .' The Mandingo's eyes looked more crossed than ever. 'I can tell you that. You just say, "I believe that there is no god but God and Muhammad is His messenger." You say that three times and you're a Muslim.'

'All right.' Lyapo repeated the words three times and smiled at the Mandingo. 'Now I'm free?'

'Free?' The Mandingo blinked.

'That's what you said, isn't it? A Muslim doesn't make another Muslim a slave.'

'Ah!' The Mandingo grinned. 'You're a clever man. But there's something you ought to know.'

'What's that?'

The Mandingo stood up and smoothed his long, indigo gown. His lop-sided smile came and went. 'I couldn't let you go free if I wanted to. You don't belong to me any more. I sold you this morning. Here is your new owner.'

He pointed a long, bony finger. Coming from the river was a thick-set man, blacker than Lyapo. There was no dry, ironic smile on his face, and no kola nuts in his huge fist; instead he carried an unpleasant looking club.

'Take me with you,' Lyapo said. 'Let me be your slave.'

The Mandingo opened his arms, a wide, submissive gesture. 'I can't do that. But I will tell you one last thing. Do you know what Muslim means? Slave of God. Eat your kola nuts.'

9

Sentinel beat her way down the latitudes. Cape St Vincent slipped away, clouds of shipping gathered off the Straits of Gibralter. Flying fish skittered across the dazzling sea and dolphins joined the ship, effortlessly running before her bows, hour after hour.

A fine Thursday dawning and the peaks of Madeira rising to the west but not a Sentinel looking at them for it was punishment day and, to the consternation of the crew, the cat had jumped out of the bag, its nine claws fully extended, and was about to scratch the back of John Rose, Able Seaman, given a dozen for spitting on the deck, blasphemy, and calling the bosun a hairy, Barbary ape; his plea that he had been seized by a coughing fit, loved the Lord Jesus, and that apes being agreeable, comical creatures, no offence could have been intended, being rejected.

Rose was given his due. The crew was assembled in full dress and best uniforms, and the drum rolled to blot out any cries of pain. Not that there were any, Rose being a hard case, with a broken nose and scarred shoulder to prove it.

Murray watched the flogging as he had watched hundreds before, his face expressionless. It was a dirty, bloody business, one he hated and wished to see abolished, and which was, in any case, slowly falling into disuse. But Brooke had forced his hand. The charges were too grave and too numerous for any lesser punishment. He had suggested to Brooke that one of the charges be dropped but the First had been adamant. And there was force in Brooke's argument that he was responsible for the working of the ship and that he must be allowed to do it in the old way, the tried and trusted way.

Rose was led away and a subdued crew shuffled off to their dinner. John, feeling sick, crawled into the ward-room where Scott and Fearnley were attacking a sea-pie with a brave show of unconcern.

'That's the way,' said Scott, sixteen years of age. 'Tickle their spines and make them jump. It's the only way to —' To what remained a mystery as he suddenly rushed on deck holding his mouth.

Fearnley, seventeen years of age, calmly watched him go and scraped Scott's pie on to his own plate. 'That was nothing,' he said. 'The bosun hardly marked him. I know for a fact that the Owner told him not to lay it on too hard. Now when I was in *Renown* I saw a man get forty-eight lashes for mutiny. You should have seen *his* back. It was like a side of —'

But John had followed Scott so Fearnley ate his pie, too.

John leaned over the side of the ship and donated his dinner to the ocean, then raised his sweating head, and looked into the eyes of Brooke. John could not go whiter than he was but he stepped back a pace, half raising his arm, and a look of genuine fear crossed his face.

'Sir,' he cried. 'Sorry, sir.'

Brooke frowned. He was not sentimental about young men, especially John, but although he demanded and got respectful deference from the junior officers and fear from the men, he was shocked by the abject terror on John's face.

John totally misunderstood Brooke's frown. There was a little spittle on the rail and he scrubbed at it with his sleeve. 'Very sorry, sir,' he cried again.

Brooke shook his head. 'Leave that,' he snapped. 'Leave it alone. Damn it, it isn't a crime to be sick.' He half-turned on his heel, then swung round. 'A flogging — it's a bloody business — but in the end the Navy's business *is* bloody. You have to learn that. We all have to. That is what discipline is about. There is nothing personal about it. Do you understand?'

'Yes sir.' John licked his dry lips.

'Very well.' Brooke nodded. 'Do your duty and it will go well with you. I — the Navy — it is stern but it is not cruel. Do your duty and it will go well with you. Carry on now, Mr Spencer.'

'Thank you, sir.' John touched his hat as Brooke strode to the quarterdeck.

In the afternoon the wind dropped a little and the sea quietened.

'Mr Brooke,' Murray said, 'we will exercise the guns, with powder.'

Murray had waited patiently for the men, even the worst duffer, to find their sea-legs before actually firing the guns. He wished to avoid the broken legs and crushed feet which could happen so easily when tons of metal crashed and recoiled on a heaving deck. The men had practised of course, running the guns in and out of the gun-ports, but that, although useful enough, had as little resemblance to the real thing as a painting of a pie would have to your real, bubbling, gravy-filled Mowbray.

The men were assembled, six to a gun, and Murray called his officers to the quarterdeck. 'Now gentlemen,' he said, 'most of our gunnery against a slaver will be fairly long range. We will shoot at the upper works, the masts and rigging, in order to disable the ship. That is a task for Mr Hayes and the long bow-chaser. But the real test of action is the broadside, ship to ship fighting it out at close range. It is highly unlikely that we will meet a slaver prepared to do that, I understand that they *run*; they depend on speed to make their escape. But we are a warship — and a Royal Naval warship at that. The broadside is our business. Now then,' he turned to the midshipmen. 'Watch Mr Cawley. He will signal you to fire on the *downward* roll of the ship. Remember that, the downward roll.'

The officers exchanged knowledgeable glances. All of them, except John, knew that the Royal Navy fired on the downward roll so that her shot would smash into the heart of the enemy. Ship-killing it was called, unlike the tactics of the French and suchlike who fired on the upward roll, hoping to carry away masts and spars. It was like the difference in boxing where your artistic pug like the Hackney Gent danced around, poking out his left, but your true bruiser, like Whitechapel Jack, got in close and drove his opponent to the ground by savage blows to the heart.

'Very well, gentlemen,' Murray said. 'Let us begin — and watch Mr Cawley.'

Silence on board. The ship rocked slightly. Murray raised his hand, Brooke took out his watch. Murray's hand came down.

'Fire,' Cawley bellowed.

One by one the starboard guns roared out, flame spurting from their muzzles, smoke billowing, the guns leaping back on the recoil.

'Port, fire!' The men rushed across the deck. 'Wham wham wham!' The guns barked as sweating men heaved and cursed, powder-boys ran backwards and forwards, the mids' voices piped high with excitement, and the acrid smoke filled the ship. The last gun roared. Men rubbed their ears and turned sweaty faces to the quarterdeck.

'Twenty minutes, sir.' Brooke said.

Murray shrugged. 'It is only to be expected.'

Brooke agreed. A rapid rate of fire could only be gained by endless practice.

'Be good enough to examine the guns, Mr Hayes,' Brooke said.

He called the officers around him again. 'Get the men to move calmly, there is too much . . . frenzy . . . about them. Keep them steady. Now, once more.'

Once more it was, and again, and again, until the crew began to find a real rhythm. Loose, level, out, run, prime, FIRE! Swab, loose, level, out, run, prime, FIRE! In and out ran the guns until men's ears ached with the roar.

The excercise over, water in great demand. 'I think we can hope to improve,' said Murray, and 'We *will* improve,' Brooke echoed, grimly.

Evening. The guns wormed and cleaned, the pleasant smell of gunpowder hanging lightly in the rigging. Dusk gathering in the east and the first unfamiliar stars of the southern hemisphere peeping over the horizon. The crew relaxed, pleased. After all . . . the guns . . . the ship wasn't some floating haystack of a merchantman. It was a man-o'-war, a fighting cock, a hard case — and watch out when it sails past, mate.

The watch on deck standing easy. Stories of Africa circulating. Jack Kemp, Able and a wizard at knots, knew for a living fact that gangs of mermaids swam about the Slave Coast and could actually pull ships down to Davy Jones's locker, which his second cousin had seen with his own eyes. Grigg, reformed drunkard and loblolly boy, who had escaped from his post in the surgeon's cockpit for an hour, had heard of flying snakes, a hundred feet long. The waggish Smith topped this with stories of talking monkeys but was outgunned by Mogger, ordinary seaman, tormented by the crew barking at him whenever he moved, who had a vague, literary memory of cannibals whose heads grew underneath their arms which the crew, although ready enough to believe in mermaids and, at a pinch, giant flying snakes and talking monkeys, found a little difficult to swallow wholly.

A pleasant evening and a wondrous night. The sea sparkling with phosphorescence, a crescent moon, and stars as bright as your true love's eyes.

A pleasant atmosphere in the ward-room, too, where the officers had invited their captain to dine off the last piglet. Talk of African waters. . . .

'If the Bight of Benin is hotter than Bengal then it must be hot.' Brooke thought that the Red Sea was the hottest place on earth, while Scott opined that Spitzbergen in the winter must certainly be the coldest. Fearnley remarked that North China

41

could be most amazingly cold, the surgeon was quite sure that Cape Horn was the windiest. Cawley remarked that the climate of the Mediterranean was pleasantly equable, but he was not taken up on it as every man present knew those waters like the back of his hand. Only John kept mum — thinking, rightly, that his trip from Northampton to Birmingham on the Great Eastern Canal was hardly worth a mention.

Murray picked John from obscurity. 'If you choose the Navy as your career, Mr Spencer, you will see the wonders of the world and the marvels of the deep, have no fear.'

'If you can get a berth,' Brooke said.

Murray frowned slightly. 'There is always a berth for a good man. As your presence shows, I'm sure.'

He bowed slightly. Brooke answered with the stiffest, slightest inclination of the head, wondering if Murray would be of the same opinion when the Tories came to power.

Jessup was conscious of the slight embarrassment. 'Well,' he cried, 'as long as the slave trade continues it would seem that there will be berths for all who wish them. And it seems that it will continue for ever. Indeed it appears to be on the increase. Why is that, I wonder?'

'It is the opening of Brazil,' Brooke said. 'Mark my words. Brazil and Cuba. And now you are on to it. Now you know why our country is so dead set against the slave trade.'

'I'm not with you.' Jessup leaned across the table. 'Why should the development of Cuba make Britain keen to stop the trade?'

Brooke was contemptuous. 'Sugar, Doctor. Our possessions in the West Indies are quite worn out. The soil is exhausted and the sugar yield is low. Cuba and the other islands are fresh. Given labour they can outstrip our plantations. That is why we are sailing along this interminable coast — to keep the price of sugar high.'

Murray was frowning and Brooke turned to him. 'I fear you disapprove of that theory, sir.'

'It is not for me to approve or disapprove of your opinions,' Murray said, 'although I am sorry to hear that you think such a sordid motive is the reason for the Anti-Slave Patrol. But in any case I think that you are wrong. I incline to the belief that it is cotton which is the reason for the increase in slavery.'

'Cotton, sir?' asked Jessup the peacemaker.

'Yes, the world is mad for cotton goods, and the looms of Lancashire mean that all the cotton grown can be used. I understand that the Americans are opening all the land they can which will grow cotton, so now slaves are being imported into the United States. It seems to me that despite what Mr Brooke says it would pay us to *allow* slavery. Lancashire would be happy to spin all the cotton the Americans can grow. It would be good business. However, it is a complex business —'

'There you have it,' Jessup cried. 'Business is the word. Where men can make a profit they will do so. It is sad but it is true.'

'Especially Cousin Jonathan,' Cawley said.

'Americans,' Brooke said with an air of intense dislike.

'Well, well,' Murray was judicial. 'There are Americans and Americans, you know. There is a strong anti-slave movement in the North.'

'Yes, sir.' As Brooke believed that the northern states were peopled entirely by grasping and vulgar merchants, whereas in the South there was a class of planters he regarded as *almost* gentlemen, his agreement was less than whole-hearted.

Murray looked at him sharply but the ship's bell rang eight bells in the first watch and Cawley stood up.

'Excuse me, sir,' he said. 'My watch.'

'I will accompany you,' Murray said.

The little party broke up. Brooke to his cabin, Jessup to his bunk, John and the other mids to their hammocks. Keverne came through to his bunk in the gunroom where he lay down and carried on reading *Pickwick Papers*, which he had borrowed from John.

Taplow and Purvis were in the gunroom, drinking rum which Keverne was inclined to believe had been stolen from the ship's stores.

Taplow grinned at Purvis. 'We're getting on, Ted. A flogging and the guns roaring. It's getting quite like old times. Much more of this and we'll be gobbling up slaving vessels like a Dutchman eating herrings. What do you think, Mr Keverne?'

Keverne, far away in Dingley Dell, grunted.

Taplow peered slyly across the table. 'What's the matter, ain't you partial to the smell of gunpowder?'

Keverne deliberately turned a page. Taplow had a niggling way of speaking which he found annoying. For some time he had had it in mind to cut the purser down to size and now, he thought, might well be the time.

'You ever seen any action?' he asked, mildly enough.

Taplow turned a delicate pink. 'No, I haven't. There's not a dozen men on board what have. Have you?'

'No,' Keverne said.

'Well then.' Taplow was pugnacious. 'What for did you go and mention it?'

'Well, it's like this.' Keverne left the Fat Boy for a moment. 'I had a drink once with a gunner that was out here three years ago in *Sunflower*, brig. They came up with a slaver at Lagos what turned and showed her teeth, so she did. *Sunflower* gave her a broadside, then crossed her stern and gave her another. It sounded like those old times you was spouting about.'

He returned to Pickwick, holding the pages close against the lantern. There was a puzzled silence which Taplow broke.

'Well, what happened?'

Keverne turned a page. 'What happened to what?'

'What happened to this here slaver?' Taplow demanded in an exasperated voice.

'Oh, that.' Pickwick came down. 'Well, I'll tell you. She struck her colours and they boarded her. And what do you think they found when the Sunflowers went below deck? What do you think, Mr Taplow?'

'I don't know.' Taplow was surly. 'Get on with it, can't you.'

'Well I'll tell you what they didn't find,' Keverne said. 'They didn't find a lot of hairy-chested pirates like Blackbeard all ready to stick them with cutlasses like pigs in a shambles. No. What they found was a hundred or two of them poor slaves what you goes on about in your comical way, and they was all chained up and those two broadsides had smashed them into jelly. And there was women and kids there as well. What do you make of that?'

Purvis, a decent, steady man, six children of his own, was grave. 'Fortunes of war, Mr Keverne. No one would want that to happen, not in a million years. But what else could they do? They couldn't let that slaver skip away.'

'You're right, Ted. It's like you say, fortunes of war. But I ain't finished the story yet.'

'Well,' Taplow burst out. 'Why don't you finish it instead of lying there, spouting and blowing like a damn great grampus.'

'All right.' Keverne, who was a big formidable man, looked steadily at Taplow. 'All right, I will. When this gunner saw them poor buggers all smashed up he felt right sick. Like he said, he hadn't never reckoned on firing a broadside into a ship full of poor devils that couldn't help themselves. Like he said, that wasn't what he was trained for. Afterwards he said to another

44

warrant officer, like it might have been a purser, and he says, ain't it a shame. Ain't it a shame.'

He paused, and Purvis nodded. 'Well so it was, Mr Keverne. A crying shame.'

'You're right, Mr Purvis,' Keverne said. 'It was a crying shame. But this bloody purser said, "It's a shame all right. We only gets half prize money on them slaves what's dead."'

Taplow scowled. 'What of it? What are you getting so holy about? That's what we're all here for, ain't it, prize money? Every man-jack on board joined for that, 'cepting maybe the officers.'

'That's as may be,' Keverne said, 'since I ain't been round the ship asking. But this gunner I'm telling you about, when he heard that purser make his little joke he turned round and hit him in the earhole, and he hit him so hard it knocked all them little purser's jokes right out of the other earhole. See?'

'Which was an offence against the Queen's Regulations,' Taplow jibbered, red with rage. 'And for which he could have got broke from the service.'

'Why, that's right enough,' Keverne said. 'But he wasn't, and he didn't hear no more funny jokes on that voyage, so it was worth the risk.'

He nodded grimly and returned to Pickwick. Stick that in your pipe and smoke it, he told himself with deep satisfaction as the ship heeled in the wind, the vast bulk of Africa drew nearer, and the splendour of the night enshrouded *Sentinel*.

10

Lyapo's new owners were a group of Benin men who had come up the river, picking up slaves. They gave the Mandingo three dollars' worth of cowrie shells, one pound of gunpowder, and ten rounds of ammunition for Lyapo. It was not much, but the Mandingo was glad to get that so he could go home. In fact he was lucky to get anything at all; the Benin men being what they were, they would have taken *him* as a slave if he had not been with a strong group of other Mandingos.

Under the Benin men there were no more dry kindnesses. They looked at their slaves with the eyes of men considering a herd of livestock and wondering what it would bring in the market. And that is what they were, dealers in livestock, big dealers. They treated their slaves like animals, although valuable ones. They were fed and sheltered, but the whip and the goad were always ready should a beast turn baulky.

The slaves were chained in groups, of twenty or thirty persons each, which were called coffles. The Benin men were short of chains so one coffle was bound with ty-rope made from grass. Lyapo thought himself lucky to be in this coffle, and luckier still to be at the end, where his neck was only jerked one way.

Not all the men in the coffle were from Oyo. Some were Bunus and Igbirras from the east. There was even a Bambara from a thousand miles away, although only God and he knew how, or why, he was where he was.

At night the Oyo men talked among themselves. All their stories were the same: shocked and bitter tales of warfare. Of Dahomey infantry, of Fulani cavalry, who had fallen upon their villages and taken them away, leaving behind them only fire, and the dead.

One Yoruba was from a large town. For him the disaster was, if no less dreadful, at least more comprehensible. 'It is the war. The great men are fighting each other, the towns fight each other. The Alafin has no power and cannot control his people. Because the Yoruba fight each other, the Dahomey and the Fulani can come into the land and do as they wish.'

In his remote village Lyapo had been hardly aware of the civil wars, but he could understand them. Men fought each other, he knew that. What he couldn't understand was why the Benin men had him, and why they were going on and on down the great river. Where were they going, and for what purpose?

The Yoruba shrugged. 'I don't know,' he said. 'But in my town they sold men for guns. Everyone wants a gun. That way they are strong.'

'Where do the guns come from?' Lyapo asked. 'Who makes them? Is it ... is it ...' Lyapo could barely bring himself to say the words. 'Is it the men who are white?'

The Yoruba shuddered, as if he had awoken to find a snake crawling over his bed. 'I have heard of them. But who could believe such a story? It is too terrible even to think about.'

It was, too. The slaves' minds went numb at the thought.

Every day the rain came, each day a little heavier. The river rose and flowed quicker, turning tawny with silt. Lyapo watched it rise. Soon there would be only one way to travel, down with the river to whatever horrors and nightmares lay waiting in that land of ghosts to which they were travelling. It was then he decided to escape.

On the banks of the river there were huge snails. Carefully and secretly Lyapo gathered their shells, pretending, to the disgust of the other slaves, that he was eating the snails. When he had a mass of shells he waited, watching the river. At last the moment came for which he had been waiting. A small canoe which one man could handle was brought in and moored next to the Benin men's canoe.

That night Lyapo began hacking at the ty-rope with his shells. The man next to him was the Yoruba from the town. 'What are you doing?' he asked.

'Be quiet,' Lyapo grunted. 'Shut up.'

The man leaned back, his eyes closed. Furtively Lyapo picked at the rope. Strand after strand severed and fell away until, just before dawn, the rope severed. Lyapo lay for a moment and then, his heart pounding, slowly, slowly, he slithered away from the coffle, down to the river. As he reached it the Yoruba shouted.

Lyapo cursed and grabbed at the canoe. It moved a yard or two, then halted. Lyapo fumbled frantically at the line which held it to the bank but by then the Benin men were on him.

The Benin men beat Lyapo. They did it methodically and scientifically, with slender canes so that Lyapo's valuable bones would not be broken. When they had finished they fettered his hands and feet, put a heavy weight around his neck, and chained him in the middle of another coffle.

Bowed down with iron, his back raw, Lyapo asked the Yoruba why he had called out.

'Why should you go free?' the Yoruba said.

'I am an Oyo man,' Lyapo said.

The man spat in the mud. 'Oyo is no more.'

'Yes.' Lyapo believed him. 'I don't know where we are going,' he said, 'but I promise you one thing. You will never get there.'

Lyapo's words came true, although not in the way he thought that they would. A day or so after the flogging the Benin men took their slaves down river in three huge canoes. At one stop, on a beach beneath a town perched on a cliff, the Benin men sold the man for salt and chickens. Lyapo watched the man being led away and wondered whether he was lucky or not. At least he was the slave of men, and not the pallid horrors which might be waiting for the rest of them at the end of their journey.

It was a long journey. The swollen river flowed on and on. The land changed. The plains were left behind. Trees became more frequent, huge cottonwoods and palas, festooned with vultures and drooping in the rain.

The trees became denser, crowding against the river in solid green walls, impenetrable and forbidding. Swallows skimmed the surface of the river, animals screamed in the forest, huge clouds of ants made their dying flight and fell into canoes.

The river changed again. Almost imperceptibly it became slower and more sluggish, turning from yellow to green, to black. There were gaps in the wall of forest as vague, meandering streams wandered from it. The trees themselves changed. Covered with heavy, dank moss they leaned sombrely over the river, fronds and creepers dipping from their branches into the black waters where purple and yellow snakes glided on their silent errands.

It was then that Lyapo gave up hope of returning to his home. The dank maze in which he found himself was as strange to him as the moon would have been. As the canoes found their way through black creeks and streams, and the birds called, he remembered the day the Dahomey men had found him by the Pool of the Leopards. He had believed then that he was a dead man and now he knew that truly Lyapo, that simple man with a wife and children, a voice in the village and a place by the fire, and a yam patch that the baboons raided, yes, that Lyapo *was* dead, as dead as if the Dahomey men had pinned him to the ground with their spears; and now, dead as he was, he was ready to enter the beckoning world of ghosts.

11

Nearing noon in Freetown, Sierra Leone, *Sentinel*, her sails reefed, rocking at her mooring in St George's Bay. Two hundred yards away *Dauntless* at her anchorage. Out towards the sandbank called the Middle Ground Her Majesty's brigs, *Firefly*, *Badger*, and *Pickle*. Inshore, by the King's Yard, *Esperanza* and *Nuestra Buena Fortuna*, slavers brought in for adjudication before the Court of Mixed Commission. Towering above them all, frigate and sloop, brigs and slavers, *HMS Hawke*, two decks, fifty guns, five hundred men, flagship of the West African squadron of the Royal Navy, a commodore's pennant drooping from her mizzenmast.

The African heat enshrouding harbour and town. On the waterfront sailors lurching from one shabby drinking-hole to another. *Sentinel*'s starboard watch, led by Dawlish and Smith, demanding to see the talking monkeys. A solitary canoe drifting across *Sentinel*'s stern, a man in it languidly offering fruit to Pike the steward who, leaning over the side, occasionally jetted tobacco juice at the vendor.

Eight black faces in *Sentinel*'s bows; Kroomen, strapping Africans taken on to assist in the heavy work on board and objects of superstitious concern to the crew. On the mainmast half a dozen men of the port watch, and Yetts, sprawled in the rigging panting for a breeze. Yetts staring enviously at the racketing sailors on shore.

'Look at 'em,' Yetts cried. 'All my mates on liberty and me confined to the ship. And for why? What for did the owner stop my liberty?'

'To stop you from awful sinning, that's why,' said Clayton, ordinary seaman and ardent Blue-Lighter. 'And because you was drunk.'

'But I wants to sin,' Yetts shouted with a deep, passionate conviction. 'I wants to get drunk again with my mates and I wants to gamble and get me a big fat —'

'Don't you say it, Jack Yetts,' Clayton yelped. 'It'll be straight to hell for you, strike me if it won't. And this heat ain't nothing to what you'll find down there in them everlasting flames what never go out — and where you won't get none of these mucky foreign fruits to suck, neither.'

'Don't fret yourself, Jack,' said Files, sailmaker's mate. 'You ain't missed much. There's nothing there but a few grog shops and about a million chapels.'

'It's all right you talking,' Yetts muttered, 'you've had your liberty. But look at that —' he waved his arm in disgust. 'My mates on shore, the owner and the first up at the governor's palace, even the mids is having a good time.'

His accusing finger pointed across the harbour to a long boat, in which John, Scott, and Fearnley were being given a tour of the harbour by a lordly midshipman off *Hawke*.

'And here,' the Hawke was saying, 'here is a sight I dare say you won't see in any other port in the world.'

He pointed to a wharf where a gang of Africans were languidly sawing a handsome schooner in half.

'Lord!' Fearnley said. 'What are they doing that for?'

'Well,' said the mid. 'That's a naughty old slave-ship, so it is. They are brought into Freetown and in there —' he gestured to a small pompous building on the waterfront — 'in there is the Court of Mixed Commission. There are two judges, an Englishman and a judge from the country the slaver reckons to sail from. They decide whether the ship is a legal prize — was really a slaver, that is. If they decide that it is then the ship is condemned. Now, children, once upon a time, officers in the Royal Navy who had money to spare used to buy the ships at auction, find a crew, and send them off to pick up more slavers. Our lords and masters in the Admiralty didn't like that, thinking it wasn't the action of officers and gentlemen, so now the ships are just sawn in half and sold off as lumber. But do not panic, little ones, we gets our prize money for them must the same.'

The suitably impressed Sentinels peered at the slipway as the longboat drifted past.

'And now,' the Hawke cried, 'we come to the King's Yard. This is where the freed slaves are kept until they can be resettled. On the left —'

As he spoke ship's bells rang across the harbour. 'Dinner time,' he sighed. 'Let us leave the slaves rejoicing in their freedom and return to *Hawke* where, in order to improve your manners, you are invited to dinner.'

The smell of mutton and peas drifted across the harbour, mingling with the rich odours from the land. On *Hawke*'s vast and spacious deck a whole file of scarlet marines clumped off to their dinner. A lieutenant, a mere fourth on such a vessel, smiled at John.

'And how long have you been at sea?'

A little self-consciously, John straightened himself. 'Four weeks, sir. And a week at harbour in Portsmouth.'

'Well, sir,' said the fourth. 'You are a lucky fellow, if I might say so. Oh yes,' he added as John raised his eyebrows. 'Captain Murray distinguished himself at the Battle of Navarino. Took a Turkish frigate almost single-handed. And your first was in the *Hampshire* when she pulled the *Comet* off the Goodwin Sands.' He peered down at John. 'The Goodwin Sands are very, *very* dangerous and there was a terrible gale blowing. Brooke swam through the surf and took a line on board *Comet*. Fifty men were saved. It was a most extraordinary, brave thing to do.'

John was astonished. That a man could be unpleasant and yet be brave, arrogant and yet be an expert in his craft, and admired by other experts, was a lesson he was still learning. He was thinking about it as the fourth, quite without seeming to, led him to the group of lordly Hawkes and humble Sentinels who were chatting together by the bell.

But that delicate touch John could appreciate. He had already noticed the contradiction of shiplife. On the one hand the rough, often brutal driving of men, officers and ratings alike, to their work, and on the other hand the easy good manners which sprang from the need of men living in close contact for long periods to rub along together.

The manners were maintained as the band of young men made room for John to join them. A steward in a white coat, as unlike Pike as one human being could possibly be from another, deftly pressed a glass of punch in John's hand and glided away as Fearnley — the *Honourable* Percival Townley Fearnley, that is, midshipman, five years at sea, wounded in action, sixteen years old, and by no means to be confused with his humble cousin in *Sentinel* — kept the conversational pot boiling.

'I was with your First in *Hecate* three years ago. Ain't his uncle Lord Keston?'

Humble Fearnley thought that he *might* be, humbler Potts was ready to swear his liver and lights that he was.

'Thought so,' said the superior Fearnley cheerfully. 'Old Keston has an estate next door to my father. He's a real old Tory, you know — Keston, that is — and they say he has Peel quite in his pocket. How does Mr Brooke get on with your owner? Captain Murray is a real Exeter Hall man, ain't he? Behold the poor African and all that. Is he not a man and your brother? I mean to

51

say, Tory meets Whig — bound to be sparks, eh?'

He looked around but met stony faces. Whatever the Sentinels thought about their officers they were not going to let the Hawkes know. They would no more have criticized their ship to outsiders than they would their own family. A loyalty to their ship and each other bound them together. It was another lesson for John that morning.

The Fourth sealed the slight breach. 'Whig or Tory,' he said, 'you must keep your watch just the same, and the rain falls on both. Still, the gods will squabble now and again, although today they are dining on Olympus.'

He pointed across the harbour. Peering over a line of trees on Mount Aureal was Government House where the gods of the squadron, the captains and first, were dining — if not with Zeus and Apollo, then with Governor Doherty and the Commodore.

At that moment the Commodore was doing his best to be agreeable to a faded and disagreeable missionary. 'No, sir', he was saying. 'I really don't know why sailors get tattooed. Perhaps Lieutenant Brooke might enlighten you.'

The missionary had no intention of being fobbed off with a mere lieutenant, but Daneleigh, the Commodore's Aide-de-Camp, came to the rescue.

'It comes from Tahiti, sir. I believe that the very first British sailor to be tattooed was a rating called Stainsby who sailed there with Captain Cook.'

'Stainsby, was it?' said Philips of *Firefly*. 'It's a strange way to achieve fame, having needles stuck into you.'

'Do the natives here tattoo themselves?' Brooke asked.

'Oh yes.' Like a relay runner taking up the baton, Bailey of *Pickle* picked up the conversation. 'The Egbas have a sort of necklace tattooed round their necks and you get the various tribal marks, cuts on the face, you know. . . .'

The conversation flowed easily on, every man at the table a past master at keeping up a ready flow of inoffensive talk, a skill acquired at countless mess-tables on countless ships over years of service.

The dinner courses came and went: soup, fish, mutton. The room got hotter and hotter, as if a madman was pumping steam into it. Sweat poured down yellow, malarial faces, wilting starched collars.

The Commodore mopped his face. 'I would give ten guineas for a bottle of iced champagne. Twenty guineas, by heaven.'

'Is there no ice here?' Murray asked.

'My dear sir!' The Commodore burst out laughing. 'Do you observe the climate?'

Murray leaned forward. 'I assure you, sir, that I am serious. I have bought ice in Calcutta where it is quite as hot as here. Yankee clippers bring it for a penny a pound. It is stored in great holes in the ground and keeps very well. The distance to here is very much less, and I am sure it would find a market. The Americans are such sharp dealers I am surprised they are not doing it.'

'I can answer that.' A dark, burly man at the far end of the table spoke up. 'On this coast there is no demand for anything but rum and muskets and there is no produce but human beings. That is your answer.'

There was a rumble from the Governor. 'Come, come, Captain Denman. There are many valuable products on the Coast: copal, palm oil, timber, coffee — I could name a dozen other articles the civilized world would be glad to have.'

'I do not doubt it,' Denman answered. 'Indeed I know it to be a fact. Why, a few years ago the Gallinas river, not a hundred miles from here, was a lively, prosperous place. Friendly people and a busy trade, quite as lively as some ports in Europe, I do assure you. Then what happens? The damned slavers arrive and within twenty years there is nothing but slaving taking place. The whole country for a hundred miles inland is a wasteland, and that devil Pedro Blanco ruling the roost. Believe me, sir, slavery smothers every other kind of trade whatsoever.'

'But why should that be?' Brooke asked.

'Profit,' the Governor said. 'It is quite simple. Men cost nothing to rear and they walk to market on their own two feet. All you have to do is to catch them. The profit on them is enormous, quite incalculable.'

Murray drummed on the table. 'But why don't the people resist?'

'Guns,' Denman said promptly. 'Muskets. It's interesting in a way. It used to be the inland tribes that were powerful, but now it's the small tribes on the coast. They have the whiphand because they are in touch with the slavers. They can get the guns and it's guns that count.'

The men around the table murmured assent. As much as any men on earth they knew that guns counted.

'But,' Brooke objected, 'but these tribes are warlike, are they not? They must be quite fearsome with their spears. After all, savages —'

Denman banged the table. 'Not savages, sir, and not very warlike either. They are not Zulus or Matabele. Most of our tribes are small farmers. They know as much about warfare as a Hampshire ploughboy. They have their own laws and customs and rubbed along pretty well until the slavers came.'

'You seem quite passionate on the subject,' Brooke said.

'I am,' Denman cried. 'I make no bones about it. It is the vilest trade that ever was in the history of the world. But we shall never stop it the way we are going on now. Patrolling won't stop your slavers running in, not with the profit they make. The only way to blot it out is to go inshore and burn the barracoons, the warehouses where they store the slaves. Wipe them out, and the devils who run them.'

There was a moment's silence, broken by the Commodore. 'Well, that's a question of policy and it isn't for us to decide that. We must leave policy to the politicians. Our job is to get on and do our duty. We need look no further than that.'

No one dissented. Duty was the word. It was what bound them together, and kept them going. And if any man did *not* do his duty the Royal Navy would sniff him out and eject him.

'Well, gentlemen?' The Governor stood up. 'I'm afraid all good things must come to an end. . . .'

His guests rose, expressed their thanks, made their farewells, slithered through the red mud of Freetown's roads to their ships, to their duty. All except Murray. The Commodore took him by the arm.

'Come along with me, Captain. I think we should have a word together before you go.'

The pomp and splendour of a flagship receiving its Commodore. Sideboys in white gloves, marines, officers . . . the ship mute; as Jehovah, followed by Murray and Daneleigh, tramped across the deck and down to his great cabin. Murray was offered wine which he refused, and tea which he accepted.

The Commodore slumped in a chair by the huge stern window. 'To business, and it can be a dirty one, Captain. No Trafalgars for us, I'm afraid. Still, we must stick at it. Are you ready for sea?'

'Quite ready, sir.' *Sentinel* had in fact been ready for sea within eight hours of her arrival in Freetown.

'Very good. Now, I think that none of your officers has

experience of this work. This is most unfortunate.'

Murray shrugged. 'My original first lieutenant was an experienced man, but at the last moment the Admiralty thought fit to replace him with Lieutenant Brooke.'

The Commodore glanced sharply across the cabin. 'You have no complaints against Mr Brooke?'

'No, sir.' Murray's face was impassive. 'He is a most competent officer.'

'I see. Well, we can give you an officer who knows the business, Daneleigh?'

'Bower, sir. He brought the *Esperanza* in. He is off *Tally*. She's down at the end of your beat, I dare say you will bump into her down there.'

Murray sipped his tea. 'Thank you. He will be a great help.'

'You will need all that,' the Commodore grunted. He had turned in his seat and was gazing through the cabin window. Grey clouds were gathering over the mountains. It was a little cooler. 'Now. You've been over the slavers, so you know what to look for if you meet one without slaves on board: extra-large cooking pots, water-butts too big for her needs, timber for a slave deck, chains — all things to look for, you know. If you do take a ship, send her in for adjudication. If you are lucky she might even be condemned.'

'And if I'm not lucky?'

The Commodore smiled. 'You could find yourself with a very large bill for damages.'

'And don't forget,' Daneleigh added, 'while you are waiting for the court's decision you pay for the keep of the slaves. It's just another little encouragement for us to do our job.'

'I see.' Murray said. 'I assure you that will not stop me doing my duty.'

A few drops of rain splashed on the window. Within seconds they had become a torrent, slashing at the glass and hissing on the harbour waters. It had become very dark. A steward hurried in and lighted lanterns. Immediately they were surrounded by clouds of insects.

'Evening rains,' the Commodore said. 'Surprising how they come at the same time every day. Not pleasant — which reminds me, your men are not to spend a night ashore. Admiralty orders. It's because of the fevers. The coast is full of them. It is the bad air, they say, *mal air* — malaria we call it.' He shook his head. 'This is a terrible place, terrible. We lose more men by disease than the rest

55

of the Royal Navy put together. But I mustn't dishearten you. You don't look disheartened, I must say.'

'No,' said Murray. 'I am not disheartened. Moses was not disheartened in the wilderness, nor was Elihu when he marched out against the might of the Philistines. And after all, do we not sail under a cross?'

'A cross?'

'Our ensign, sir. It carries a cross.'

'Yes.' The Commodore and Daneleigh exchanged glances. Daneleigh gave a little cough, the discreet naval cough.

'Captain, I think the Commodore would like to warn you about ships flying American colours.'

'Quite, quite.' The Commodore shook himself like a great dog. 'Now, Murray, you show . . . zeal . . . commendable — most admirable — meritorious, but, *but*, be very careful with any craft under American colours. Be very careful indeed. The rest don't matter but the Americans do. Clear?'

It was quite clear. Murray knew perfectly well that the Americans did not allow their ships to be stopped by a foreign power. They had gone to war with Britain over just that point in 1812, and the Royal Navy had one or two bloody noses to remember it by.

'But still,' Murray opened his hands. 'You don't mean to say that if I come across a slaver flying American colours I can do nothing? Not even board her?'

He stared incredulously at the Commodore, whose gaze was fixed on the ceiling. 'Sir, that would mean that any rascal could run up the Stars and Stripes and roam the seas as free as a bird.'

Daneleigh coughed again. 'It is illegal for an American ship to deal in slaves but they maintain that their own warships will deal with them.'

'How many vessels do they have on patrol?'

'At the moment . . . none.'

There was a silence. Quite a long, thoughtful silence. The Commodore laughed sharply. 'Did you ever hear the story, Captain, of the man who was ordered never to drink alcohol? No? Well, he went into a public house and asked for a glass of water. The barman asked if he wanted brandy in it. The man said no, he didn't, then turned his back. Of course, he said, if you were to put a drop in without me knowing, that would be different.'

The Commodore paused. The rain drummed on the deck. Insects crackled and flared in the lantern, something squeaked and scuffled in the bulkhead.

'Quite different,' the Commodore said. 'Sail tomorrow, if you please.'

Daneleigh accompanied Murray to the ship's gangway. 'I will bring your written orders over tomorrow, but you will be at the end of the beat, in the Bight of Benin. Most of the action is down there nowadays. There is one other thing you might like to know.'

'Yes?' Murray turned, the yellow light of the ship's lights picking out his hard features.

'Some of these slavers are hard cases, and we have heard of a fast clipper that came out from Havana. She has a bucko Yankee skipper called Kimber and he has been heard to say that if he meets a British man-o'-war he will blow her out of the water.'

'I hope to meet her,' Murray said. 'I profoundly hope to meet her. What is her name?'

'They call her *Phantom*,' Daneleigh said. 'The *Phantom*. Good-night, sir.'

Bower arrived at the crack of dawn the next morning. A stocky young lieutenant with two years' service on the coast under his belt. Murray renamed the head Krooman, refusing to have him called Frying-pan and naming him Noah, for he had a delicate repugnance to giving a heathen a name from the New Testament. Thomas Atwell, gunner's mate, found a spider in the bread-room, a truly appalling spider, as big as a plate and with more hair on it than the bosun, causing a minor panic among the crew.

Daneleigh came over with Murray's orders: '"You are to patrol the area between longitude four degrees east and ten degrees east, diligently looking into and searching the several creeks and lagoons, apprehending any vessel or vessels which, in our judgement, are indulging in or are about to indulge in, or have indulged in, the trading of slaves . . . and herein fail not at your peril, et cetera, et cetera."'

'A mere five hundred miles of coast,' Daneleigh said, smiling. 'Good luck, sir, and good hunting.'

Daneleigh away, the anchor cleared, the tide drawing *Sentinel* out to sea, following *Dauntless*'s wake, and bound for the Bight of Benin.

12

Two thousand miles from *Sentinel* the Benin men were edging out of the maze of lagoons. The arching trees unclasped their boughs. The water of the stream was brackish. The stream itself widened into a river. There seemed to be small islands on the river, small islands with slender trees on them. Then Lyapo realized that one of the islands was moving and that there were men on it. The Benin men took their canoe downstream past one of the islands and Lyapo realized that it was a boat, a canoe, an enormous canoe with huge poles sticking up from it. He shook his head and looked away and saw a muddy bank with a stockade of logs jutting from it like teeth from the jaws of a dead man.

At one end of the stockade was a tower with a man in it. As the Benin men drew near he raised a long brass trumpet and blew a wailing call. Men in red robes came from a gate, carrying muskets. One raised his gun and fired it into the air. The Benin men back-paddled and one of them stood up and called across the river. Another musket banged and the slavers took their canoe into the bank.

What happened next was familiar. Lyapo was prodded and poked, his teeth were examined and his eyes. Then he was driven inside the stockade and chained to a long rail which ran the length of a huge hut.

Lyapo knew that he had been sold again but it did not matter to him. He was already dead and what happened to him was beyond his control. Only his brothers in the fetish society could help him. Only they could make him rest. But he didn't even worry about that. Since he was dead it did not matter.

There were many other ghosts in the stockade. Hundreds of them. The male ghosts were chained to the rail, the women ghosts and the children wandered about freely. Near Lyapo was the ghost of another Yoruba. It spoke to Lyapo. It said, 'Brother, let us break our chains and kill the guards and escape.'

Lyapo laughed. He was amused at the thought of a ghost speaking so to another ghost. But the Yoruba was angry. 'Don't you understand?' it cried. 'We are going to be sold to white men. They will take us far away and eat us. Do you want to be eaten?' But Lyapo just laughed again. What was the point in talking to a ghost?

The next few days were strange ones for Lyapo. Sometimes he was hot, so hot that he thought he was burning. Then he felt cold. His bones ached and he shivered and moaned. Often he floated in the air, high over the stockade and the forest. Everywhere he looked he saw lines of captives, endless lines of men and women, in canoes or creeping through the forest, all in chains and all weeping. High in the air, Lyapo waved at them. He waved and called, asking if any of the captives had seen his wife, but none of them ever had.

As he shook and sweated in the barracoon, as the fever shook him so that he trembled from head to toe and his teeth rattled, Lyapo remembered the little green snake and then he understood why there were so many ghosts. A dead man could only be put to rest by having his name spoken at the shrine of the fetish. But the snake had told him that the pots of the Yoruba would be smashed and their sacred trees cut down. If the shrines were destroyed then the dead could never be put to rest. Even a ghost could understand that.

Lyapo was treated well, for a ghost. The owner of the barracoon, a slave-dealer who was half Spanish and half Ibo and whose mother had been a slave, gave orders that he was to be well treated. He was unchained and wrapped in a good woollen blanket from Yorkshire, and a woman brought him chicken and palm-wine. After all, Lyapo was a very valuable animal.

After a last, rending shake, the fever left Lyapo. He awoke to find the barracoon almost empty. A few relics were left, a dozen or so listless, sickly slaves. But Lyapo, although weak, was clear-headed. No longer a ghost but a man, a man in shackles, a man without a wife or home, owned by other men, but still a man.

The barracoon filled again. Slaves were brought in, ones and twos, dozens, hundreds, chained to the pole, given cassava and plantains, flogged perhaps, until their time came and they were driven through the gates of the stockade, down the muddy bank, into canoes, and down to where the forest and the river ended.

Lyapo's turn came as well. Down the river he went in a canoe full of terror and tears and mourning. The river widened, the banks fell away, and Lyapo heard a noise. It was a strange noise, a roar, like the cry of an animal; but muted, distant, perhaps more like a sigh than a roar, and perhaps more like the passing of the wind in the trees than either. Except that there were no trees. Instead there was a stretch of still water and beyond that a line of white surf crashing on a sandbar — and beyond that, nothing.

Lyapo thought that he was looking at a hole in the earth, for beyond the surf was merely that vast grey expanse which went on for ever. He was afraid that the canoe would go into the hole but it swerved and turned a little. Lyapo saw that at the edge of the still water was a canoe, but a huge canoe, like the floating islands he had seen on the river. This canoe, too, had poles sticking upwards from it, poles bigger than the tallest tree Lyapo had ever seen, and with white cloth hanging from them.

The slavers tied up against this vast vessel and, in a welter of blows and curses, the slaves were driven up a ladder. Lyapo was the first on board and as he stood on deck, weak, shaken, terrified, he saw an awful thing. Something was looking at him, tall and thin with pallid skin and the head of a bird, a huge beak, and yellow fur on top of its skull; and staring bleakly forward, two terrible blue eyes.

13

Sentinel two weeks out from Freetown. The Grain Coast left behind, Cape Palmas rounded, and the ship beating down the Ivory Coast. To port, the unvarying strip of forest unreeling and the Atlantic surf roaring on the beach, day and night.

Days of heat and boredom, and never a sail in sight. Sudden torrential rains, implacable sun. The huge, glossy-brown cockroaches which had joined up in Freetown swarming everywhere. Another giant spider found in the fo'c's'le. Ginger and Tiger killing rat after rat by the water-butt but the rats still multiplying.

Stupefying days, but good ones for John. Time for him to learn his craft; learn the ship from clew to earing, stem to stern, and every rope and spar on her. And his books, too. Keverne a good teacher: tables of latitude and longitude, sines, cosines, trigonometry, the tables of the stars, the use of the sextant. John an apt pupil, enjoying mathematics and navigation, catching up on Fearnley, overtaking Scott, and leaving Potts in his wake.

Supernatural nights. Vast stars and a sea dripping crimson with phosphorescence, lightning forever flickering on the horizon. In the bows Martin Docherty, late of County Armagh and Her Majesty's prison, Liverpool, playing the accordian to an appreciative audience of Kroomen. In the waist, lying on a coil of rope, Bob Carlin, carpenter's mate, a Blue-lighter but much respected for his steadiness, waved a horny hand at the heavens.

'The wonder of God's handiwork,' he said. 'Behold it and then tell me there ain't no Creator, Zeb Dawlish.'

'Which I've never denied, Bob,' said Dawlish, easily. 'Which I wouldn't even *like* to hear denied.'

'Then why don't you come to Jesus?' demanded Jimmy Grey, Able Seaman. 'Get rid of that dunnage of sin you're carrying about so that you're weighed down port and starboard and can't steer a straight course.'

'Yes, Zeb,' Carlin said. 'Do a bit of praying and holy reading. I've got a little book what's specially written for mariners.'

'Well, I'll tell you what,' Dawlish said. 'I ain't much of a one for reading. Books is a lee shore for me. But why don't you go and do a bit of converting with them Kroomen over there.'

'Which I'm going to do,' Carlin said earnestly. 'They speaks a bit of English and it says in the Gospel, preach the word to all nations. That's when the disciples was sent out to foreign parts,' he added helpfully.

'Well, you're in luck then,' said Smith, 'seeing as how you've got the heathen on board with you. Go on, now. Let's see you start.'

Carlin grinned. 'You wouldn't have me disturb men listening to a bit of music, would you?'

''Fraid they'll eat you?'

'Now, now.' Carlin shook his head. 'Don't make a mock of them. They seem a decent set of lads. Ready and willing.'

'I'll give 'em that,' Smith said. 'But looky here. I thought them blackies was all slaves and treated something cruel. But in that Freetown they was walking about the same as you and me. Some of them had got shops!'

'What about that, Bob?' Yetts asked.

Carlin shoved an enormous plug of tobacco in his mouth. 'If you'd come along to the prayer meetings now and then,' he said indistinctly, 'you'd have heard what the owner told us. There ain't no slaves there in Sierra Leone. Them blacks is what the Navy's gone and freed. They gets taken there and given a bit of land.'

'Why don't they send the buggers back home?' a voice demanded.

Carlin turned. 'If you'd got the brains of a mackerel, you wouldn't ask that. What's the good of sending them home? They'd just get made slaves again, wouldn't they?'

'Aye.' Yetts stretched. 'Well, when are we going to catch some of them slavers, that's what I wants to know.'

There was a murmur of agreement but Carlin shook his head. 'There ain't no slaving along this coast. The slavers is all round what they call Lagos and the Oil Rivers. All this stretch got cleaned up by the Navy, so the slavers has to go east. And that's where we picks 'em up.'

'*If* we pick 'em up.' Yetts said, '*and* if we don't pick up a mouthful of that mal air first.'

'Don't worry, Jack,' Smith said. 'You've breathed worse in Limehouse.'

The moon disappeared behind a cloud. Rain swept the crew below deck. An inky night and lightning flashing on the horizon. The crew beat their hammocks, fearful of finding a spider there waiting for them. Dawn, grey and melancholy. Off the port beam

62

Cape Three Points, and to starboard a ship.

Intense excitement. Even the hardest case left his hammock to line the rails. Dawlish, eagle-eyed, declared her to be a brig, French-built and worth five hundred pounds easy, not counting her cargo.

The brig was remarkably coy, showing no signs of wishing closer acquaintance with *Sentinel*. In fact, in a clumsy, lubberly, dago sort of way she began to reach out for the south as if looking for sea-room.

'Give him a gun, Mr Brooke,' Murray snapped.

Hayes lumbered for'ard. The long bow-chaser cracked out its flat challenge: heave to — or else.

Even then the brig showed an inclination to run, but *Sentinel*'s bigger spread of sail took her down upon it. In less than an hour she was in long-hailing distance, her mainsail was down, and she hove to, as submissive as a puppy.

'Eight hundred quid,' said Dawlish. 'Two months' pay. Say two hundred slaves on board, another thousand — three months' pay. And all for free.'

Not the dreams of avarice perhaps, but enough to make your pocket bulge for all that. Plans to spend it rife already, from Brooke who rather fancied a new cocked hat to John Rose thinking of a gigantic, comprehensive booze-up — and all to be dashed as a clear, English voice hailed them from the brig.

The voice issued from the lungs of Hugh Byam, sixteen years old, midshipman HMS *Wicklow*, who, when Murray and Brooke climbed aboard, heaved a sigh of relief — as well he might, having command of the *Lustra*: slaver, caught red-handed, and carrying on board one hundred and eighty restless slaves, a prize crew of six (three down with fever), and, battened down in the fo'c's'le, nine villainous slavers breathing fire and brimstone.

The fire and brimstone were extinguished abruptly as Dawlish, Smith, Rose, and the mighty Rafferty went below and knocked the slavers down like nine-pins, their blasphemies offending Murray's ears and hence, by extension, his crew's; but a little sulphur smoked on the deck as Murray glowered at Byam.

'Why did you not heave to at once?' he demanded. 'You heard my gun and saw our colours.'

'Yes, sir, but, I beg your pardon, sir, out here — it pays to be careful.'

'Explain yourself,' Murray snapped.

'Well, sir. You could have been a slaver, sir. They fly what colours they wish, they would fly the flag of the Swiss Navy if they felt like it. And if you was, sir — a slaver, I mean — I couldn't have done much to stop you taking the vessel, sir. It has happened.'

Murray was somewhat mollified. 'Where was she taken?'

'Coming out of Lagos lagoon, sir.'

'And what colours did she have then?'

Byam smiled. 'Oh, American, sir.'

'But you took her?'

'Oh yes, sir. We could see a crowd of dagos on board.'

'And did she have American papers?'

'Yes, sir.'

'But what did you do then?' Murray asked.

Byam's smile broadened into a grin. 'Chucked 'em overboard, sir.'

'Chucked —!' Murray was staggered. 'You threw her papers — but —'

'They all have them, sir,' Byam said. 'They have two sets of papers, their own and Yankee. They get them in Havana. Usually they have a Jonathan on board who pretends he's the master, but you can tell. It's experience — begging your *pardon*, sir.'

'Well bless my soul,' Murray said.

A busy morning. Every man on *Sentinel* being taken over to see a slave-ship with your actual slaves on it — and coming back grim-faced, even Brooke. Even Taplow.

Only Bower was unmoved. 'It's quite a good vessel,' he said. 'And only a hundred-odd slaves. I've seen craft smaller than that with twice as many blacks on board — and with Yellow Jack loose.'

The ships parting, parting, a cable-length, a mile, ten, gone. *Sentinel* about her business, beating down the coast. Day succeeding day. Freak weather, contrary winds, and only the steady current moving *Sentinel* at all.

More days slipping away, time creeping past on leaden feet. The ship's bell, thirty minutes which passed like thirty hours, another bell: men yawning in the waist, in the bows, on the quarterdeck, in the masts; the ship yawing to and frow, and Keverne looking up from the charts, looking down again, smiling a little and going on deck to announce that *Sentinel* had arrived in the Bight of Benin.

Fever on board. A dozen men shaking in their hammocks,

Fearnley one day saying, 'My word,' and going down as if pole-axed and so the Navy placing its hard shoulder on John and using him instead and, among the dizzy spars, as Brooke's rasping voice drove him on, so John learned to drive others; if not wearing the uniform of command, at least touching its hem. But it was in the hold, on all fours, that he first tasted the ambivalent flavour of true command.

As the days had reeled away and food and water were consumed, the balance of the ship altered slightly. To get the best from *Sentinel* her stores needed to be altered a little. Doing that was a thankless, wearisome task, and two of the worst men on board were told off for the job — they and John.

John scrambled down into the hold followed by Keeley, an insolent ruffian, and Green, a gangling near-idiot. The hold was less than five feet high, crammed with barrels of pork and beef and flour and lighted only by the smokey glow of an oil-lamp. It was suffocatingly hot and from the foul water in the bilge beneath them drifted a sewer smell, made worse because a barrel of pork had sprung a leak and a disgusting, stinking mess of foul liquid had oozed from it.

Within minutes John was covered in filth and dripping with sweat. Ruefully he thought of his visions of officers in immaculate blue and gold, posing elegantly on a snowy quarter-deck. . . . To make matters worse, as he tugged and heaved at the barrels with splintered finger-nails, and as the rats squeaked and scrabbled in the darkness, he knew that the men were idling and he was not very sure of his ability to make them work harder. Of course he could report them to Brooke but that would not get the job done any quicker, and he now knew enough about the Navy to understand that running whining to a superior officer was no way to gain respect — from either the men or the officers. No, *leading from the front* was the Navy's answer; the willing, cheerful acceptance of responsibility and a readiness to put your own back into the hardest work. Which was all very well, but what happened when you did — as he was doing now — but the men did not follow your example?

He turned around. Keeley was sprawled on the deck and Green was grinning vacantly at him. Trying to force his voice into a baritone, John growled, 'Get up here and lay into your work.'

Keeley sighed, insolently, and slowly crawled forward.

'Jump to it!' John's voice cracked a little.

On all fours, Keeley glared at John like an enormous dog in a kennel. 'It's a bit awkward getting past you, like . . . sir.'

John leaned back and Keeley and Green shoved forward and, in a desultory way, began tugging at a barrel.

'We ought to have made a whipping for this,' Keeley said.

'Never mind a whipping,' John cried, horribly aware that he did not know what a whipping was. 'Just get on with it.'

Keeley shrugged his bare shoulders and muttered something to Green, who sniggered idiotically.

'What was that?' John demanded. 'What?'

Keeley turned, insolence and contempt on his hard face. 'Just said there's a right old stink down here.'

It was a blatant lie, and John knew it, but what he didn't know was what action he should take. Almost without thinking he blurted out, 'Stow your gab. Any more talk from you and I'll have you up before the captain. Now get on with it.'

Keeley gave John a long challenging look, then turned and heaved at the barrel. As he did so he muttered a curse and scrambled backwards.

'For Christ's sake!' John's voice cracked with rage. 'What is it now?'

Keeley moved further back. 'There's something behind that barrel,' he said. 'It ran over me.'

'A rat,' John said. 'Don't try telling me you're afraid of a rat.'

''Twarn't no rat,' Keeley muttered, licking his lips. ''Twas some bloody crawly thing.'

A pulse flickered in John's temple. 'Don't say you're afraid of a God-damned insect.'

'Yes I am.' Keeley rubbed his face. 'Anyway, it warn't no ordinary insect. 'Twas a bloody great thing as big as a rug.'

John took a deep breath. 'Are you going to move that barrel?'

Keeley shook his head. 'No,' he said, flatly.

'All right.' John gave up. 'We'll have the first down here then.'

He began to crawl to the hatch, but as he did so Keeley said: 'If an insect's nothing to be afraid of, why don't you move the barrel?'

And that held John. There was a basic justice in that demand which he could not ignore. It was, in fact, what the Navy meant by leading from the front, if anything did. The trouble was that John was genuinely horrified by large insects, and absolutely horrified by huge spiders. Those already found on board had given him bad dreams and the thought of facing one on his kness, in the shadows behind the barrels, was worse than his worst nightmares come true. But Keeley's eyes were on him, and

Green's too. His mouth as dry as a kiln, and his heart pounding, John picked up a loose stave. 'All right,' he said. 'All right. Move that barrel and I'll get the bloody thing.'

For a moment Keeley paused, his eyes on John. Then, slowly, he reached a long arm and tilted the barrel towards him and from the shadow darted a *thing*, a horror, a nightmare of dank fur and too many legs and an air of appalling alertness. John's stomach heaved as he raised his stave, slashed at the horror, and missed. He struck again as it scuttled sideways, caught something pulpy — and again, and again, then turned away, bile and vomit dribbling from his lips.

'There's your God-damned insect,' he spat. 'Now move those barrels or I'll have your back flayed off you.'

Keeley stared at him, then nodded. 'Right you are, sir,' he said, and heaved the barrel clear as if it was made of paper. And as he did so, as he moved his bulk, John saw, by the hatch, the cold face of Brooke.

An hour later, the work done, John had washed and changed and was standing in the waist of the ship, still trembling a little, when Brooke called him aft. John stood obediently before the first who, as ever, stared bleakly into some mysterious space known only to him.

'You have a certain horror of insects, do you not?' Brooke said.

John's gorge rose again. 'Yes, sir.'

'Yes.' Brooke nodded, fractionally. 'Tell me, did those two worthless idlers give you any trouble in the hold?'

'No, sir.'

'You have no wish to bring any charges against them?'

'No, sir.'

'Very well.' Brooke nodded a dismissal but, as John moved away, he gave a little cough. 'I have no great love of insects myself, Mr Spencer. Good night to you.'

An enormous moon rising over Africa. Its steady, tranquil light shining on the darkness of desert and savannah, on rivers, lakes, swamps, mountains, and forests, on its creatures, prowling or sleeping, and on all the people of its immensity; the living and the dead, the oppressed and the oppressor, slaver and slave.

The moon rising higher, trailing a glittering finger across the delta of the Oil Rivers, touching a black slave-ship lying in a green lagoon, dappling five hundred miles of ocean, and resting a silver finger on the sails of *Sentinel*.

Hardly a man below deck, both watches sprawled in the waist, the quarterdeck crowded, and over the whole ship a sour whiff of discontent.

In his cabin Murray reached out for the ship's journal. As he removed it a cockroach darted from the bookshelf. Murray clicked his teeth with disgust. There seemed no possible way of ridding the ship of the insects, nor of the rats. Even the best efforts of Ginger and Tiger, and a bounty of twopence for ten tails, could not keep them down.

He was well aware of the discontent on board, and he knew very well what was causing it. Heavy, endless labour was one cause. In the fickle, fitful breezes, coming from this quarter and from that and never the same two minutes together, the crew was never at rest; forever trimming the sails, adjusting the spars, heaving and hauling on ropes. Back-breaking toil, wearing the men's nerves thin. And boredom. Boredom and hard work and all in the sticky, humid heat which did not even dry out of the men's clothes. It was a good job the Kroomen were on board. Their labour had been invaluable.

He opened the journal. Another flat, obscene insect scuttled from its damp pages. The entries, written up from the rough log in Fearnley's best copperplate, told the ship's story: changed sail, shifted sail, light airs, changed sail, variable winds, altered sail. And punishments were mounting. Three men in irons for drunkenness, five men waiting to go into irons for insolence, refusing an order, fighting, and another man flogged for striking the bosun's mate.

In the dim light of the lantern Murray's face was grim. The punishments were cracks in the tight unity of the ship, and the cracks were becoming bigger. One of the names in the journal was of an ardent member of the prayer-group, and it was there for drunkenness. He closed the journal and replaced it in the book-rack. As he did so there was a long, quavering cry from the mast-head, someone roared on the deck, there was a clatter and crash of feet outside his cabin, a bang on the door, and John rushed in.

Murray raised his eyebrows, his face impassive.

'Sir,' John could hardly get the words out. 'Sir, strange sail in sight!'

'Oh?' Murray leaned back in his chair. 'I thought perhaps the ship was on fire. Now report properly.'

John went bright red. 'Sir, Mr Cawley's compliments and there is a strange sail reported.'

'That is better,' Murray said. 'Do not run, Mr Spencer. Running leads to confusion. Orders become garbled. Suppose you had fallen down the companionway and broken your neck? The report would not have reached me. Now be so good as to report to Mr Cawley that I shall be with him directly.'

'Aye aye, sir. Thank you, sir.' John slowly backed away. Murray waited a moment or two, then deliberately climbed on deck.

In the few minutes which had passed the atmosphere had changed as if a fresh nor'-easterly had blown away any disaffection. The crew was on its feet and there was an excited buzz.

Cawley stepped from the shadow of the mizzen-mast into the silver of the moonlight and touched his cap.

'Mast-head reported a sail, sir. Ten points on the starboard beam.'

'Has anyone else seen it?'

'No, sir.'

'Very well, bring the look-out down. Mr Scott, up to the mast-head — you too, Mr Spencer.'

The mids raced up the shrouds as the look-out plummeted down the backstay. Murray looked at him closely. He was called Rogers, a responsible, middle-aged seaman.

'Quite sure you saw a sail, Rogers?'

Rogers touched his forehead. 'Sure as can be, sir. 'Twas just a flicker but it looked like a sail. It was up moon, sir.'

'Distance?'

Rogers paused, thinking before he spoke. 'Couldn't rightly say, sir. On the horizon, sir.'

Murray turned away. From his mast-head, a hundred feet up, the visible horizon was thirty miles. But still up moon, and with such a moon, and a blaze of stars, and to starboard, looking out to sea, it was conceivable that the flicker of a sail might be spotted by a sharp look-out.

'Ask Mr Scott to report,' he said.

Potts bellowed and Scott's voice answered from the blackness. 'Nothing, sir.'

Murray leaned against the bulwark and considered. Taking the ship in search of a vessel which might or might not exist meant sailing off his course and, more importantly, having to claw his way back on to it. But there was no real doubt in his mind. Nothing could be better for the morale of the crew than to come up with a ship, any ship. Even a chase would be good. . . .

'Bring her head round, Mr Cawley,' he ordered. 'Let's find her.' Then, the only man on board to do so, he went below to his humid cabin and the cockroaches, for it would never do for the Captain to be seen suffering from such human weaknesses as curiosity, excitement, and impatience.

Sentinel crept through the night. The maddening little breezes called cat's-paws played teasing games among the sails, and the watch on deck, willing enough now, pattered up and down the chequered decks trimming the yards. The moon reached her zenith, began to fall, crossed *Sentinel*'s stern. The deck emptied, the watch changed, men slept, the stars in the east began to fade.

Brooke took over the dawn watch. Heavy ochreous clouds were massing over the sullen sea. Potts handed over the watch.

'We've lost her, sir,' he said.

Rain came, lashing the sea into a froth, reducing visibility to a hundred yards. Wrapped in his tarpaulin by the for'ard mast, Dawlish wiped his face. 'We've lost her,' he growled.

Under his feet in the gun room Keverne, eating a breakfast of mouldy ship's-biscuit, shook his head. 'We've lost her,' he said.

Pike took the Captain's breakfast in. 'No butter, sir,' he said, 'no milk, the bread's all green, that bacon smells terrible. And we've lost her — if she was ever there. Sir.'

Murray ate in a gloomy silence. Rain hammered on the deck and that, too, seemed to be saying, 'You've lost her, you've lost her.' And the bacon *was* bad.

There was a muffled cough outside. The door crept open and John appeared. In a sepulchral voice, as if he were trying to set the world's record for speaking slowly, he said: 'Mr — Brooke's — com — pliments — sir — and — there — is — a — strange — sail — in — sight, — if — you — please — sir.'

The ship was a two-masted schooner without a flag. She was lying about six miles off, half hidden by scudding rain.

'Beat to quarters, Mr Brooke,' Murray said, more for the sake of giving the crew practice than from any thought of serious action. The drum rattled, the crew raced to their battle-stations, and there was about them a touch of swagger, a sense of *élan* as the men felt for the first time what they truly were — the crew of a man-o'-war.

At no great pace *Sentinel* stole down on the schooner. For John, at his station at six and seven guns, the pace was maddeningly slow, but no power on earth could make the wind blow faster. Standing on tiptoe, clicking his fingers, John began to acquire the greatest of all sailor's gifts, the talent for patience.

A mile slid away. Every telescope was trained on the schooner and there were puzzled faces on the quarterdeck.

'They're a set of lubbers,' Cawley said. 'Look at her mainsail, it's hanging like washing on a line. They'll lose it if they don't watch out. What's the matter with them?'

'Drunk most likely,' Keverne said. 'Look at that!' The schooner bucked suddenly and set her masts shivering. 'She'll carry all away.'

'Whoever they are they're no more sailors than a pack of Shoreditch tailors.' Brooke snapped. 'What does that man at the wheel think he's up to? Can't he see our signal?'

Murray was thinking the same thing. 'Give her a shot across her bows,' he said. 'Let's see if they're deaf, too.'

The long eighteen cracked out. A ball whistled across the mile separating the two ships and splashed a hundred yards ahead of the schooner's bows. The man at the wheel turned his head. Another man came on the deck, stumbled to the rail, and waved.

'Drunk.' Murray clapped his telescope to. 'Mr Brooke, please go over and look at that ship. Take six men and Mr Bower. Any resistance and you may use force.'

The jolly-boat was brought alongside; six men, your real hard-case, on-report brawlers, cutlasses slung over scarred shoulders, swarmed over the side. Bower and Brooke followed them. The oars were unshipped and the boat splashed away from under the shadow of *Sentinel*'s guns.

Absolute silence on *Sentinel* as the boat drew alongside the schooner, every eye on Brooke as he went over the side. The man at the rail lurched forward and grabbed at Brooke, hard-case Rose felled him with a blow. Two more Sentinels grabbed the man at the wheel, others dived below deck. . . .

'What the deuce —?' Cawley said. The Sentinels were moving about the deck of the schooner in a confused manner and Brooke was making strange gestures.

'Take her in,' Murray snapped.

The quartermaster spun the wheel and *Sentinel* swung in to the schooner.

'What is it, Mr Brooke?' Murray hailed.

Brooke cupped his hands and leaned over the side of the

schooner, 'Blind,' he yelled. 'They are all blind, sir.'

'Blind!' Murray drummed his fingers on the ledge of his cabin window. Half a mile away, a safe half a mile, the schooner — *Nuestra Señora del Mar* — lay hove-to, trailing a sea anchor.

'Yes, sir,' Brooke, his face paler than it had been an hour previously sipped some claret. 'Eight men on board, seven stone-blind and one nearly so. He was the one at the wheel. They are Spanish, out of Rio, but the master speaks English.'

'My God,' Murray said. 'My God.'

'Yes, sir. Just what I felt.'

'But two hundred miles from land . . . and the whole crew! Have some more wine.'

Murray was as shaken as Brooke. He peered through the window at the schooner. 'Jessup should be back, soon. Perhaps he can tell us something. You say she had called in somewhere?'

'Yes, sir. She sailed from Brazil and went into Whydah. She picked up a dozen slaves there, then sailed for Bonny. She took another fifteen on board and was going on to Brass for more when she ran into one of our cruisers. She slipped into a creek and unloaded the slaves but the cruiser sent her boats in after her. Anyway, she cut and ran and got clear — she's a fast vessel, sir. But then their eyes started to go. She tried to beat back to the coast, but it was too late. They've been drifting for a week.'

Murray raised his arm in a queer, sacramental gesture. 'Drifting and blind. Imagine it! Well, I see Mr Jessup is coming back.'

Jessup, portly, breathless, was heaved on board, squeezed into the cabin, and accepted a glass of claret.

'It's blindness, sir. No doubt about it. The corneas are seriously affected.'

'I —' Murray was about to say, I see, but decency prevented him. 'Yes, but what is the disease which causes it?'

Jessup coughed, not a discreet, naval cough, but a portentous medical one. 'Ophthalmia, sir. I make no doubt about it. Ophthalmia.'

'And what,' Brooke asked, 'what does that mean?'

'Why, why —' Jessup puffed a little. 'It means damage to the cornea.'

'Blindness, you mean.'

There was a cold silence for a moment. Jessup mopped his brow. 'I can only say what I know. These tropical diseases . . .

there are things we have only just begun to understand.'

'Yes.' There was an edge to Brooke's voice which suggested that he would not be at all surprised if there were things about *European* diseases Jessup did not understand.

Murray frowned. 'But surely in England people suffer from this disease.'

'Yes, sir,' Jessup said. 'But diseases differ.'

'And is the disease infectious?'

'Highly so,' Jessup said. 'Most highly so.'

'And how does it spread?'

Jessup spread his hands helplessly. 'We really do not know, sir.'

'Mr Jessup,' Murray was impatient. 'I need to know more than that. Do men ever recover from the disease? They do? Good. Now what can we do to make that vessel safe?'

Jessup was unexpectedly prompt. 'Burn her.'

'Burn her!' Murray was profoundly shocked. 'Mr Jessup, I am taking that ship as a prize, but until she is legally condemned by the Court of Mixed Commission in Freetown she is the property of her owner. Do you think I can go around burning other people's property? Good heavens, man, what would become of the world if we went around doing that? Now, what else can we do?'

Murray listened to Jessup's suggestions, then sent for Fearnley. 'Mr Fearnley,' he said. 'I am taking that vessel as a prize and sending her into Freetown. There are no slaves on board but there is a crew of eight. I am putting a prize crew of five men on board with an officer. The officer I have chosen is you.' He paused and cleared his throat. 'As you may know, the crew is diseased. Have you any questions?'

Fearnley sat bolt upright in his seat. 'Will I be rejoining the ship, sir?'

'Of course, of course. The Commodore will arrange for you to be sent back down to our station. You should be with us again in a matter of weeks. I am most anxious to have you back. Most anxious.'

Anxiety was not confined to Murray. His voice trembling so slightly that it needed sharp ears to detect it, but trembling nonetheless, Fearnley whispered:

'Er, the disease, sir. . . .'

'Yes.' Murray leaned forward in a fatherly way. 'Mr Jessup says we must smoke the ship out and douse her with vinegar.

73

You should pay strict attention to cleanliness and keep the slavers locked away. Do not come into contact with them. I understand your apprehension, Mr Fearnley, but we must do our duty. The ship is manifestly a slaver and must be sent for trial. I am sorry your first independent command should be like this, most sorry, and I am sure that Mr Brooke concurs. Do you not, Mr Brooke?'

Brooke did not concur at all. Fearnley had his duty to do and if he had not been chosen, someone else would have had to do it. Murray's fawning was underbred, vulgar, ungentlemanly, and he despised it. However, he nodded brusquely and expressed his good wishes.

The officers went on deck, where a sullen crew was assembled. Although the boarding party had been ordered by Brooke not to say one word of conditions on the schooner under pain of death, flogging, and having their rum stopped, every man on board knew that the prize was infested with some filthy, noxious, bone-rotting devil's disease without a known cure and that if a man was to go within a mile of the ship then he would be struck as blind as ten bats.

Brooke ordered the prize crew to one side: Farley and McGittigan, released from irons and wishing they were still in them; Gray, Blue-lighter, whose last-minute, fervent prayers remained unanswered; and Jack Smith.

Like men condemned to the gallows they collected their belongings and went over the side, watched by their silent mates. Smiling bravely, Fearnley followed them. They bent sullenly at the oars and splashed away. Only Dawlish yelled, 'Good luck, Jack.'

Murray turned to Brooke. 'Let us get under way, Mr Brooke.'

The ordered rush of relieved men, the creak and groan of timber, the wind raising its voice among the rigging, the ship on its new course to the Oil Rivers.

In the afternoon Murray sent for John. He stood nervously before the Captain, wondering why he had been sent for.

Murray looked piercingly at John. 'Mr Spencer,' he said 'you came on board as a gentleman volunteer. By now you will have realized that such a creature is scarcely worthy of human consideration. I will tell you frankly that I had grave doubts about taking you on this ship and, what is more, if you had shown yourself to be a mere idler I would have dropped you off at Freetown. Is that clear?'

It was by no means clear to John but, wisely, he did not say so. Instead he raised his chin an inch higher and said, as smartly as he could. 'Aye, aye, sir.'

Murray sucked his teeth for a moment, his terribly sharp grey eyes, that seemed to look into the distance and also to be focused on the person he was speaking to at the same time, drilled into John. 'Aye,' he said. 'Well, Mr Keverne gives me excellent reports on your navigation, and Mr Potts says that you are most willing to learn the working of the ship, and I have carefully noted that you go about your duties in a cheerful, willing way. But that, by itself, is not enough. A clever fool can learn the tables of longitude, and an idiot can be cheerful and willing. But there is more than that to making an officer of the Royal Navy. Much more. Much more.'

He paused and swivelled a little in his seat, his icy gaze directed through the cabin window where *Sentinel*'s wake troubled the sluggish waters of the ocean. Silence. John, who had flushed at Murray's remarks, felt the blood drain from his face. Was this it, then, he wondered? Had cheerful willingness and assiduous attendance to his duty been for nothing? Did he not possess that mysterious something, at which Murray was hinting, and which alone made a man worthy to carry the Queen's commission in her Navy? For a second John had a vision of himself stooped over a desk in a counting-house in London, trudging there through the dirt and fog, trudging back home, back to some anonymous room, oneself anonymous in it. . . . His eyes smarting and his cheeks white, he stood at attention. 'Yes, sir,' he said.

The ship's bell rang, boots clumped outside the cabin door as the marine sentries changed guard. Ginger looked through the skylight and gave an encouraging 'miao'.

Murray gave a little '*tsiss*' between his teeth and Ginger flickered away. Murray raised an eyebrow. 'Command,' he said, with a rare flash of humour.

John smiled too, although he was not sure quite what he was smiling about. And his smile vanished when Murray's did.

'Command,' his captain said. 'Command. Any fool can run about a ship threatening the cat, but it takes a wise man to command without it.'

Another silence; the silence, that is, of a captain's cabin on a small ship, where hardly a rat could move without him hearing it — if he wished. Murray coughed.

'I will say this, Mr Spencer. Mr Brooke has given me an excellent report on you. Yes —' waving away John's instinctive gesture — 'he has told me that you know when *not* to report men for punishment. That is an act of judgement beyond your years. Because of that, because of the reports made on you by your superior officers, and because — and only because — I am an officer short, I have decided to rate you a midshipman. Yes.'

Murray raised his head, and the grey eyes rested on John. 'Let me emphasize that your rank is temporary. You will be an *acting* midshipman. An *acting, unpaid* midshipman, but a midshipman just the same, and if you attend to your duties in a satisfactory way I promise you I will rate you regular. That is up to you. Do not let it take too long.'

John opened his mouth but Murray cut him off. 'A mark of rank for a midshipman is a dirk. Do you possess one?'

'No, sir.' Although Mr Radley had provided John with all things necessary for his voyage, a dagger was not among them, perhaps because he had not been fully convinced that John would need one.

'I thought perhaps not.' Murray opened a drawer in his desk. 'Take this,' he said, and handed John a gleaming, silver dirk.

'Thank you, sir,' John said. 'Thank you very much.'

Murray shook his head. 'Do not thank me, Mr Spencer. That dirk belongs to Mr Fearnley. He asked me to pass it on to you.' He stood up, towering over John. 'The Navy is full of tradition, tradition and symbol. The tradition is a great one; regard the passing on of this dirk as a symbol of that tradition. You will not go far wrong then. Dismiss, Mr Spencer.'

14

As John, torn between pride and embarrassment, walked the deck of *Sentinel* sporting his dirk and with a deep blush on his cheeks, three hundred miles to the north the ship called the *Phantom*, lying deep off the Brass River, shook her sails free and in silence, without a light showing, slid from her mooring.

Beautiful in the starlight, she left the dark banks of Africa and headed for the open sea. On board, shackled in pairs, she had one hundred and eighty men, fifty women, and thirty children. It was an excellent cargo, which had cost around twelve thousand dollars and would sell for something like one hundred thousand dollars by the time it reached Carolina. It could be smelled a mile away.

Lyapo lay on the slave-deck of the ship, part of a living carpet of men crammed into a space fifty feet long, twenty feet wide, and fourteen inches high. In a coop in the bows were the women and children. Most of the slaves were Yoruba or Ibo. Already there had been fighting as men struggled for an extra inch of space.

Lyapo lay under a hatch and thought himself lucky. The hatch was covered with a huge iron grating but the night air could filter in and he could catch a glimpse of the stars.

A shadow crossed the grating as a man walked across it. On the deck someone shouted, a harsh, angry cry — or so it seemed to Lyapo, although he had no way of telling. For all he knew, it was a cry of joy. The pale creatures stalking about their enormous boat were more alien to him than the stars blinking their white eyes in the night sky.

Alien, but no longer monstrous. Lyapo had no doubt that the beaky creatures with their piebald skin were men; horrible, deformed men perhaps, but men just the same. He had no doubt either that the men had some horrible end waiting for the slaves. In the barracoon, interpreters had spoken to the slaves. 'You are not going to die,' they had said. 'You are going to another country to work, that is all. You will grow fat there.'

Some slaves had believed the interpreters, eagerly snatching at any tale on which they could feed their dreams of some kind of hopeful future. Others were openly sceptical. Lyapo was one. He did not believe anything, certainly not that he was going to a happy land. But he did not believe either, as he once had, that he was being taken to a slaughterer's like a goat to be butchered and sold for meat.

It was suffocatingly hot in the hold. Sweat poured off Lyapo and gathered in a pool beneath him. He tried to turn on his side. The man on his right muttered angrily and dug his elbow into Lyapo's side but the man on the left, to whom Lyapo was shackled, lay absolutely still.

Lyapo peered at him. He was a man without an interpreter. A stranger from some remote and fantastic tribe. How had he arrived on the ship, Lyapo wondered? Where had he come from, this man with a face like a piece of carved wood and teeth filed into dagger-like points?

But although the man was as fantastic to Lyapo as the creatures who had enslaved them both, he knew what was happening behind the mystery of the man's mask. The stranger was willing himself to die. He was severing his links with this world and wandering on a journey to the gates of death, for only through those gates could he return to his homeland.

'Brother,' Lyapo whispered. 'Brother, I. . . .' he would have liked to say something, to say that he understood, sympathized, would remember the man and make a sacrifice to him at his own fetish. But what was the point? The man could not understand him and, Lyapo thought, when would he see his own fetish again?

The ship shuddered and trembled as she met the first long roller from the sea. Along the slave-deck there was a mutter of alarm and the rattle of chains as the men moved, uneasily. *Phantom* shook again, lifting her bows and crashing them down. There were more cries of fear. The man on Lyapo's right cried out and dragged himself up, crashing his head on the planks above him. Another wave took *Phantom* amidships. She heeled, tilting over at a crazy angle. There were howls and shrieks, hoarse bellows of rage. Men clawed at each other, kicking and pummelling as the world lifted up and down, up and down.

Seasickness quietened the slaves in the end. Each man was too absorbed in his own wretchedness to attack his neighbour. Many of them believed that they had been poisoned and, as they vomited, whimpered last petitions to their gods; others merely wished to die as quickly as possible.

With her cargo of misery and filth, *Phantom* bore steadily

south. By dawn, as the morning rain had lashed her decks, she was a hundred miles from land and, as Kimber her master believed, through the cordon of the British anti-slave patrol.

As the rain pattered across the sea and the sun burned up the morning mists Kimber came on deck, his yellow hair hidden under a straw hat and a Cuban cigar jammed in his mouth. In the galley huge copper pans simmered, and the smell of boiled yams drifted across the ship.

'Right,' Kimber ordered. 'Bring 'em up. Feeding time.'

The grating was dragged aside and a seaman, a pointed stick in his hand, crawled into the hold. On his hands and knees, in the filth and vomit, he drove the slaves out on deck.

Weak with nausea and shackled in twos, the slaves found it difficult to move. Slippering and slithering, they crawled to the hatchway and were heaved out. Some slaves were too sick to move. The sailor lashed at them and prodded them with his stick. Lyapo tried to wriggle from his place but was held by the man with the pointed teeth. A snarling, red face covered with ginger hair thrust itself against Lyapo and the stick cracked against his ankles.

'Yes,' Lyapo shouted. 'Yes, I'm coming. I'm coming.'

He dragged himself sideways, spitting out bile. The weight of the man with the pointed teeth pulled on his leg. The stick cracked across his chest and into the face of the man.

'He's dead.' Lyapo cried. 'He's dead!'

And dead he was. The man, with his carved face and blank eyes which had first opened on some fantastic, gibbering rain-forest and had closed in the darkness of a Baltimore clipper, was dragged on deck, together with a young Ibo who had choked to death on his own vomit.

Kimber stared at them and exploded with rage. 'God dammit!' he roared. 'God dammit! Prime field hands worth five hundred dollars in South Carolina — six hundred once we knocked those shark's teeth out of that devil there. Two dead, and we ain't been at sea twelve hours.'

He swung on his heel. 'Throw them overboard. And you —' he pointed to a man. 'Get below and clean that deck out.'

The man, a creole from Cuba, stared back sullenly. 'You been down there?' he muttered. 'Look at the state of him.' He pointed to the red-faced man. 'It's like ten pigsties.'

Kimber hooked his thumbs in his belt. 'That's why I'm sending you.'

The man flushed. 'I ain't no pig.'

'Is that so?' Kimber took a menacing step forward. 'And I was just thinking that all you needed was a ring through your nose and you'd get a prize in a hog show. Now git.'

The man went, backing away not only from Kimber's cold blue eyes but also from his bucko mate, Gavell, six feet three inches and the terror of Baton Rouge.

Kimber leaned on the rail as the slaves were fed. Most of them were too sick to face food, but a crack of the whip across their shoulders persuaded them to try. The last slave crammed down the last yam. Kimber spat his cigar over the side.

'Set 'em dancing,' he ordered.

The bewildered slaves were dragged to their feet and made to shuffle about the deck. 'Jump,' Gavell bellowed. 'Jump. Up! Up! Up!'

Dizzy with sickness, ashamed of his nakedness before the women, Lyapo jumped and jumped as if his life depended on it. Up and down the slaves went, a hose-pipe gushing water on them. Up and down they went in a grotesque, terrible parody of a dance.

'Shake 'em up,' Kimber cried. 'Shake 'em up. Shake the fever out of them. Ain't no more Goddam niggers going to die on me.'

The slaves were rammed back below deck. The day set fair. Although the inimical sun began its sullen climb, a steady nor'-east breeze kept *Phantom* driving south, down to where the trade winds blew and where a ship could pick them up and be wafted clear all the way to Cuba. But by eleven a copper-coloured cloud began to form to the east. By twelve it had grown larger, poised ominously on the horizon.

Gavell joined Kimber by the rail where the master habitually lounged.

'Seen that?' he said, jerking his thumb at the cloud.

'I've seen it,' Kimber said. 'It's a tornado cloud. But no need to worry. Before that breaks up we'll be out of here. Crack on the sky-sail.'

The sky-sail, a tiny scrap of canvas, was bent on the very peak of the mainmast. As it billowed, adding the last, fractional touch of speed to the ship, Kimber clapped his hands together.

'That's what I like,' he said. 'I do like to see a vessel just so with every sail set. Yes siree, a sky-sail never did any harm a-tall.'

Which was where he was absolutely wrong. For, fifteen miles away on the very rim of the horizon, Rafferty on *Sentinel*'s mainmast saw the flicker of the sail, glinting against the great copper cloud as sharply as a fragment of broken glass. It was an hour after that before the lackadaisical look-out on *Phantom* saw *Sentinel*'s topmasts, and by then *Sentinel* had cut off four of the miles separating them and there was no way they could avoid meeting.

''Cos you see,' said Potts, high in the rigging with half the crew around him, 'there ain't no way he can avoid it.'

'But what if she runs?' observed John, with the air of deep sagacity his new rank had conferred on him.

Potts smiled, the smile of a seaman who might not be your Isaac Newton when it came to mathematics, but who had the logic of sail and the strategy of the seas bred in his bones. 'Which she can't run because she's got nowhere to run to. She can't go east because there's nothing there but the Skeleton Coast, and she won't want to go back to the Oil Rivers because of our patrols and on this tack she can't pass us. No. She's a rat in a trap, my lad. A little rat in a great big trap maybe, but a trap just the same.' He grinned. 'I'll bet her Master can't believe his eyes.'

Kimber couldn't. He stared incredulously at the distant ship, hardly bigger than a cork on the horizon but a red splash of colour on her mizzen stating plainly that it was a British man-o'-war.

'Goddamit,' Kimber spat. '*Goddammit*! What in hell is a warship doing down here?'

Gavell joined him, dangling his huge, hairy arms over the rail. 'John Bull in person and as welcome as Horace Greeley in Alabama. What you aiming to do?'

Kimber scowled. 'If he tries to stop me I ain't going to play kiss-in-the-ring, that's for sure. Muster the crew.'

The men gathered in the waist. Kimber casually lit another cigar, blew a cloud of smoke, and pointed to *Sentinel* — now seeming rather larger, about the size of a bottle.

'Boys,' Kimber said. 'This is where you earn your keep. That vessel yonder looks like a British warship and it looks like she wants to come a-visiting, but I reckon we'll keep the door closed. He's got no more right to stop us now than a Dutchman, but if he tries there's no call to worry. I know that class of vessel. She's what the Limey's call a sloop-o'-war, carries maybe ten-twelve guns. Just the same as us boys, just the same as us.'

The crew peered over their shoulders, and it was clear that not all of them thought that the taut, menacing ship bearing down on them was remotely like their own vessel. One of the crew rubbed his hand across his mouth.

'You mean that is a regular British warship?'

Kimber raised his telescope and peered through it. 'Yes, it looks more like one every time I take a peek. It's just like one of those King's Navee ships that we knocked the hell out of in 1812. You want to take a look?'

The man shook his head. 'I don't know anything about 1812 but you ain't fixing to fight, are you?'

Kimber pushed his hat back. 'That notion had crossed my mind. You any objections?'

The man looked around, uneasily. 'I didn't sign on to fight no regular warship, that's for sure.'

'Oh?' Kimber looked carefully at the end of his cigar and brushed the ash away. 'What did you sign on for?'

'To pick up a passel of slaves.'

'You thought that, when you signed on for double wages? You thought that, when you knew that half this crew were trained gunners? Well, that's all right. You're a nutmeg-chewing, free Connecticut Yankee and you don't have to do no fighting. You don't even have to stay on the ship. You can go right over the side and swim straight home. Take your pick. Anyone else want to head for home?'

No one did. At least, they didn't want to swim there.

'Right,' Kimber said. 'Run out the guns.'

Sunlight flickered on metal. On *Sentinel* Murray slapped his thigh. 'Surely he can't mean to fight? Beat to quarters, Mr Brooke.'

There was the slightest, most momentary hesitation before Brooke touched his hat and passed on the order. As the drum rolled, Murray took Brooke by the elbow and led him to the taffrail.

'Do you have any doubts — any reservations — about my order?' he asked in a low, intense voice.

'Do you mean to challenge that ship, sir?' Brooke was equally intense.

'Indeed I do,' Murray snapped.

'And do you intend to use force?'

'If necessary.'

'Sir,' Brooke leaned forward, his voice even lower. 'She is under American colours.'

'Do you think I am not aware of that?' Murray's eyes were sharp with anger. 'She is a slaver, I am convinced of it. Do you think I will let the ruffian sail past without even a challenge?'

'There is not a shred of evidence that she is a slaver,' Brooke hissed. 'And if we halt an American ship, God knows what it could lead to — a war, even.'

'Nonsense!' Murray turned away. Behind him Brooke beat his fist on the rail.

'Our orders,' he said stubbornly.

Murray swung back on his heel. '*My* orders, sir. And I will interpret them as I see proper. Now attend to your duties — and I will trouble you not to blaspheme. That is all.'

Brooke went down the ship and Murray gazed at him bleakly. Did the fellow really think that he was going to let a ship go past him without even a challenge? Preposterous!

But *Sentinel* was trim, there was no doubt about that, and the credit was due to Brooke. The crew looked fit and confident as they stood by the guns, and the transition from the daily routine to action-stations had gone with impressive smoothness. Murray only hoped that if it came to a fight the men would be as hard as they looked.

He looked across at the distant ship. It would be at least an hour before she came in long-shot range, longer still before she could be hailed.

'Mr Brooke,' he called. 'The men may stand easy at their stations and they may eat.'

Cold pork and biscuit for the crew. Rum and prayers to follow. The Blue-lighters refusing the rum, the hard cases taking both on the reasonable grounds that neither could hurt you and both might do you good.

Murray strolled along the deck, having an encouraging word with his men. By John, standing by his guns, he paused. The lad had a rather strained rigidity which he found disturbing.

'Are you quite well, Mr Spencer?' he asked.

John touched his cap. 'Quite well, sir, thank you.'

Murray stooped. 'May I ask what you are doing?'

Without batting an eyelid or moving his head as much as a fraction John said, 'Keeping an eye on Mr Cawley, sir.'

Murray looked at Cawley, who was leaning casually on number one gun. 'And why are you doing that?'

'Orders, sir.'

'Orders?' Murray was mystified. 'Orders to stare at Mr

Cawley? Who gave you that order?'

'You did, sir.'

'I?' Murray wondered if the sun had got to the lad.

'Yes, sir. You said that at battle-stations I must watch Mr Cawley. For firing the guns, sir.'

'Ah!' Enlightenment gleamed in Murray's eyes. 'Yes indeed, and most commendable that you should bear your orders so firmly in mind. But we shall not be firing the guns for at least an hour, if then, so I think that you might, er, divert your eyes from Mr Cawley. Have you had your dinner? No? Indeed you must. Go below and have some. That is an order. And Mr Spencer.'

'Sir?'

Murray coughed. 'It is not unmanly to say a private prayer before battle. Have your dinner.'

John darted into the gunroom, crammed a piece of cheese in his mouth, swallowed it in one great gollup, and reappeared at his station before Murray had reached the quarterdeck. But oddly enough, in that brief space of time the strange sail seemed to have come very much closer, as if, after the long, slow morning, time had speeded up. Less than a mile or so now separated the two ships, and through a telescope it was quite possible to see on the stranger a man by the wheel. A tall man, with a cigar in his mouth and yellow hair gleaming in the sunshine.

The wind dropped for a little while. The ships lay rocking on the waves, the great copper-coloured cloud towering over them and a vast rainbow arching across the horizon. Then the wind blew again.

Murray took a last glance along his ship. Without orders the men had risen and were standing by their guns. By the mainmast the Kroomen had gathered.

'Send those men below,' Murray ordered. There was no justice in keeping them on deck where they might be injured in a fight not of their seeking.

A mile, half a mile, five hundred yards. Men licked their lips and wiped their brows, wondering why they were standing by a cannon and not by a bar in a Portsmouth pub.

Three hundred yards and Murray raised his speaking-trumpet. 'Heave to,' he called. 'Heave to. This is Her Majesty's ship *Sentinel*. Heave to.'

From *Phantom* came a faint cry, hardly distinguishable, more a howl or a taunt, but certainly defiant. The black ship came on its unswerving course. Murray bellowed, 'Mr Hayes, put a shot across his bows.'

But as Hayes reached for his slow match there was a surge of movement on *Phantom*, men raced across her deck, there was a flurry of sails. She swung round sharply, showing her black side to *Sentinel*, and even as Murray roared a warning his voice was obliterated by the thunder of *Phantom*'s guns.

15

Phantom's broadside slammed into *Sentinel* like the beating of huge hammers. Mogger went down screaming with a three-foot splinter in his side. A marine grunted with disbelief as he looked at what had once been a hand. The mainstay of the mizzen-mast parted with a vicious *twang*, lashed across the deck, and smashed Hackney, ship's boy, into the scuppers.

'Fire!' Murray roared. Cawley dropped his arm. 'Fire!' Potts bellowed. 'Fire!' Scott screeched. 'Fire!' John screamed, his voice cracking into a piercing treble.

The deafening roar of *Sentinel*'s guns. Tongues of flame flickering from brazen mouths. Acrid smoke, the clamour of the gun-carriages trundling back and forward, shot whistling overhead, crunching into the sides, and the shrill voices of the midshipmen: 'Loose, level, out, run, prime, FIRE! Loose, level, out, run, prime, FIRE!'

Sweating men peered through the gun-ports, catching vague, confused glimpses of masts and spars, flames, green water, sudden, dazzling shafts of sunlight. Weeks and months and years of drill proved their worth as, in the ear-splitting din and the blinding smoke, the gun-crews answered to the steady orders — loose, level, out, run, prime, FIRE! Hours passing, days, a lifetime.

On the quarterdeck Murray leaned over the rail, peering into the gunsmoke. *Phantom*'s arching sails were trembling and the enormous spars that carried them were slowly shifting round.

'She's veering off, sir,' Keverne cried.

'Yes.' Murray beat his fist on the rail. From being side by side with *Sentinel*, *Phantom* was swinging away. Already, with her clipper lines, built for speed, she was slipping away, showing the curve of her wake as she headed north.

'She's running,' someone called, and a ragged cheer went up.

'Silence!' Murray cried. He climbed into the shrouds. Already *Phantom* was half a mile away. Hayes was still blazing at her with the long bow-chaser, but more with hope than expectation.

Murray jumped down to the deck. Was the enemy really running? Was she taking to her heels, racing back to the coast to hide in some lagoon? If so, *Sentinel* would never catch her. His ship was built for sturdy service in the battering weather of the

Atlantic but he was facing a ship built for speed.

'Hard a-starboard,' he rapped out.

Shock on the quarterdeck, dismay, disbelief. Stunned silence among the guns. A last bang from the eighteen-pounder like an exclamation mark. Turning to starboard meant that they were heading south, away from the enemy. Brooke took a step forward, but halted before Murray's savage glare.

'There is damage to the ship, Mr Brooke,' Murray snapped. 'Please attend to it. Mr Cawley, see to the men. Mr Hayes, see to the guns.' A steady rattle of commands; the wounded being taken below to the grizzly cockpit, where Jessup did his best; the Bosun splicing the backstay, Taplow writing up the log, Purvis sounding the ship for leaks; a stolid marine ringing the ship's bell, for all the world as though it were a dull Sunday in Portsmouth. But sullen faces all round as *Sentinel* bore away south and her enemy reached north and Murray, as solitary as a man can possibly be in this world, stood braced against the rail, his telescope trained on *Phantom*'s masts.

Three masts showing as *Phantom* curved away. Three masts, the copper cloud glowing between them, three masts — and then, quite suddenly, only one as the ship ran due north and her three masts stood in line ahead.

Murray's face set like stone. On what happened next his career depended. Indeed his life, in any meaningful sense. He had not believed *Phantom* was going back to the coast but that she was going to swing round in a great circle and then race back south, dodging past *Sentinel* like a boxer, slipping past a straight left and using her speed to break out into the vastness of the South Atlantic, while *Sentinel* floundered in her wake.

That was why Murray had taken his ship south. He too was sailing on a great curve, which would bring him back to meet *Phantom*. If he was right — *if* he was right — he would have done more than his duty. If he had judged wrongly, then all that waited for him was court martial for cowardice in the face of the enemy, and he could be shot for that. A British Admiral had been shot on his own quarterdeck for a lesser charge.

Murray accepted his position. It was the Royal Navy's bargain: supreme power, and supreme responsibility. Still he watched the masts of *Phantom* like a hawk. One mast visible, one mast, *Phantom* sailing away and away, taking his life with it, and then. . . . And then — three masts. Three masts, and one mast again as *Phantom* completed her circle and came charging back.

And *Sentinel* completed hers, the wakes of the two ships forming a gigantic figure-of-eight as Murray's great gamble was rewarded.

He stepped back from the rail. Discipline or no discipline, a cheer went up from the men, and Brooke touched his cap in genuine admiration. 'Bravely done, sir,' he cried.

Murray formally touched his own cap. 'Thank you, Mr Brooke. Be good enough to bring the men back to their stations.'

The rainbow arched across the copper cloud as, to the shattering roar of the guns, the two ships collided again. Darkness and fire and blood. The sky turning amber, lightning flashing and, louder than the guns, louder than all the guns in the world, the roll of thunder crashing across the heavens. Shrill young voices cracking with fatigue, men slipping on bloody decks, the wind rising and the sea mounting.

The sky turned dark, maroon, and the rainbow was uncannily bright. 'Mr Brooke,' Murray roared. He jabbed his finger at the sky. 'We must get alongside — tornado — these signs — we must board her.'

Brooke waved an acknowledgement and dived into the inferno of the deck. 'Bring her head round,' Murray ordered the helmsman. 'Lively now.'

Sentinel swung her noble bows and leaned into *Phantom*. Murray drew his sword. *Phantom* was beaten. He knew it. She looked half a wreck, her rigging shot to shreds, one vast yard-arm dangling crazily, and her rate of fire dwindling. One rush would do it, one tearing, howling, smashing charge across her deck. He raised his sword. From the smoke of the deck a line of men arose like demons; Blue-lighters and hard-cases and with them, breaking all regulations, the Kroomen.

'Now!' Murray roared.

And then from nowhere, like some fearful, invisible animal, a wind leaped upon the ship. *Sentinel* reared, her sails cracking. A last blaze of fire came from *Phantom*. Someone screamed behind Murray. The wheel was a shattered stump and so was the helmsman. Without steering, *Sentinel* swung madly. More stays parted. The mizzen-mast gave an ominous groan. But *Phantom* was not twenty yards away. Another dazzling flash of lightning, every detail of the enemy picked out with startling clarity, and on its deck the man with the yellow hair.

Murray swung his sword as if, across that gulf of water, he could hack down his enemy and all he stood for. But even as he did so, with a wrenching, splintering crack the mizzen-mast tore itself from its socket and, in a tangle of canvas and rigging, crashed across the deck.

Murray woke in his cot with a blinding headache and a nagging pain in his shoulder, and found Pike's face six inches from his own.

'Glory be!' Pike squeaked. 'You're alive!'

'What?' Murray raised himself on his elbow. 'What?'

Pike gave a horrified cry and pushed him back. 'Never,' he cried, 'never. You ain't to stir an inch, surgeon's orders — being as how you'm be at death's door, sir, and begging your pardon.'

'Nonsense,' Murray wrestled free from Pike's grasp. 'Get me some coffee and my cape.'

'But which coffee I can't do, sir,' said Pike, wrapping the cape around Murray's shoulders. 'Seeing as how the galley is all smashed to smithereens by that wicked, God-rotted slaver. Take a drop of brandy instead.'

Murray swallowed the brandy and lurched on deck to the debris and devastation of battle. The mizzen-mast was gone, leaving an odd blank in the afterdeck. Spars and yard-arms splintered, rigging severed, canvas flapping in the wind, raw white scars in the timbers and ugly, sickening, brown smears everywhere. Chaos, confusion, but beneath it the steady discipline of the Navy asserting itself. Every man at work, and the craftsmen coming into their own; the carpenter, sailmaker, armourer, bosun, caulker; stitching, hammering, splicing; men below and aloft. *Sentinel* was being wrenched and tugged back into shape.

A stir as Murray arrived on deck, and a mutter running the length of the ship. What did that mean, Murray wondered, pleasure or anger? The resentful growl of a battered crew, or pleasure at seeing the Captain alive?

Brooke came striding aft. 'Are you well, sir?'

'Well enough.' Murray stared grimly at his battered ship. 'We took a pounding.'

'Yes, sir.' Brooke's voice was flat, without emotion of any kind.

'You have the repairs well in hand. I congratulate you.'

'Thank you, sir.' Again that flat, expressionless voice.

'Perhaps we should go below,' Murray said. 'Ask Mr Cawley to take the deck.'

'Mr Cawley is dead, sir.'

'Oh.' Deep sadness in Murray. Cawley gone. Cheerful, friendly Cawley, ever willing, well liked by everyone, twenty-three years old.

In his cabin Murray slumped in his chair and waved Brooke to sit.

'The state of the ship?'

'Nothing we can't handle, sir. We are making a little water but the Kroomen are handling that at the pumps. The rigging is knocked about but the worst damage was the mizzen-mast. We're fixing a jury-mast now.'

'Yes.' Murray nodded. 'You have taken a knock, Mr Brooke.'

'A scratch, sir. I am perfectly well.'

Brooke's wound didn't look like a scratch. His face was cut to the bone and the stitches were crude. He would be marked for life, Murray thought.

'Take some wine,' Murray said. 'As a restorative.'

Pike brought in a bottle of claret and two glasses. The two men drank. Murray sipped his wine and put the glass down.

'What happened?'

Brooke clenched his fist, the knuckles showing white under the tanned skin. 'We were almost on her, sir. Five more minutes and we would have had her. She was beaten, beaten. There was hardly a gun firing. We had her in the palm of our hands.' Brooke's face was flushed and his voice trembled a little.

'Yes,' Murray prompted. 'And then?'

'Well, sir,' Brooke downed some wine, greedily, as if suffering from a great thirst. 'The wheel was hit, I suppose you saw that, but we had enough steerage to carry us on to the enemy. And then the mizzen-mast came down. It had been hit a couple of times. You went under it, sir — and then the storm — the tornado came.'

Brooke took another drink. The purple claret shook in the glass as he raised it. Murray looked at him keenly. Was the man suffering from the exhaustion of battle? 'The storm,' he said.

'It simply erupted, sir. I've never seen anything like it, even in the China Sea with the typhoons. It simply drove us apart. We fouled the enemy's bowsprit — carried it away — but there was no possibility of boarding her, none at all.'

Murray nodded. A helpless ship, no steering, an exhausted crew, a storm of terrible power, one senior officer to carry the burden. He thought of Cawley again. . . .

'What is the butcher's bill?' he asked harshly.

'Three dead, sir, nine wounded, then there are the minor injuries. I've logged them, sir.'

'Did the men behave well — after I. . . .?'

'Yes, sir. Exemplary.'

'And the enemy?'

'The last I saw of her she was afloat and driving north, sir. The mast-head reported a sail at dawn, after the storm. It's possible it was her.'

'Maybe,' Murray agreed.

'She was no ordinary slaver,' Brooke burst out. 'She had trained gunners aboard, and plenty of them.'

'Yes,' Murray agreed with that, too. But what would the Navy think? What would it think of a well-manned sloop being beaten off by a slaver manned with the scum of the earth? Murray could almost hear the voices. 'A Queen's ship, regular man-o'-war, twelve guns, eight men, beaten off by a dirty slaver. *Cowardice*.'

It wasn't a pleasant prospect. Men had been broken for less. His career could well hang in the balance and even the three dead, proof of a bloody fight, might not be enough to tip the balance his way. And then he realized why Brooke was so nervous. Of course, he had been in command at the crucial moment. In command and bearing sole responsibility, with the slaver not a hand's breadth away. There would be many an eyebrow raised at that and many a harsh, unyielding voice to say, 'And a storm blew up! A convenient storm if you ask me. Comes along just in time to prevent the crew jumping aboard a bloody deck to fight it out hand-to-hand with desperate men.'

Brooke knew perfectly well what was going through Murray's mind. And he knew, too, that if when Murray came to write his dispatch to the Admiralty he chose to lay a certain stress here and there, nothing obvious, of course, he could clear himself of all blame by suggesting that the slaver was ready for the taking but that his First Lieutenant — in *command* — had let her slip through his fingers. And Murray was a Whig, and his friends at the Admiralty and in the Government were Whigs, too, and to skewer a Tory on a charge of neglect of duty would be meat and drink to them.

Yes, a few strokes of the pen and Murray could clear himself and destroy Brooke, and both men knew it. But Brooke kept his face impassive and his voice cold. Let Murray write what he wished. He had done *his* duty.

Murray stood up. 'Thank you, Mr Brooke. I will join you on deck as soon as I have dressed.'

So that was that. Brooke stood up, his face a mask, and went to the door, but Murray halted him.

'We must make arrangements for the burial. Please attend to that. And, Mr Brooke.'

'Sir?'

'I might just say that I will be pleased to recommend you for your gallant conduct.'

The burial of the dead. Murray facing his men, prayer-book in hand, the wind ruffling his hair.

'"I am the resurrection and the life, saith the Lord: He that believeth in me, though he were dead, yet shall he live. . . ."'

The whine of the wind in the rigging. A hoarse whisper from Keverne to the helmsman — 'Keep her steady, blast you.'

Murray's calm voice continuing. '"I know that my Redeemer liveth, and that he shall stand at the latter day upon the earth . . ."'

The clump of a marine's boots. The bell ringing five times: half-past two in the afternoon watch.

'". . . Therefore, my beloved brethren, be ye stedfast, unmoveable, always abounding in the work of the Lord, forasmuch as ye know that your labour is not in vain in the Lord. . . . We therefore commit these bodies to the deep, to be turned into corruption, looking for the resurrection of the body, (when the Sea shall give up her dead,) and the life of the world to come, through our Lord Jesus Christ. . . ."'

The last words. Murray nodding to the bosun, the planks tilting, the bodies sliding down into the ocean, twisting and turning as they sank into the darkness of the abyss: cheerful Cawley; Mogger, no longer to be barked at; Atwill, gunner's mate, Blue-lighter, gone to meet his Maker; and Timothy Hackney, ship's boy, died two hours ago, orphan, twelve years of age, his tiny body in its shroud looking like a pillowcase.

Dismissal, back to work. Every man who could spare a glance looking north, for *Phantom*.

16

The tornado had driven *Phantom* eighty miles to the north, where she was rocking on a burnished sea and trailing a tangle of wreckage behind her, like a sea-bird with a broken wing. She, too, was hard at work, patching her damage and burying her dead.

Eighteen bodies thrown over the side, where the sharks thrashed the water and the sparkling foam turned red. Kimber, with a murderous rage in his heart, strode the deck, driving on his men with fists and boots. *Phantom* a combined charnel-house and lunatic asylum.

Gavell, wet to the waist, climbed over the side. 'We took a pounding,' he said. 'I've plugged the worst holes but we need to get at them from the inside. Should I roust them niggers out?'

Kimber's smouldering rage exploded. 'You've got the brains of a woodpecker. You think we can bring them slaves up here? We got to get this deck clear. Goddammit, they come up here now they could rush us clear off the deck, take the ship like that.' He snapped his fingers.

Gavell was sullen. 'If we don't get them holes plugged and another of them tornadoes comes up we won't have no ship at all,' he muttered, but he backed away just the same.

Little by little, like a botched and bungled amputation, the ship was cleared of debris. By noon she had some kind of sail set and her deck was clear. Kimber ordered a cannon loaded with grape-shot to be trained on the main hatchway, armed his men with muskets, then spat on his hands.

'Right,' he said. 'Let's get them up.'

Four men stepped forward and lifted the heavy grating. For a moment there was silence and then a wave of noise built up from the hold. An appalling, baying howl, as if the cover of hell had been opened.

The men jumped back and dropped the grating. 'Holy Jesus,' one cried. 'What was that?'

Kimber strode forward, a pistol in each hand. 'Open that hatch,' he ordered. 'Jump to it. They can't get out.'

Reluctantly the men heaved the cover aside. Again the baying roared from the hold. Kimber had a glimpse of faces contorted with rage and fear. Lyapo's was one of the faces, and he saw

Kimber too. He clawed upward through the grating as if he could smash his way through the iron and drag Kimber down into the hold, drag him down and rend him, tear him to pieces. The slaves had been sealed in the suffocating heat and darkness of the hold for eighteen hours. For them the fight had been hours of incomprehensible terror, of gigantic bangs and crashes. Three of *Sentinel*'s shots had smashed clean through *Phantom*'s side and swept across the slave-deck. Men had been killed and mangled, and they were still down there in the darkness.

And now the men who had subjected them to their ordeal were staring down at them through the grating, and it was that sight which evoked the bay of hatred.

Even Kimber was shaken by the fury of the slaves. He stepped off the hatch. For a moment he was tempted to leave the slaves in the hold but they had to be fed and given water, and there was the overriding necessity of getting to the holes in the side.

'All right,' he said. 'We'll do this carefully. Just remove that grating a mite.'

The grating was dragged to one side a little, just enough for a man to wriggle through. The slaves were dragged out and driven into the bows. The women were brought up, and the children, then the maimed and the dead. There were nine dead and a dozen more so mangled and badly wounded that they were worthless. When Kimber saw them his rage boiled over again.

'Throw them overboard,' he roared. 'Thirty thousand dollars! Thirty thousand dollars gone. That Goddammed Britisher —' He stared across the sea as if his bleak gaze alone could seek out *Sentinel* and destroy her.

Behind him Gavell, still surly, wanted to know what course to lay.

'Due south,' Kimber said.

'Due south?' Gavell was incredulous.

Kimber swung round. 'Mister, are you going deaf?'

'You mean you ain't going back to the coast?' Gavell stared at the battered masts and spars. 'You ain't really thinking of taking this vessel across the Atlantic? Without putting in for repairs?'

'That's right,' Kimber said. 'All the way.'

'You ain't serious.'

'Ain't I just, though.' Again the black rage shook Kimber. 'I took a vessel from the Gallinas river to Cuba with two hundred slaves and five men to handle the ship and we used bedclothes for sails. Now git.'

Gavell turned sullenly away. The rest of the crew were equally sullen but none of them were ready to meet Kimber's eyes.

'Get them yams fished out and feed them slaves,' Kimber ordered. 'And rig the pump and water them.'

Two men went to the pump which brought up the water from the tanks. The pump clanked, water spouted out. In the hold hammers and mauls thudded, the yams boiled, and wind freshened a little. In the bows, under a ring of muskets, the slaves crouched, looking with hatred at the seamen, and the seamen looked with hatred at them.

The pump stopped its clank. One of the men working on it went over to Kimber. 'Something wrong, skipper. No water coming up.'

'No —' Kimber strode across the deck. 'Get going.'

The men jerked on the handle, a feeble trickle of rusty water came from the pump. Then it stopped.

Kimber exploded in a fit of profanity. He did not need the carpenter's report to tell him that the tank was holed and that for the past eighteen hours water had been gushing from it, nor Gavell's looming presence to inform him that now, without water, he would have to run for the coast. But as he listened to the carpenter drone on he felt like raising his pistol and shooting the man dead where he stood. With a huge effort he mastered himself.

'All right,' he said. 'Lay a course for the coast.'

Night came. Clouds blotted out the moon and the stars. *Phantom* crept through the darkness like a thief in the night. In the stern Kimber leaned on the taffrail, staring unwinkingly over his cigar. Somewhere out there, in the vastness of the seas, was the warship he had fought. He felt a bitter satisfaction. Not many men could have done that, he thought. Fought off a regular man-o'-war, that was something.

He flicked his cigar away. It streaked through the darkness like a shooting star and then disappeared. He turned and made his way along the ship. As he walked across the hatchway a terrible stench drifted up to him, but he didn't even notice it. It meant no more to him than the smell of penned cattle to a farmer.

Lyapo saw the dark shadow cross the grating. He heard the footsteps clump away and guessed who was making them. Most of the men on the ship went barefooted but Lyapo had noticed that two of them always wore stiff, heavy footwear. They were the ones who gave the orders, they were the *bale* and the *janata*: the chief and his right-hand man. The other men on the ship were afraid of them, just as he himself was. Yes, fear. It filled the ship like a foul odour that one could almost taste and smell.

Down the hold there was a sudden, savage squabble of voices, cries of pain, yelps, thick animal-like voices growling. Lyapo knew what was happening. There was a group of Yorubas who had forced their way down there. It was a foul place to be, away from what little air and light found their way into the slave-deck. But beyond that darkness the women were kept in their cage. Lyapo leaned back, his shoulder brushing the man next to him. The man spat something sharp and venomous and dug Lyapo in the ribs with his elbow. Lyapo smashed back, driving the man to the deck. This is what is happening to us, he thought; we are turning into beasts, lying in our own filth, snarling and snapping at each other. A sour taste flooded his mouth. Beasts, he thought.

Seventy miles away, *Sentinel* was also reaching north. John doing his watch, and finding out that putting on the Queen's uniform meant putting on its responsibilities as well as its privileges; staying on your feet until dawn, and no sympathy wasted on you by men just as tired.

Long, leaden minutes ticking past, the glass turned every thirty minutes, the log written up with every shift of wind. Sudden, galloping bouts of work, long periods of utter blankness.

It was very confusing. John had imagined a battle would be a great and glorious affair. He had had confused images drawn from story-books of bright swords flashing in sunlight, of vivid heraldic colours, red and blue and gold, and afterwards smiling admirals offering congratulations! But for all he had seen of the fight he might as well have been down a coalmine. Great clouds of smoke had hidden the enemy from his sight and he had spent a good deal of the time coughing. The most vivid memory he had was one of the thunderous noise. That and of men dying but not, as he had imagined, dying nobly, wishing their comrades well, and then lying down quietly and going to sleep; but dying screaming and blaspheming, and *moving*, writhing and twitching. Just to think of it made John sick — and sick he was, spewing out his supper over the side. And now here was the ship sailing through the darkness as if nothing had happened.

And yet just that routine was a relief. The order of ordinary life was asserting itself. The ring of the bell seemed to say time is passing, memories fading. Every half-hour that slips away takes with it the horrors of yesterday. Forget that and the men who died. Keep your watch, do your duty. Tomorrow is another day.

17

Dawn. Little more than a grey gleam under the clouds, but cheering, like the hot coffee brought by Pike to the quarterdeck. Brooke, stern and shaven, was taking the morning watch when Murray appeared; all hats off, all hats on, the ship present and correct. A new day, and the dead of yesterday already half forgotten. Eagle-eyed Rafferty spotted debris on the starboard bow.

The debris was a tangle of smashed timber and rigging with a scorched sail lashed to it.

'What do you make of it, Mr Brooke?' Murray asked.

'Odds on the slaver, sir,' Brooke answered. 'But. . . .'

'It's about where it ought to be if it is,' Keverne observed somewhat ungrammatically. 'Say she made thirty or forty miles on us yesterday —'

'Yes,' Murray didn't want a debate on the matter. He was convinced that it was jetsam from *Phantom* and it merely confirmed what he believed to be true, that the slaver had run for the coast and would be hiding there. 'Please come with me, Mr Keverne,' he said and went below to his cabin.

He took a chart from the locker and laid it out on the table. 'Now, Mr Keverne. I think that this slaver has gone due north. After that fight I do not believe that he is in any position to try anything fancy, but we are. What I intend to do is sail west a little to get to leeward of him. When we make our station I shall beat down the coast and with luck flush him out. Pray plot me a landfall a little east of north.'

He went back on deck. Brooke touched his cap. 'The bosun has asked permission to auction, sir.'

'Very well.' The auction was for the sale of the dead men's belongings. It was a healthy custom. The breaking up of the gear helped to end any maudlin sentimentality and the money raised went to the dependants. 'Yes, noon at the mainmast, conditions permitting. Where is Mr Bower?'

'Having breakfast, sir.'

'Roust him out when he has finished or if the weather clears, whichever is the sooner. Mr Keverne will give you the new course in a moment or two, but I think we can clap on some extra sail now.'

Bower had time to eat his breakfast but only just, for, by the time he had eaten his last sliver of rotten boiled beef barrelled two years earlier, the mists rose; revealing a grey smudge to the north which was Africa and, coming from it in a brisk, business-like manner, a brig. A brig-of-war, too, but a friendly one, carrying the red ensign and, after hovering a little to assure herself of *Sentinel*'s good intentions, very happy to come alongside and exchange courtesies.

The ship was *Hornet*, twenty-five men and four six-pounder cannon which looked as dangerous as pop-guns. Her Master, Rutherford, was a short ramrod of a lieutenant, nineteen years old but hard-bitten in every sense of the word, having just spent six weeks on boat work off Lagos.

'I see you've had a run in, sir,' he said cheerfully. 'I hope you had good luck with your prize.'

'Unfortunately not,' Murray said. 'She got away.'

'Oh!' Rutherford glanced at the stony faces of *Sentinel*'s officers. 'She got away. . .?'

'In a tornado,' Brooke said icily.

'Ah!' Rutherford nodded vigorously. 'A tornado.' Quite by chance he rested his hand on a great white scar on the rail. 'They can do a fearful lot of damage. Indeed they can.'

'A slaver did the damage,' Murray said, 'and killed three of my men. Now, perhaps you will join me for breakfast.'

Hornet's watch off duty had joined the Sentinels for their breakfast, and were being rather less tactful than their Commander.

'Got away?' asked a long, sinewy gunner's mate. 'Clear away, from a sloop?'

'It was this tornado,' Dawlish muttered. 'How could we help it?'

'She did all this damage, a slaver?'

'She was a tartar,' Smith growled. 'Stood up to us broadside for broadside.'

'Oh aye?' The gunner's mate winked broadly at his mates. 'What were you doing, blowing kisses?'

Carlin glowered. 'We ain't in no mood for joking. We got three dead and a dozen injured.'

The Hornets whistled in amazement. 'And what are you going to do about it?' they demanded.

'I know what I'd like to do.' Dawlish clenched his extremely large fist. 'But it's up to the Owner, ain't it?'

The owner was drinking coffee in his cabin with Rutherford and Brooke. Rutherford spoke, respectfully as became a young lieutenant addressing a captain, but firmly as became a man with two year's experience on the Coast.

'Well, I'm not really surprised, sir. What's happening is that we've swept all the easy stuff away. Now we're meeting the real hard cases, ready for a fight, especially the Yankee vessels. Was that an American ship you fought, sir?'

'She had American colours,' Murray said.

'She would, sir. You can't run up a lagoon without meeting one.' He scratched a sore on his chin. 'Of course, not all of them are American, but you can bet your boots most of them are. I tell you, sir, blockading is no good. It just don't work. We would need the whole fleet out here, and the slavers would get through then. The only way to stop the Trade is close the markets, seal off Brazil and Cuba and the States, and go in and burn the barracoons.'

'Just what Captain Denman said,' Murray observed.

'Captain Denman — that's the man,' Rutherford cried. 'He's got the idea. Well, I must be off, sir.'

'Yes, indeed.' Murray rose. 'May I ask what your orders are, Mr Rutherford?'

'Yes, sir. Back into Whydah to see what Da Souza is up to.'

'Oh yes, Da Souza.' Murray led the way on deck. Already the sun was beginning to burn with a terrible, steady glare. Murray put his hands on the rail and looked across the blinding waters to the dark, obscure line which was Africa. 'Da Souza,' he whispered.

'Yes, sir.' Rutherford joined Murray. 'He has quite an empire in Whydah, huge barracoons, the Dahomeys provide him with slaves, thousands of them. They say Brazil was built because Da Souza provided its labour.'

Murray shook his head. 'What monsters that shore breeds.'

'It certainly does, sir. Crocodiles, manatees, spiders as big as —' he almost said as big as your head, but thinking it would not be wise to refer to a commander so, pointed his finger at Rafferty '— as big as his head. Well, goodbye, sir.'

Goodbye, goodbye; Rutherford and his Hornets off to Whydah where the busy slave-ships, so elegant and so beautiful and small, like toy ships on a mirror, waited for Da Souza's tearful cargoes. *Sentinel* edging north-east against the current, making her landfall off Akassa, off the delta of the Oil Rivers.

18

The coast of the Oil Rivers. Banks of mud, sickly yellow and mauve. Secretive creeks winding their black ways from the interior. The land, if it was land, and the water, if it was water, sweltering in the sickly heat, and fever written all over it as plain as the nose on your face.

Seamen on *Sentinel* looking at the coast with disgusted contempt.

'Call that a country?' Docherty said. 'Mother of God, I'd swap the boiling of it for a sow in litter.'

No dissent. Yetts spat over the side. 'Like looking for a needle in a haystack,' he said. 'That slaver could be anywhere up one of them creeks.'

General agreement. Four hundred miles of swamp and lagoons, innumerable nooks and crannies; why, you might look for a slaver for years — *years* — and never come within ten cables' length of her. But one dissenting voice: Parkin, Able, late of the *Beagle* (Fitzroy commanding, and a pack of civilians on board forever catching things and cutting them up, leaving a trail of nasty stinks everywhere, but an easy berth notwithstanding and a good master despite his testiness) — five years on the one voyage, and knowing tropical waters like the back of his hand — shook his rugged, ragged head.

''Tain't every creek that will take a vessel. And she'll need water, won't she — for all those slaves? No good lying in a mangrove swamp for that. And if she has run for shore — I say *if* she has, then she'll have gone to the nearest place, won't she? So she can't be all that far away. I daresay the Owner had that in mind?'

The Owner had. He did not believe that *Phantom* could be more than a hundred miles away. And those deceptive streams, those mysterious tunnels, dark holes in the sombre wall of forest, how many of them would take a clipper drawing at least eight feet of water? But still, the rat-holes need a ferret to sniff the rat out.

'Mr Brooke,' he called. 'We will have the longboat made ready.'

Forty men bent their backs at the labour of heaving the boat, all twenty feet and two tons of it, off its skids and over the side.

'Mr Purvis!' The carpenter ran forward. 'Please sound the boat and make sure she is ready for the voyage. Mr Hayes! Mount the nine-pound cannon. Fifty pound of fine-grain powder, thirty mealy-white, thirty cartridges and shot. Six muskets, twenty rounds each. Mr Taplow, provision the boat for thirty days. Mr Keverne, please check the compass — Bosun, the rigging and sails'; the rattle of commands and the brisk exercise of skills to make one boat ready for one month's voyage.

'Mr Bower!'

'Sir.'

'Mr Bower, I want you to take command of the longboat and sail ahead of us, looking for this slaver. I am choosing you because you are familiar with boat work. I know you have had an arduous tour of duty already, but you will understand I have no alternative.'

Bower understood perfectly well. The moment he had seen the men rush to the longboat he had known he would be chosen to command it. Not that he really minded. It was *command*.

'Aye aye, sir,' he said.

'Good,' Murray nodded his approval of Bower's prompt reply. 'Now I want you to search the creeks. You know.'

'Yes, sir.'

'Very well. Now, you are not to attempt to take a ship of force unless in your judgement it is advisable.'

Bower appreciated that remark. It confirmed him in *true* command. Once he was in the longboat his judgement and his alone mattered, but it was reassuring that his lord and master thought so too.

Murray gazed along to a line of men steadily moving across the deck, each carrying a burden from the hold to the longboat.

'I shall sail down the coast behind you. If necessary we will rendezvous at longitude seven off the Bonny river. Arrive there in seven days' time. Wait three days. If I do not arrive, carry on to the Isle of São Tomé and join *Dauntless*. Choose four seamen and take two Kroomen.'

'Aye aye, sir.' Bower dodged off to check his stores and to wrangle with Brooke about the best men to take; Brooke being perfectly happy to shuffle off on to the longboat the worst idlers on board and Bower being stubbornly determined to take only four good men.

The longboat provisioned, watered, charts, compasses, sextants, cannon, muskets, shot, cutlasses . . . everything counted twice and signed for. The seamen ready to go over the side.

Bower reported to Murray that he was ready to sail.

Murray called Bower to him. 'Have you picked your men?'

'Yes, sir.' Brooke and he had come to an amicable arrangement. Two good and two bad.

Murray nodded. 'I have decided to send Mr Spencer with you. He needs experience in boat work and I will be glad to see him in the charge of an experienced officer.'

Bower was ready to take the ship's cats with him if Murray wished and so he merely touched his cap and moved off. Murray called after him, 'I do not believe in cosseting, Mr Bower.'

'Just so, sir,' said Bower, who did not believe in cosseting either.

John was rousted out and, instead of lying in his hammock full of plum duff and cheese, it being blessed Tuesday, found himself on a hard plank, soaked with spray within ten minutes, hard tack and water to look forward to, and taking it philosophically as all part of a sailor's life.

So did every other man in the boat. Yetts and Dawlish in fact had volunteered. Cobber, who never, ever, volunteered for anything, had been fobbed off on Bower as a crack fleet-gunner and accepted his orders with a shrug of his scarred shoulders, as had Rose. As Rose said, taking the tiller for his trick of steering, it was better by a sight than being on an open boat in the North Sea in the middle of winter — *which* he had done, and the frost and snow so thick you looked like that there Santy Claws the Germans went on about.

The longboat glided away from *Sentinel*, its long, triangular sail picking up every breath of air. There was a sparkling exhilaration as the boat slipped over the long rollers and a rainbow glittered in the bow-wave. Even the heat seemed less intense. There was an agreeable feeling of holiday, of escape from the tight routine of the ship; and a faint smack of excitement, a tang of danger, like mustard on an old sausage.

Bower laid down his course to take the longboat close inshore, and within an hour they were within a long pistol-shot of the shore and could smell its dank, fetid odour. Bower shortened sail.

'We'll ease along,' he said. 'Keep your eyes peeled for a lagoon or a creek.'

An added dash to the holiday mood. The men peering eagerly into that dark line of green, looking for a break in its dreary, interminable length.

Time passing, the sun rising, the boat glided on. Now and then a wave broke over the side and splashed the crew; pleasant, refreshing, reviving — until the sun evaporated the water and left a layer of stinging salt.

By then, the holiday spirit was ebbing away rapidly. Especially in John, whose lips had begun to crack. He went to the water-cask and was quite surprised to have Bower call him back and to be told sharply that he had already drunk his ration.

'And you will see to it that the men stay clear of the cask,' Bower added, sounding most remarkably like Brooke.

The coast went on and on interminably; muddy headlands, vestigial capes, bays and rivulets, all backed by forest and swamp. At noon Bower and John took the sun's height, balancing awkwardly on the rolling boat.

'More by God and guess than good work,' Bower said as he wrote up the rough log. 'Let's eat.'

Biscuit, a bit of cheese, water. Dawlish was finished his meal and sat in the thwarts looking at the coast.

'It's a solemn country,' he said, shaking his head. 'What's behind all those trees? Do you know, sir?'

Bower shook his head. 'Not really. You find fishing villages here and there, and on the rivers, on the Bonny and the Brass, there are biggish places, small towns. But beyond them —' he shrugged.

'Has any white men been up there, sir?' Dawlish asked.

'Oh yes, Clapperton, Mungo Park. They say the land gets dry up north, and a man called Lander reckons he came all the way down to the Oil Rivers on a huge river. Maybe that's what the Oil Rivers are, the delta of one great big river. But nobody knows.'

Yetts finished his cheese. "Bout five or six years ago, I was up in Liverpool town — I was on a merchantman — that was afore long service came in, sir,' he said apologetically. 'There was two steam-ships fitting out to come to these parts. The *Quorrah* and, and, I disremembers the other name, like.'

'The *Alburkah*,' Bower said.

"Twas something like that,' Yetts agreed. 'I know it was old Laird what built them. He's got a yard in Birkenhead. Do you know what happened to them, sir?'

'Yes. Forty-eight white men came out and nine got back. All the rest died.'

'Pheoo!' Dawlish whistled. 'No wonder they calls it the white man's grave. What really is these diseases, sir?'

Bower shrugged. 'No one knows.'

'So it's all a bit like a mystery, then,' Yetts said.

'Yes,' Bower handed over the tiller to Rose. 'It's a bit like a mystery, all right.'

The afternoon wore away. They found two or three creeks, but none of them large enough to take a ship the size of *Phantom*. Grey clouds formed, the first heavy drops of rain began to fall. Bower took the boat out to sea.

'Ain't we going ashore for the night, sir?' Dawlish asked.

'No we ain't,' Bower said. 'That's a strict order. And if you'd spent a night up one of those creeks you wouldn't want to either.'

'You ain't been breaking orders yourself, sir, have you?' Yetts asked, a friendly grin taking the edge off any insolence the question might otherwise have had.

'No,' Bower said. 'I got stuck up the Bonny one night. Get the sea anchor out. We'll do two-hour watches.'

The boat tugged at the long canvas sleeve. Bower and the men were asleep in minutes, the Kroomen in seconds. John held the first watch, keeping the bows of the boat facing the waves. The clouds drifted away and the stars shone down. Surf broke on the shore with a sound of distant trains. Something, a dark shadow, bumped against the boat. A shark's black fin broke the silver phosphorescence of the sea.

John clutched the tiller a little tighter. A long way from Northampton. A long way from damp English fields, homely cows, slow-speaking farmhands, and the pealing of church bells. He wiped his cracked lips and rubbed his salt-caked head, weary-eyed but vigilant, keeping his watch under the African stars.

Two hours, Yetts taking the watch; another two, Dawlish taking over; two more, Bower up, taking command, running the boat back to shore, rounding a muddy headland — and finding a creek large enough to take three *Phantoms*.

Across its mouth the creek had a bar, a bank of mud brought down by the stream. The sea broke against the bar in a tumult of surf and from the sea it would have seemed quite impassable. But at the edge of the bar, curving around it like a sickle, was a channel of black, still water.

'Well, well,' said Bower. 'A nice little old passage. Just right for a wicked old slaver that knows the coast. Right, let's go a-sniffing. Break out the muskets, Mr Spencer. Cobber, stand by the gun with Rose. Unship the oars, lads. Dawlish, try your hand on the sounding-rod.'

Yetts and the Kroomen sweating at the oars, the boat splashed up the channel. Dawlish, balanced in the bows, deftly swung the sounding-rod and measured the depth of the channel.

'No bottom,' he called. 'No bottom. No bottom.' A deep channel. Deep enough for *Phantom*, deep enough for *Sentinel*, deep enough for a frigate if she wanted to try her luck.

The channel narrowed, widened, narrowed again. The bar was left astern and the tumbling Atlantic, as the boat crept into the mouth of the creek. The creek was full of mist and it was difficult to see more than a few yards. But through the mist loomed strange shapes, fantastic, contorted arms draped with grey, hair-like fronds. And there were noises, a steady splashing, as though it was raining heavily (although there was no rain), and the hum and whine of millions of insects.

As the boat progressed up the creek, the mist rose. Mangroves trailed their fronds in the water, dank plants raised fat, mauve fingers from the mud, green ooze bubbled, and little creatures, something like fish, leaped from the mangrove roots into the stream making that strange splashing noise. It was very hot, and the mosquitoes were clustering on the men in clouds.

'Jesus,' Dawlish slapped at his face. 'It's like the end of the world.'

'Stow your gab,' Bower snapped. 'I don't want any talking.' He bent over the side of the boat and scooped up some water. It was brackish, but not disgustingly so. From somewhere a steady current of fresh water was flowing down to the sea. And the swamp was changing. Muddy banks were beginning to appear, small islands of firm ground, and here and there a cabbage-palm had found a footing.

Two more hours of solid slog at the oars. And then there was no more river, merely a maze of channels, some larger than others and running with fresh water, but none large enough to take a ship.

'Well, sod it,' Yetts cried. 'All that for nothing.'

'Not for nothing,' Bower cried. 'You ought to know better, Yetts, a prime seaman like you. We know that slaver ain't here, don't we? We can save some other boat wasting its time.'

'Aye aye, sir,' Yetts said, his voice strongly suggesting that he didn't care if ten thousand sailors wasted their time rowing up the creek.

'All right then.' Bower mopped his face. 'I spent six weeks on this duty with a boat crew, and never a peep out of any of them. Lay on the oars and let's get downstream.'

The boat was swung round and as its bows pointed downstream there was a noise, a rather hollow sound with a flat echo, like a man clapping his hands.

'That was a musket,' Bower said.

The men in the boat sat very still but there was no more noise, only that one eerie bang echoing from the wilderness of mud and water.

Bower broke the silence. 'Where away?'

Cobber assumed one of his rare speaking roles. 'Two points off the starboard beam,' he said, spat a long stream of tobacco juice at a toad, and relapsed into a wooden silence.

Bower looked at the others who nodded their agreement. ''Bout a mile off, sir,' Yetts said. 'Somewhere in that muckheap.'

'Yes.' Bower slaughtered some hundreds of insects browsing on his neck. Two points off the starboard beam meant downstream and somewhere off to the right, in (as Yetts had expressed it) the muckheap of the swamp. But who could be in there with a musket? A native? It seemed unlikely, but at all events it needed investigating.

'All right,' he said. 'Let's take a look. Silence now.'

The longboat drifted downstream, needing hardly more than an occasional nudge from the oars to keep her moving. The men were tense and alert; that sinister bang meaning, however improbably, that there were men somewhere, not too far away, perhaps watching them through the fringe of moss dangling from the mangroves.

But sharp-eyed though the men were, John saw it first. Or rather, he thought he saw it first, and he reproached himself for not saying it first. As it was he certainly said it second because one of the Kroomen saw it, too, through his remarkably sharp brown eyes, and he spoke first too, through his remarkably white teeth.

'Cap'n,' he said. 'That no look right.'

And it didn't either, because *that* was a great branch which had been lopped off and jammed across the entrance to a sidestream.

Bower leaned over and tugged at the branch. It moved quite easily. Behind it was another branch, and behind that another. 'Now, now,' he said. 'What a clever old slaver he is, to be sure. And what a cunning one. Well, let's go and take a peep. Cobber, load that cannon.'

A sinister little journey up the stream which, after a few

hundred yards, opened out into a large lagoon, half a mile long and five hundred yards wide; at its end an agreeably high bank of mud, tied up to which was *Phantom*.

'Oh Lord,' Bower whispered. 'Lordy me. Time for us children to run back to Pappa. Back oars, you Sons of Wrath, and any man who splashes gets two dozen.'

Like a cat backing from a dog, showing its teeth all the way, the longboat slid back and, as silently as it had come, slipped away downstream.

'And now,' Bower cried. 'Row like all the devils from hell. But I do wonder what clever old Johnnies like that were doing bangin' off a musket.'

Although, as a matter of fact, the explanation of that was simple, and absurd, and tragic.

19

After the fight, Kimber had known exactly where to take *Phantom* to replenish his water. The knowledge of quiet creeks and streams where a slaver could lie up safe from the prying eyes of the Royal Navy was part of his stock and trade.

On arriving in the lagoon Kimber had put the slaves over the side, chained in coffles of twenty. They daubed themselves with mud as a shield against the mosquitoes. Plastered as they were they sat huddled on the bank, hardly distinguishable from it, hopeless, passive, and cowed. But not all.

Among the slaves there were some who had kept their wits about them and who realized that they had returned to their own country. Lyapo was one of them, and it was clear to him that the ship had returned for repair. Any fool could see that, and any fool could understand that once the ship was ready it would sail again — and when it did, Lyapo felt in his bones, he would never see his own land again.

A boat came down the lagoon laden with casks. Lyapo watched carefully as the boat tied up to the ship and the casks were hauled on board. The small boat had made several trips, and each time it had unloaded the casks had gone back into the boat. This time they weren't. They have finished, Lyapo thought, soon we will be driven back to the filth and the darkness.

He looked at the men in his coffle. One or two looked undefeated. Perhaps together they could think of a way to get free. After all, there were hundreds of slaves and not many of the other men. Surely something could be done. Something.

Lyapo licked his lips. He was no fool. In fact he was a shrewd, capable man, and respected as such in his village. That he knew nothing about Europeans or ships or cannon was beside the point. He knew a great deal about farming, quite a lot about animals, and a good deal about men. And that was his problem. He was young, and in his village young men did not make plans. They sat back as the old men, the wise men, spoke, and only then did they make their own tentative proposals. But as the Mandingo had told him, that was in the old days, and the old days were gone.

He took a deep breath. 'Brothers,' he said. 'Brothers, what are we to do?'

It was not the opening he had intended. It was hardly masterful or commanding, but it was a beginning, and beginnings led somewhere. Not that this one seemed to be doing so for the men stared at him, as if by speaking he was breaking some profound law. And perhaps I am, he thought, but he blundered on just the same.

'This —' He pointed to *Phantom*. 'This, soon they will take us away on it. We must do something before we are put down in that hole.'

At the end of the coffle was an elderly Yoruba, sour-faced, his arm raw with ulcers. 'Do?' he said. 'Do what?'

Lyapo did not know how to answer him. 'There are many of us,' he said, 'and few of them. Do we let ourselves be driven back like goats? By a handful of men?'

The Yoruba spat contemptuously. 'Men with guns against men with chains on their legs. Young men, pooh! That's what young men do, speak without thinking —'

Another Yoruba joined in. 'That is right. Young men are like empty pots, they may be big but there's nothing inside them. In my village. . . .'

Lyapo was amazed. Here they were, plastered with mud, sitting in the middle of a swamp, chained like dogs, and the two Yoruba were carrying on exactly as the old men did in his village. Just as if they were sitting outside a hut in the sunlight. There was something admirable about it if you looked at it in the right way. An indomitable refusal to accept defeat, to be turned into other than what they were. But, Lyapo thought, we must change. Change, or be wiped from the face of the earth.

But the old man had not finished. 'Do you think that you are the only man with eyes in his head? That . . . that big canoe has been taking water on so that we can go where we are going, and —' the old man pushed his sour, sore face into Lyapo's — 'there is nothing we can do about it. Nothing at all!'

Lyapo shook his head. 'We must do something. We must.'

'Must! Must!' Abruptly the old man changed his tone of voice. 'I don't want to be taken away either,' he said reasonably. 'What do you suggest? Even if we capture that thing there, what would we do with it?'

'I don't know,' Lyapo said. 'Perhaps we could run away.'

The old man opened his mouth showing one or two old, yellow fangs. A strange, creaking noise came from his mouth. 'Run away?' The creaking grew louder, and Lyapo realized that the old man was laughing! 'Run,' the Yoruba cackled. 'Run! All chained up together, running together — through this —' He waved his hand at the morass around them and cackled again, louder. Another man in the coffle laughed with him, then another. Soon every man in the group was laughing, even those who could not speak Yoruba.

A man in another group called over and asked what the laughter was about.

'It's a madman,' the old Yoruba cackled. 'We've got a madman who says we should run away through this swamp. All of us, with chains on our legs!'

Amazingly the other men laughed too, and those with him. The joke passed around the slaves. A madman . . . run through the swamp . . . chains. The laughter spread. Yes, even in the depth of their misery men laughed. Ha, ha, ha! Hee, hee, hee! Ho, ho, ho! Even Lyapo began laughing. Even he saw the comedy, hundreds of slaves running through the swamp with their chains clanking. Hundreds of slaves! Everyone was laughing, Yorubas, Tivs, Ibos. Screams and whoops of laughter, screeches from mud-daubed faces, laughter because men's eyes had grown dry with crying, laughter from the Pit.

On *Phantom* the sailors stopped working and stared down at the slaves. They laughed too, viciously, mockingly, bending their knees and jumping up and down, scratching their armpits like monkeys. From the quarterdeck Kimber looked down with a cold eye.

'You see that,' he said to Gavell. 'Them niggers is as happy as pigs in clover. They're always laughing once they gits settled down. I've seen 'em in the cotton-fields in Georgia, all laughing and singing and having a good time and all. Goddammit, they have a better time than them cracker farmers down there. Then those Goddamned abolitionists and those hypocritical, long-nosed Britishers come along and tries to stop us making an honest living a-buying and selling them.' His voice quivered with righteousness. 'Stands to reason they ain't human. Look at them. Would a human being laugh iffen he was in their position? Anyway, get that crew back to work. I want to get the hell out of here tonight.'

Gavell turned to his slave-driving of the crew. The slaves stopped laughing, and wondered why they had started. Lyapo lay back. Well, he thought, he had tried. Nothing had happened, but he had tried. It began to rain.

But one man hadn't laughed. He was an Ibo from the Oil Rivers, married with two wives and four children. One day his chief had told him that he had broken a tribal law and offended the village god by killing a chicken on a certain day. Because of this he had been sent to Chukwa, the Long Oracle of the Aro people.

The Ibo had never heard of the law which forbade you to kill chickens on a certain day, and he certainly didn't want to go to the Long Oracle, which was a snake which lived in a cave and swallowed up wrongdoers, but he had been given no choice in the matter. Four large men had taken him and, when he protested, had hit him on the head with a club. Since then he had suffered from terrible headaches, and he believed that Chukwa had swallowed him and that he lived in another world.

If nothing else persuaded him of that then the laughter did, although it did not sound like laughter to him. It sounded like the howling of demons, and when the men fell silent the howling continued in his head: Ha, ha, ha. Hee, hee, hee. Ho, ho, ho. Ha, ha, ha. Hee, hee, hee. Ho, ho, ho.

The demons were still in his head when the slaves were driven on *Phantom* in the late afternoon. The embarkation was done by experts at the trade and there was no chance of escape, or of rushing the crew. They were taken aboard in groups, surrounded by muskets, and deftly stacked on the slave-deck. Lyapo's group went aboard, then another, and then it was the turn of the Ibo with the demons in his head.

He shuffled awkwardly, sideways, up the gang-plank with the demons hooting away in his head, laughing and yowling as a seaman bent down to release the long chain which ran through his fetters. The chain was not easy to release, and the seaman fumbled with it for a while. 'Hee, hee, hee,' cried the demons, 'ho, ho, ho.' The Ibo looked down and, instead of the seaman's hands running over his feet, he saw two huge spiders. Huge spiders with red fur on them. The Ibo was horrified, a man with spiders instead of hands, and the spiders were running on his feet. He screamed. Or rather he thought that he screamed. He opened his mouth but no sound came out of it, none at all, and anyway the demons were laughing so loudly that they would have drowned out any scream he uttered; Ha ha ha. Ho ho ho. Hee hee hee.

The Ibo tried to stamp on the spiders, but with his ankles shackled he could not raise his feet. So he bent down and grabbed the sailor by the throat and squeezed.

The sailor gurgled. Gavell jumped forward and tried to drag the sailor clear, but the Ibo was very strong. Another man struck at him with a club but it was difficult to get a clear blow through the other slaves. The Ibo squeezed and squeezed, then threw the man away and grabbed at another seaman. But that man had a musket, and as the Ibo came for him he raised the gun and fired. The Ibo fell, the laughter of the demons fading as he fell, and the echo of the musket-shot reverberating among the green shades of the mangroves was the last sound he ever heard before he finally did go into another world. And that was the shot which Bower and his men heard.

Six hours later *Phantom* left the lagoon. Towed by her boats she went silently down the dark river and, as she came within sight of the moonlit sea, the boats of *Sentinel*, lying in wait and manned by sixty Sentinels, came from the shelter of the mangroves and rushed her and took her as easy as kiss your hand, mate.

20

Deep satisfaction on *Sentinel*. In the waist of the ship, among the seamen, profound and expansive pleasure at revenge exacted, honour satisfied, and prize money as good as in your pocket. The arithmetical Dawlish much in demand. On the quarterdeck, exultation. Every officer's face wreathed in a smile. The shadow of dishonour quite gone; glorious success, distinction, Murray's neat little plan working perfectly and every man doing his duty nobly. The Yankee skipper shot neatly in the shoulder by Brooke, his bucko mate measuring his six feet three on the deck after a blow from Rafferty's mighty fist, and only two casualties among the Sentinels: Jack Kemp, ordinary seaman, bitten in the ear and losing his front teeth, and John Spencer.

In the excitement of the fight John had run full-tilt into *Phantom*'s spare anchor and had a gaping wound on his forehead. Jessup had stitched it in a nautical sort of way, so that it looked like a patched sail, and had left John feeling most unheroic and looking feebly up at Brooke.

'A nasty gash.' A touch of human warmth in Brooke's voice and across his icy face a smile, like a glacier dividing. 'Are you sure that it wasn't a cutlass slash?'

'Yes, sir. I ran into the anchor.'

A long pause from Brooke. A measured, thoughtful pause.

'Are you *quite* sure? In the dark, you know . . . fluke of an anchor . . . easy to mistake . . . an arm wielding a weapon . . . confuse it. . . .'

'Oh, quite sure,' John piped.

'*Quite* sure?' A hint, a shade of exasperation in Brooke's voice, but another feeble although still obdurate denial.

Brooke departing, replaced by Scott. An admiring whistle at the sight of the wound, and frank and open envy: 'A jolly good wound, it should leave a really good scar' — replaced by incredulity as John insisted that he had bumped his head on the anchor.

'No, no, *no*. A cutlass wound, ferocious slaver, nine feet tall, gave you a whack.' Scott tapped his head in a meaningful way. 'Wounded in action — in *action*, facing the enemy. Very good for the reputation.' Scott exiting, still hissing — '*Cutlass* wound.'

But on deck no one was thinking of John as Murray, flanked

by his officers, faced Kimber. In his best uniform and with a sword buckled at his side, Murray looked the very type and symbol of the victor, and his face was like the wrath of God. Not that Kimber, his arm strapped, seemed daunted by the blue and gold and scarlet, and the dazzling perfection of the quarterdeck.

'You've a lot to answer for, Captain,' he spat. 'Just what in hell do you think that you're playing at?'

'None of your insolence,' Murray rapped out. 'And none of your blasphemy. In the name of Her Majesty Queen Victoria I formally apprehend you and your vessel, its crew and cargo, and I am sending you to Freetown under guard, there to await trial.'

'Trial!' Kimber exploded. 'Goddammit, it's you that should be on trial, chasin' me half-way across the Bight of Benin and killing half my crew. What Goddam charge do you think you can bring against me? You want to charge me, you'll have to send me into New York, and if you think that an American court is going to find me guilty after what you've done you're crazier than you look in that Goddam fancy dress. You think you can hold an American citizen on a slavery charge?'

In a quite expressionless voice, Murray said: 'Captain, I have warned you against taking the name of the Maker in vain on my ship. Blaspheme again and I will have you gagged. I wish you to have no doubt in your mind about that.'

Kimber nodded. 'I reckon you would, too. Well, mister, I'm looking forward to getting back to civilization. The sooner I get there, the sooner you will be broken from your command. I can't wait to see it.'

A little breeze blew from the creek, bringing with it the sickening stench of *Phantom*. Murray raised a white-gloved hand to his mouth. Over the glove his eyes were chill and remote.

'I very much doubt whether you will ever see that, Captain, because I am not sending you for trial as a slaver.'

Kimber thrust his head forward, like a dog ready to bite. 'Then just what charge are you taking me on?'

Murray lowered his hand and placed it on the silver pommel of his sword. 'I am charging you with piracy on the high seas. You will be tried in London. When you are found guilty you will be hanged at Execution Dock, and I doubt if even your government will raise any objection.'

The ship had gone very quiet. Men stopped their work and lifted questioning heads. A bird called, a strange raucous cry, and landed on the mainmast cap. Kimber threw his head back and laughed, a mirthless, contemptuous laugh.

'Mister, you're crazy. Plain tarnation crazy. You've got a crazy man here, you know that, crazy as a coot.' He looked around at the crew and found faces that might have been carved from stone. 'Piracy, what sort of charge is that?'

'A fatal one,' Murray said. 'Captain, you are a stupid man. Had you shown any colours but American you would have been sent into Freetown. You would have lost your ship but you would have gone free. Had you surrendered under the American Flag I would have been obliged to send you to New York where, as you so rightly observe, you might well have gone free. As it is, you chose to open fire without warning on a national ship going about its lawful business. That is piracy, Captain.'

He turned to Brooke. 'Take the captain to his own vessel. He is to be kept under close arrest. If there is any sign of trouble clap him and his crew in irons. That is all.'

Kimber back to his ship, Murray following with Bower and Noah in a boat bristling with armed men. Murray strode to the hatch and peered down. Faces, oddly chequered by the sunlight, stared back up at him. There was a flash of eyeballs and teeth, but not a sound. The hold was as silent as a hedge full of birds when a hawk hovers over it.

'Mr Bower,' Murray ordered. 'Form up your men around the hatch. We must get the slaves up. If there is a rush, do not shoot unless it is absolutely necessary. Now. Noah.'

'Sir.' Noah stepped forward and gave a splendid and wholly unlawful salute.

'Do the best you can, Noah. Try and explain that we are friends. I don't see that there is anything else we can do. Right. Let's have the hatch up.'

The unbroken glare of the sun beat into the darkness of the hold. Food, thought the slaves, and they prepared themselves for the difficult squeeze on to the deck. At the rattle of chains the Sentinels brought their muskets to the ready.

'Easy,' Murray called. 'Come on, Noah.'

Noah obligingly lay on the deck and stuck his head into the hold. 'Does any here speak Krio?' he cried.

There was a ripple of movement among the slaves.

'Krio,' Noah repeated. 'Come on, somebody here must speak it.'

Somebody did. In fact many did. Along the Oil Rivers Krio was

116

widely used and most people from the Delta knew a little, but only one man, an Itsekiri from Brass was bold enough, and unbroken enough, to answer.

'All right,' Noah wriggled a little further into the slave-deck. 'Now listen. We're your friends. Your friends, see? We're not bad men, not slaver men. We're going to make you free!'

A complete silence. Those who did not understand Noah were dumb through fear. Those who did were silent, because they could not grasp what he was saying. Free? they thought, how could they be free? The slaves turned their minds away from the thought as a man might turn to avoid a cruel practical joke.

Murray called to Noah anxiously. 'Noah, are you all right?'

'Oh yes, sir,' a muffled voice came from the slave-deck. 'But these men, they're stupid, sir.' Noah's head popped up suddenly. 'I've told them. I said you are all free, but they don't say nothing.'

'Well,' Murray shrugged. 'I suppose we must bring them up, then.'

The slaves came blinking into the light. One or two gaped at Murray and his amazing cocked hat, but the rest did not spare a glance as they hobbled and shuffled forward to their place in the bows. There they all stood, filthy, naked, flakes of dried mud falling from them, looking at the men in blue and gold who might, for all they knew, have fallen from the moon. The Sentinels stared at them, too, with pity and contempt and seemed as if they would stare all day, until Murray spoke.

'Mr Bower, set the armourer to knocking off those shackles, if you please.'

The armourer set to work, the fetters opening with an ugly rasping sound. Ankles revealed, raw, scabbed, bleeding. Jessup and his loblolly boy busy with Blue Ointment, tutting over ulcers and sores. The women were brought up and, at Murray's scandalized order, hastily sent down again until every spare scrap of cloth had been brought over from *Sentinel* and the decencies were preserved. A growing babble of noise, men chattering, chuckling, laughing. The mirage of freedom was becoming tangible, solid, real! Grinning Sentinels handed out yams, sour-faced Phantoms scrubbed the slave-deck with vinegar.

Lyapo ate his yams and dived under the pump Murray had rigged up. How light he felt without his fetters. He felt as if he could float, float like a feather, drift away from the ship, across the swamps and forests, up the great river, and back to his home. He stepped from the pump and joined a group of Yorubas. The sour old man was among them, but even he could not spoil the savour of the moment.

The Itsekiri stepped forward and spoke to Noah. Noah nodded and went to Murray.

'He asks where they are going, sir.'

'Ah,' Murray slapped his thigh. 'Tell them that they are going to Freetown . . . to a fine city. Tell them that they will be cared for and given land. Just tell them the truth.'

Noah had a deep respect for Murray, whose grim courtesy he recognized and respected, but he regarded the instruction as so wildly impracticable that it could only be meant humorously. 'Yes, sir,' he said, 'I'll tell him that.' Turning to the Itsekiri he said, 'You are going to go home, back to your own village. It takes some time to get there, you have to go on this ship for a while, but then you'll be happy again.'

'I've told him, sir,' he said. 'He'll tell the others.' After all, he thought, only an idiot would tell two hundred men that they were being taken to a town two thousand miles away and that they would never see their homes again.

'You made it quite clear?' Murray asked.

'Yes, sir!' Noah saluted and smiled, a large confiding smile, which had won the heart of many a girl and broken the heart of many a man who had tried to cheat him, and been cheated himself.

'Thank you, Noah,' Murray said. 'Carry on.'

Murray returned to *Sentinel* and sent for Brooke. 'Please select a prize crew,' he said. 'Ten seamen and two Kroomen. I know it is a lot for a prize but there are two dozen prisoners on the slaver, let alone a hundred or so slaves. We will be a little short-handed for a while, but we must get used to that. Anyway, I hope we may expect Mr Fearnley and his men back before too long. Now, command.'

'Yes, sir.' Brooke rubbed his chin. With Cawley dead and Fearnley away, *Sentinel* was not over-endowed with officers. 'It is a problem. There is the boatwork to consider, and if we take more prizes. . . .'

'Suppose we send a good petty officer,' Murray said. 'The bosun is a reliable man. Didn't he hold a commission once?'

'Thomas? Yes, sir. He left the service and lost his rating. He is a sound man.'

'Well?'

Brooke did not like the idea. After all, if men got it into their

118

heads that they could roam the seas without officers, who knew what other ideas about rank and its importance they might not get into their heads? Look what was happening in England: every Tom, Dick and Harry demanding a say in the affairs of the country.

'I have to say, sir,' he said, 'that I do not approve. There should be a commissioned officer on board.'

Murray did not disagree. He hated slavery and, indeed, oppression of any sort, but his view on rank and authority were quite as sharp as Brooke's. 'Suppose we send Mr Spencer,' he said.

'Spencer!' For once Brooke was shaken from his cold, aristocratic composure. 'Sir!'

Murray nodded. 'He is a trifle raw, I agree, and he is hardly what either of us would call a regular officer, but he has the making of one, do you not agree?'

'Well. . . .' Brooke turned his head a little, showing his fine profile. For a moment he hesitated and then an innate honesty made him speak, although reluctantly. 'Yes, sir,' he said. 'He has.'

'Well then?'

'Sir, he is only fifteen.'

Murray smiled. He had a curiously bright smile, which shone the brighter because of its rarity. 'How old were you when you first took command, Mr Brooke?'

'Twelve,' Brooke said, without smiling. 'But if you will excuse me, sir, that is nothing to the point. I had been at sea then for two years — and I was in command of a gig, with four men in it, and we were rowing about Portsmouth harbour.'

'Command is indivisible,' Murray said. 'You were as much in command of your gig as any admiral with a fleet ever was. And you will remember, Mr Brooke — not, I am sure, that you need reminding — Lord Nelson was full post-captain at the age of nineteen and was in command of a brig.'

'Well. . . .' Brooke rubbed his chin. 'He is only an acting midshipman.'

'I am ready to rate him full,' Murray said. 'But allow me to say this. Rank is an actuality — every man must obey his superior or pay the consequence — but it is also a symbol. Did you ever hear of Captain Andrews? You did. He died before he got on to the admirals' list but I served with him in *Naiad*, frigate. He was as mad as a hatter. He believed that he was the Archangel Gabriel and, I do assure you, he spent the entire voyage in his cabin blowing on a trumpet. He was no more capable of commanding the ship than a Tom o' Bedlam, but he was the lawful captain and every single order on the ship was reported to him. Actually the voyage was extremely smooth.'

The bumps and bangs of a happy ship about its work. Men laughing, Potts's healthy bellow shaking the sky-light, the sacred bell again measuring the day.

'I shall, of course, put Thomas on board with him,' Murray said.

Well, Brooke thought, well, it would keep the experienced officers where they should be, on the ship. 'The other middies won't like it,' he said.

Murray raised an eyebrow and smiled, crookedly. 'I hardly think you and I need worry about the feelings of midshipmen, Mr Brooke.'

The naval rush. Ten men told off to join the prize. John, amazed, staggered, disbelieving, rated full midshipman, on pay and rations, and acting master of *Phantom*. Murray whispering in Thomas's ear, and the bosun coming as near to winking at his captain as he dared. Brooke having an equally quiet word with John, emphasizing that every officer who had ever lived or breathed, or was ever likely to live or breathe, depended entirely and totally on the wisdom, experience, and judgement of his bosun, especially when that bosun was forty-two, with twenty-eight years' experience at sea, and the officer was fifteen years with three months in the service.

John quite understanding; modest, humble, retiring. But as *Phantom* cast off her tow and set her sails he strode the poop, Brooke's second-best telescope under one arm; bearing, he rather thought, more than a passing resemblance to — well — if not *quite* Lord Nelson, then at least to Captain Murray . . . or Brooke . . . or, well then, Samuel Potts.

21

Phantom reaching south in search of the easterly winds; short-handed, with reduced sail, and not showing her true speed, but even so throwing up a satisfying bow-wave — although the dolphins keeping her company were merely dawdling. John on the poop, dirk at his waist, telescope under his arm, and deep, satisfying joy in his heart.

Next to him, Thomas respectfully touched his hat. 'Were you thinking of shortening sail, sir.'

John paused for a judicious moment, an eyebrow raised, his lips pursed.

'It might be as well, sir,' Thomas said. 'Get snug for the night. It's a bit like a merchantman, but we are short of hands.'

John nodded. 'Yes, pray attend to it, Mr Thomas.'

With hardly more than a murmured order from Thomas the men swarmed aloft and reefed the topsails. Amazingly sensible the men were, John thought, quite amazingly so. Jolly good men, all of them; sound, reliable seamen. He took a deep breath.

'I think I shall examine the ship, Mr Thomas.'

'Just so, sir.' Not by a flicker of a muscle did Thomas betray his feelings at John inspecting the ship for the fourth time in the twelve hours since they had parted from *Sentinel.*

John wandered along the deck, the men good-humouredly showing him the deference they might have given an admiral of the fleet, had one wandered on board. In the bows John looked at the slaves. Amazingly sensible they were too, sitting quietly under their awning, eating and drinking in an orderly way, not interfering with the working of the ship, and no squabbling among them even though there were so many of them crowded for'ard and refusing to go in to the slave-deck.

By the forward mast there was a ladder which ran into the main hold. John slid down it. At its foot was a brawny seaman armed with a musket and cutlass.

'All well, Hardwick?' John asked.

The man touched his forehead. 'Oh aye, sir. There was a terrible lot of cursing before but they've quietened down, like.'

They were Kimber and his crew. Murray had offered them the freedom of the deck if they would be chained. Kimber had contemptuously refused, so Murray had ordered them battened down for the voyage. Now they were in the old fo'c'sle with the door sealed by three-inch oak beams.

'Very well. Keep a sharp watch now.' John climbed back up the ladder. Night was sweeping in across the ocean, stars hanging like lanterns in the darkness over Africa. John suppressed a yawn as he climbed on to the poop.

'All is just so, Mr Thomas. Just so.' He leaned on the rail, his eyelids drooping after a long day.

'Would you be thinking of turning in, sir?' Thomas asked.

'Turning in?'

'Commanding officer's privilege, sir,' Thomas said gravely. 'I always remember Lord Nelson saying to me what a pleasure it was to be able to go below and turn in when night came.'

'Lord Nelson,' John said. 'You mean *Lord* Nelson?'

'The very one, sir,' replied Thomas, who had been seven years old when Nelson died. 'He always told me that one sure, certain, sign of a good officer was him getting his head down. Ready for tomorrow, like.'

'Well . . . I was thinking of turning in,' John said quite untruthfully, as he had been about to examine the ship yet once more. 'I'll go below. Let me know if there is anything to report.'

Thomas's emphatic 'aye aye, sir' rang pleasantly in John's ears as he went down to Kimber's cabin, six feet high, eight feet wide, twelve feet long; vast, spacious, airy after two months in a hammock by a corner of the breadroom. And a long, full night's sleep too, the first for many a week, since quite astonishingly neither Thomas nor his relief found one single reason to disturb him.

Dawn and a full sea running. A little rain. The wind veering easterly, freshening a little. Joe Baker, ordinary seaman, entering with a mug of coffee. A moment's dawdling under the blankets — oriental luxury — and then the remembrance of the responsibility of office. John leaped to his feet, dressed, and, clutching his hat, telescope, and dirk, dashed on deck to find a stolid rating at the wheel, two look-outs posted, and Thomas coming up from his breakfast.

Nothing in the sky, nothing in the sea, nothing to write in the log. The slaves fed, the crew fed, food lowered into the fo'c'sle to Kimber and his men, and such a barrage of profanity coming from that venomous spot that Thomas threatened to withhold the rations. But that apart, a pleasant, sensible ship, and a pleasant sail on an agreeable sort of day. Uncertain winds, to be sure, but fresh, with a few scattered rain squalls on the horizon. And coming out of one of them, with something of the air of a wolf prowling after a lamb, a handsome, rakish schooner.

The schooner was the *San Felipe*, owned by a Spanish-American syndicate, sailing from Rio de Janeiro, and feeding the vast Brazilian market with slaves from Biafra. Her Master, Da Silva, was a Portuguese from Peniche although, being wanted there for double murder, he had not troubled it with his presence for fifteen years.

Although Da Silva was a slaver by trade, he was not averse to a little piracy if it came his way. However, that could be a dangerous game: the most innocent-looking vessel might turn out to be stuffed with ruffians quite ready to capture *you*. And not only ruffians were dangerous. Only the previous year Da Silva had tried to take a little Dutch snow which was trading, quite lawfully, in tobacco with Cuba, and had found it full of stolid Dutchmen who were quite ready to fight all day, and all week if necessary, and who had given him such a pounding that he had been forced to run into Guadeloupe for extremely expensive repairs.

Consequently, when Da Silva saw *Phantom* he was ready to be careful. The ship was obviously American-built and he had no wish to take on a Yankee slaver, Americans being worse than Dutchmen when it came to a fight. On the other hand it was just possible that the ship was flying the British ensign quite legally, in which case it was a prize with, probably, only a small crew on board. It was certainly worth looking into.

'Run up the French colours,' he said to his mate, 'and give them a gun.'

On *Phantom*, Thomas spat on his hands. 'If she's French I'll kiss my elbow. More like a bloody slaver with fifty men on board. Cut for twelve guns, ain't she? Well, give her a gun back, sir, show her we've got teeth too. And best get the slaves below.'

There was not much deference in Thomas's voice now. John wisely threw any pretensions to command aside and ran forward, although getting the slaves below deck was easier said than done. John pointed and gesticulated, but it took some ungentle pokes from the Kroomen to get them moving and the crack of the long eighteen to persuade them that below deck was the place to be. But as they shuffled to the hatch Thomas roared down the ship.

'It might be a good idea to keep some of those blacks on deck, Mr Spencer. Those that have some clothes on. Give an impression of a full crew.'

'Aye aye —' John cut off the 'sir' just in time and hastily sorted out a dozen slaves, Lyapo among them. By the time he had finished the ship was looking taut. Muskets and cutlasses had been issued, and the slow-matches by the guns were smouldering in sinister fashion.

'That's the best we can do,' Thomas said. 'We can just about fight two guns if it comes to it, which please God it won't. Let's hope she's not a tartar like this one was. And let's hope the wind holds.'

Every man on deck looked up at the sails. They had a satisfying curve, and as long as that curve held *Phantom* could snap her fingers at the schooner. And for an hour or two the wind held in a gratifying way, leading Baker to observe, before a scandalized crew could prevent him, that they were away and clear. Whereupon the main topgallant sail gave an ominous flap.

'Which you are a screw-gutted sea-horse,' a voice said bitterly. 'Now see what you've gone and done and.' All Baker's sullen protestations that he didn't mean no harm, did he, couldn't bring the wind back into *Phantom*'s sails, and she lay as becalmed as a ship could be.

The schooner was becalmed, too. But by three in the afternoon a capricious breeze was playing about the sea, first touching *Phantom*, then the schooner. However, the schooner was the winner at the game. She certainly had more men than *Phantom*, and could handle a greater spread of sail. By four she was less than half a mile off but the wind died away again and she lay, idly, rocking on the waves.

'We might be all right at that,' Hardwick said, but Thomas shook his head. Men were moving about the deck of the schooner, and experienced eyes on *Phantom* knew what they were about. John's eyes were not experienced, but Thomas's were vastly so.

'She's breaking out a boat,' he said. 'Man the sides.'

A boat left the side of the schooner and bobbed its way towards *Phantom*. Thomas took John's telescope, grunted, and took John aside.

'There's a dozen men in that boat,' he said. 'I don't reckon that they're up to any good. But I was wondering. Suppose we gave them arms —' He jerked his thumb at the slaves who were still on deck. 'If we mix 'em up among the men we'll make a decent show of force. What do you think, sir?'

John looked at Thomas sharply. It was the first time in hours that Thomas had used the formal title, and for the first time that afternoon he had asked permission for an order. John knew why that was. Thomas had taken over the working of the ship directly. That was only sensible. A fool might object but no one else would, not even the Lords of the Admiralty, if they ever got to hear of it. But to place arms in the hands of Africans, of men who might take the ship . . . that was a decision only an officer could take. And John took it.

He walked to Lyapo and held out a cutlass. It was an act of enormous confidence and one which only a man of great experience, or a youth of little, could have committed. 'Here,' he said.

Lyapo looked at the cutlass and at the youth. Why was he being given a sword? What did the youth want? The boy said something and pointed to the distant ship. He shook the sword and shouted, bang! bang! Lyapo understood. The boy wanted him to take the sword and fight against the men in the other ship. But still he did not take the cutlass.

John clicked his teeth with vexation. 'Slaver,' he cried. 'Slavers. Bad men.' He pointed to Lyapo's ankles and shuffled his feet.

Lyapo understood that, too. But how could he tell if what the youth was suggesting was true? Maybe the men who were coming across the sea were not wicked men, perhaps they were friends. And in any case, what affair was it of his? It was true that the men on this ship treated him better than the other men, those who were locked away, but what did that mean? Perhaps these new men would treat him better still. He decided to refuse the sword and stepped back a pace. Then the youth put his hand lightly on his arm.

It was a gentle touch, almost beseeching, almost affectionate. It was the first time Lyapo had been touched in that way for two months, and the gesture moved him. He looked into the boy's eyes, and the boy smiled. That was the first smile Lyapo had seen since he had left the Mandingo, and the touch and the smile implied a common humanity which the offer of the weapon made explicit. Without thinking more, Lyapo held out his hand and took the cutlass.

'Take a sword,' he said to the other Yorubas.

'Why should we?' one asked.

Lyapo hesitated. He could hardly say that they should take weapons because a boy had smiled at him. Instead he waved his hand at the schooner. 'The men there will come and put chains on us again,' he said.

'How do you know?' a man asked.

Lyapo felt a sort of despair in his heart at the question. How could he *know*? He shook his head. 'All I know is that these men have freed us,' he said. 'Now they give us weapons. What would you have us do? Throw the weapons down and wait? I am tired of being a goat. Now I think that I will be a man again. Make your own choice.'

He turned away and went to the side of the ship, joining the men there. And after a brief moment he was joined by the others, so that there was a fair show of force waiting for the schooner's boat when it came within hailing distance.

The boat had twelve men in it. They were a mixed bunch, mainly Europeans but with one or two dark skins among them and one obvious Chinese. A man was standing balanced in the bows. He was tall and dressed in a blue jacket and a white shirt. Under his hat his face was dark, but whether that was natural or a suntan it was hard to tell.

'What ship are you?' the man hailed.

John opened his mouth to reply, but Thomas nudged him. 'Don't say nothing, sir. Let them do the spouting.'

The boat came in a little closer. 'I am French ship,' the man cried. 'French ship of Government, you savvy?'

'We savvy,' Thomas called. 'What do you want?'

'I want to see your papers,' the man said. 'You got to stop when Government ship say so.'

'Tell it to your granny,' Thomas roared. 'This is a British prize. Look at our colours.'

'Ah,' the man balanced easily on the thwart as the boat edged in a little nearer. 'Anyone can show colours. You look like slaveship to me. You better tell me. You better show me papers.'

'I'll show you the back of my hand if you ain't careful,' Thomas cried. 'Now shove off. Vamoose, see, and pronto.'

The man in the boat turned and muttered something. In the stern the Chinese stood up with a boathook.

'Watch 'em,' Thomas said. 'Hardwick, keep your eye on that Chinee. If he tries to hook on, let him have it.' He turned back to the boat. 'Keep your distance now, we've warned you.'

126

The boat was very close in now. A dozen hard and scarred faces looked up at *Phantom*'s rail. 'I got forty — fifty more men,' their leader called. 'I don't want no trouble but you better be careful. I'm Government ship, French Government.'

John put his hands on the rail. In a high, clear voice he cried: 'Ici un bateau britannique. Ici un bateau sur la protection de la Reine de Grande-Bretagne. Comprenez?'

The man grinned. Under the shadow of his hat his teeth glinted like an assassin's knife; 'Oh, monsieur,' he jibed. 'Such a clever boy. Where you get that bad cut on the head? I come aboard, I got doctor here.'

John leaned forward. 'Messieurs —' he began, but the man suddenly cried harshly, 'Atacar!' The men at the port oars heaved and the boat crashed into the side of *Phantom*. The Chinese slammed his boathook into the rigging and the men in the boat jumped to their feet, cutlasses magically appearing in their fists.

'Hardwick!' Thomas yelled. A red face shot up over a hammock, a musket cracked out, and the Chinese's face turned into something scarlet and unpleasant. The man fell back into the boat as muskets rattled along *Phantom*'s side. A hand came over the side and a black arm wielding a cutlass slashed at it. John bit his lip, swung his pistol up, and took deliberate aim at the leader. The boat was sliding away from *Phantom* in a confusion of sprawling men and splintered oars. John leaned outwards as far as he dared in order to get his shot in, but a hand clamped on his shoulder and dragged him back. 'Get your head blown off, sir,' a voice cried. 'They've got muskets out.' To give point to the remark, something whined past them and smacked into the mast.

Thomas rushed to the stern with a musket, but the boat was already a hundred yards away. He rapped out an order and the helmsman brought the ship around a little. Cobber and his crew heaved at the long nine, trying to train it on the boat, but by the time they were ready it was well away and their shot skipped harmlessly over the waves.

Da Silva climbed back on board his ship and rubbed his chin. The ship was certainly a British prize, and he was inclined to leave it and get on with his business. On the other hand, it was a valuable ship and crammed with slaves. He had carefully counted the men lining the side and had made out no more than eight or nine. That was not many men both to sail a ship and fight her. The Blacks he did not take into consideration. But the white men were regular seamen, trained to fight, and the big man, the one who had spoken so violently, clearly knew his business.

But still . . . but still . . . ten men against thirty. He turned and gave an order.

22

San Felipe came down slowly on *Phantom*, the reflection of her masts reaching out across the brazen sea. At half a mile she tried a ranging shot which splashed harmlessly two hundred yards wide and a hundred yards short. Old Cobber, crouching across the long nine, cackled derisively.

'We'm be all right as long as she aims at us,' he said and fired back. His shot cracked into *San Felipe*'s rail and sent a shower of splinters whirling across its deck, blinding her best gunner.

Thomas slapped Cobber on the back. 'That's the way,' he cried. 'But keep your shot up, aim for her rigging.' And, spitting on his hands, Cobber did so, regarding shooting like this as no harder than shying coconuts.

A pleasant breeze blew up, ruffling the golden sea. On the burnished waves both ships began a delicate and deadly dance, *San Felipe* swinging in a wide circle around *Phantom*, *Phantom* turning inside the circle, keeping her unprotected rear well tucked in and her teeth bared at the slaver. Round and round the ships went, their guns banging out; ragged broadsides from *San Felipe*, two guns from *Phantom*, Cobber's long nine and the deeper bark of Hardwick's carronade. Cobber made good practice, judging the range and the elevation to a nicety and making every shot tell so that *San Felipe*'s rigging began to wear a tattered look, like unravelled knitting.

But there was nothing sensational or dramatic about the fight; merely the ships, neither of them large, circling slowly, at times hardly moving. The only noise the fitful wind and the banging of the guns, like slow, irregular hand-clapping.

Now and again *San Felipe* got a blow in. A shot hit the damaged mainmast, making it shiver, another made a neat hole in the longboat and a third smacked into the bows, just above the waterline — but in the sweat and rush of handling the ship and supplying the guns, that went unnoticed. And all the time, from three, to four, to five, as the sun slid steadily towards the horizon, Cobber chipped away at *San Felipe*.

By five o'clock Da Silva had had enough. Two of his guns were dismounted, he had half a dozen injured, one man dead, and the rest of his men were edging away from their stations and clustering behind the ship's boats. It would be only a matter of time before they refused to face the deadly accurate fire from *Phantom* and scuttled below deck. Da Silva was a philosophical man and, what was more, he was a businessman. He was ready to risk his capital, the ship, but only in expectation of a good profit. He no longer thought that he would make one with *Phantom*, so he was prepared to cut his losses and get on with his business. Besides, it would be dark in a matter of minutes, and he did not think his crew was up to a fight then. Shrugging his shoulders he turned to the helmsman. 'Bring her away,' he said.

And so an unsensational end to the day. *San Felipe* running north, to a contemptuous cheer from *Phantom*'s crew. Smiles all round; Cobber the hero of the day and promised as much rum as even he could drink when they got to Freetown. Thomas shaking hands with John, the crew shaking hands with one another, even the slaves recognizing a victory when they saw one and grinning away, their white teeth shining in the sudden night. Yes, a wicked vampire of a pirate fought off, beaten away by good gunnery, a steady crew, and masterful seamanship by Thomas; and, what's more, hardly a scratch to show for it — in the excitement of the moment, no one caring much about the shot from *San Felipe* which had hit *Phantom* in the bows.

But that shot had hammered a splinter from the side, and that splinter, a foot long, had killed Baker who had been on guard over the fo'c's'le. And Kimber, listening to the fight, had heard Baker fall and heard, too, his dying grunts and, taking his chance, had smashed through the battens and, with his men, was about to come roaring on deck.

Which he did, catching the Sentinels in that treacherous moment of complacency and congratulation; Kimber shooting Thomas dead on the spot with Baker's musket, and Gavell chopping down Old Cobber with a backhanded slash of Baker's cutlass. Within seconds the deck had been cleared. Sentinels and slaves were clubbed down with oaked billets, and those who weren't were rushed to the taffrail at the stern. For a few seconds there was a savage, confused mêlée there as desperate men snarled and struggled at close quarters. John had his dirk out and stabbed at Gavell, but before he had made a feeble, token blow, he was hammered in the side of the face, the stars of the night were joined by several hundred more, and he went backwards, over the rail, into the sea.

John was only half-conscious as he hit the water, less like a

130

young midshipman than a lump of debris, the remnant of a carcass thrown overboard to the sharks. But it was the thought of the gulping, snuffling sharks that gave him strength. He splashed out blindly, moved a yard or two, and struck against something hard.

What John had hit was the jolly-boat towed behind *Phantom*. It was not large and its sides were not high, but although John could grasp its sides he could not drag himself over them. Twice he heaved his head clear, but each time he was dragged back into the terrifying sea. Something brushed against his legs and he had a vision of a shark gliding past him, turning, coming back, its vast mouth gaping — John gave a little moan, his hands slipped from the boat. For a moment he held on with his fingertips and then, as he let his hand fall backwards into the waves, a powerful black hand clamped on his wrist and heaved him into the boat.

That long arm from Africa belonged to Lyapo. He, too, had gone overboard in the savage mêlée and had picked up the boat as it drifted past him. In the bows he had found a cutlass and had chopped through the tow-line. He had heard the bumps and bangs against the side of the boat as John had struggled to board it, and he had seen the hands clutching the side. For a moment he had been tempted to chop at them. He had even swung the cutlass over his shoulder, but he had not been able to bring himself to swing the blade down. Then he had recognised the youth who have given him a sword on *Phantom*, and had hauled him to safety.

The boat rocked perilously as Lyapo dragged John over the thwart. Lyapo grunted with alarm and jammed John into the bottom of the boat. After a moment the boat steadied, and Lyapo crept up to John. In the faint starlight the boy looked horribly pale and his eyes were closed. Lyapo touched John's face. It was cold and clammy. He wondered if the boy was dead, and felt regret, regret and sorrow but also fear. But his fear was not of the dead. In his bloody journey he had long since lost that. He was afraid of being alone, of being left solitary on this vast stretch of water. And besides, he was quite shrewd enough to understand that this boy knew about boats and water. Conceivably he could take them back to land.

Phantom was lost in the night. There was no moon, and the stars showed only fleetingly through grey cloud-wrack. The tiny boat rocked on the waves, insignificant, meaningless, a mere speck of debris on the vast ocean.

John sprawled in the boat exhausted and shocked. His jaw throbbed, the sea-water he had drunk made him feel sick, and blood was trickling from the corner of his mouth. A wave swept over the gunwale and slopped across his face. He gave a little cry of alarm and held out his arm defensively. But even as he did so he began retching, vomiting into the bilge. Then he rolled over, into the vomit, and fell unconscious. He looked very small in his blue jacket with its bright brass buttons.

After an hour or so he awoke to a sky streaked pink. 'I'm asleep on watch,' he thought and lurched forward in a panic. For a moment he stared, bewildered, at the boat and at Lyapo, who was slumped in the stern. John was terribly thirsty and had a vicious headache, and there was something wrong with his left eye. It was closed, and he had to force it open with his fingers. He struggled up, leaned over the gunwale, and splashed water on to his face. There was a crust of brown scum on his jacket where he had been sick. He splashed that with water, too, and rubbed at it with his sleeve. It was then that he fully realized what had happened.

'I have lost my ship,' he whispered. 'My first command, and I lost her.'

To his horror, he found himself crying. What would Captain Murray say? And Brooke? And all the men on *Sentinel*? He rubbed the palm of his hand across his eyes and his snivelling nose. A long way now from the pride of command and the glory of uniform. A long way, too, from the comforting presence of grown men who knew what they were about, and how to do it.

He looked around helplessly. The sullen waves rolling towards him seemed enormous, seen from such a tiny craft. A larger wave struck the boat. It yawed wildly and water poured over the side. John shook himself and lurched down the boat. He grabbed Lyapo. 'Move!' he croaked.

Half-asleep, Lyapo rolled to one side as John seized the tiller and brought the bows into the waves, steadying the boat. Lyapo made to stand but John waved an imperious hand. 'Down!' he cried. 'Get down!'

Lyapo understood the gesture if not the words and crouched, holding the side of the boat, looking upwards at John, glad that he had saved the boy and waiting, himself, to be saved.

John wiped his mouth on his sleeve and licked his lips. He looked at the boat. There were four oars, a cutlass, a tin baler, and the big black man. Suddenly he burst out giggling. Now I'm in command, he thought. Now I'm in true command.

Lyapo grinned with John, his teeth glinting in an amiable, companionable way. But why was the boy so happy? he wondered. Perhaps he knew something that made him cheerful. If so, Lyapo would very much have liked to know what it was. He was hungry and thirsty, there was no shelter in the boat, and the sun was beginning its remorseless climb. He pointed to the sun and to his mouth.

John nodded. He nodded but he did not know what to do about the sun, or about water. To the north the rains had been frequent, but here there was no sign of the heavy, grey clouds which brought the torrential downpours. The sky was a clear, bright blue and already the day was hot. It suddenly occurred to John that he might die soon.

The thought of his death concentrated his mind amazingly. He stopped his snivelling and his hysterical giggling and began to think. He guessed that they were about a hundred miles from land, but the rains certainly extended fifty miles out to sea. That made them fifty miles from life.

He scrambled past Lyapo, got the baler, and began emptying the boat. When they got to the rain-belt it would be important to have the boat as clean as possible so that rain-water gathering in it would not be spoilt by the salt-water. After a moment or so he gave the baler to Lyapo and tried to make a mast with the oars. But after a few attempts he gave that up. There was no way of strutting the oars, nor of stretching his jacket across them.

Still, he thought, that was not too bad. They did have oars. If they rowed they could travel, what — two, three miles an hour? At that rate twenty hours would take them up to the rains. Surely they could manage that, a mere day's rowing. After all, Captain Bligh had journeyed four thousand miles in an open boat. What was fifty miles or so compared to that? He took off his belt, strapped it around the tiller to try and keep a reasonable heading, fixed two oars in the rowlocks, took a seat, and grasped an oar. He waved to Lyapo, who joined him at the thwart. Then, side by side, they began to row.

The sea was calm, and after the first hour they had rowed three miles. After the second hour they had rowed another two. By then John's hands and arms and legs were knotted with cramp. His lips were cracked into bloody fissures, and his tongue was like a small, shrivelled piece of wood.

Lyapo was in no better shape. He was bigger and stronger than

John but his hands, soft from disuse, were skinned and sticking to his oars in a bloody glue. But in the third hour, their coats wrapped around their heads, they were still rowing; forward, back, forward, back, forward, back, in a state of trance, numbed, raw, bleeding; but rowing.

Then John began to hear voices; men hailing from distant ships, Brooke's voice snapping out an order. Docherty's accordian, the shrill calls of children at play, and, increasingly, the delicate splash and gurgle of a stream. Lyapo was thinking of water, too, especially the water he had wasted, thrown casually away after sipping a mouthful from a yellow gourd, or poured over his head to cool himself after working in the clearing. He thought, with incredulity, of the times he had actually refused water. Then he, too, began to hear sounds: the splash of a bucket in the cool village well, the drumming of the rains on the thatch of his hut, the deep murmur of the great river.

Now and then they rested, slumped over their oars, the breath rasping in their scorched throats; each rest grew longer and when they recommenced they rowed more slowly, the strokes of the long unwieldy oars becoming shorter, less powerful, until at times they were merely stirring the water.

Then, as the fourth hour began, John's arms simply stopped moving. He stared at them as though they belonged to somebody else. Around the boat the sea lapped, tinkling musically as the waves broke against the bows. What a lot of water, John thought. He turned to Lyapo. 'Four-fifths of the earth's surface is covered in water,' he mumbled. Then he fell forward, his head banging on his oar.

Lyapo stared dully at John. He, too, was near to collapse. His face was shrunken and his fine, mahogany skin was grey with salt, as if he had been covered with wood ash. Is this the end? he thought. Have I come to it at last? Am I to die here, on this salt sea, where my spirit will be blown away by the winds, never to be found, so that I shall spend the rest of time wandering the wastelands of the world, friendless and alone?

He looked at John, and rage flared in his breast. 'His kind brought me to this,' he thought. 'He and his kind.' He raised his arm to strike John, then let it fall. What was the point? Death had come for both of them. He laid his head on his oar and drifted off into a comatose sleep, as the little boat rocked and swayed on the purple sea.

23

Something moved in the boat. Something flapped and scuffled against the timbers. Another flapping noise and a touch on Lyapo's shoulder, a cold and clammy touch. Death on his only visit.

'I am ready,' Lyapo said. He turned and there, staring at him, goggle-eyed, its thin mouth open, was a fish.

Lyapo looked down, unable to believe his eyes. A fish in the boat! A long, elegant fish with delicate, elongated fins and shimmering colours, red and blue and gold. And even as Lyapo gaped at the fish, another tumbled over the gunwale and thrashed around the boat, and another, striking Lyapo in the chest.

Salvation. John roused by Lyapo, who thrust the cold fish in his hands, the fish full of watery juice. Five flying-fish in the boat. Squeezed, chewed, chomped at like oranges, sucked down to the last bone, giving pints of juice. The sun falling away to the west, a little breeze blowing, cooling, inspiring. John and Lyapo back at the oars, swinging away, backwards and forwards, the sun dawdling on the horizon, a bird landing in the bows, snow-white and innocent — and a blur of movement from Lyapo. He and John rowing on with bloody mouths and bloody hands, bloody thighs and bloody buttocks too, the sun going down abruptly, the southern sky glowing with stars, but none to the north. John resting, falling on his back, and seeing no stars to the north and the stars above his head going out one by one; and then a faint tapping on his cheeks, a tinkling in the baler, and the rains were coming.

Torrential rain. Within minutes John and Lyapo were more concerned with baling water out of the boat than drinking it. But water, pints of it, quarts, great, bursting bellyfuls of it, and then the nightmarish sleep of exhaustion. Through the hours of darkness the boat drifted, but its movement was not at random. John and Lyapo in their long-heroic row had brought the boat north, to the edge of the Benin current, and that was slowly dragging them north-east, to Africa. In fact, lying asleep in the boat, the two survivors were travelling as fast as they had been the previous day, labouring at their oars.

By dawn the skies had cleared. Lyapo woke and shook John. His sleep had not made John feel better. He felt as if he had a huge leaden hat screwed on his head, and it took him minutes to open his fingers. There was water left in the baler. He took a mouthful, and handed it to Lyapo. He drank in his turn and then they turned to the oars.

The menacing sun rose again. Backwards and forwards went the oars. The blood flowed from their hands and buttocks. The water in the baler went down — and down — until there was none. Little left in the boat, either, and that so contaminated it was undrinkable. No flying-fish, no birds, and the horizon shrouded with a subtle, evanescent mist.

John's hands were so numb that he no longer held the oars, his fingers were hooked over them like claws. None of his joints would bend and he rowed upright, moving as woodenly as a puppet.

Lyapo was no better off. He had long since stopped thinking whether the boy next to him knew what he was doing. He heaved and hauled, although for what reason he did not know. Indeed he would have stopped long since but for the fact that the boy was rowing, just as John would long since have surrendered but for the fact that Lyapo was rowing. And so both kept at their work although, in truth, for much of the time they were merely zig-zagging crazily across the blazing face of the sea.

Then, by noon, when the sun's rays were like an iron bar across their necks, John heard noises again. This time it was not the cries of yesterday but the sound of the train his mother had taken him to see as a special birthday treat. But it was strange — there were many trains, one after the other, roaring past; a train, silence, another train, another. And the trains were coming closer — closer — John raised his head slowly, as if it weighed a ton, and saw a line of white breakers where the surf broke on the coast of Africa.

The coast was a mile off, the dark line of trees just visible behind the white breakers as the boat rose on the swell. John rose and staggered to the tiller. Just a mile away, land and safety. Just a mile away, and only the sparkling white foam between them and it. Lyapo raised his fist; 'Tawata,' he said. 'Tawata.' Land.

Yes, land, but John knew enough of the coast to be aware of the danger in the dazzling foam barrier which broke so elegantly on the creamy shore. Fleetingly, incoherently, the thought crossed his mind that they would be better staying out to sea and running down the coast. Sooner or later they would find a creek where they could land in safety, or, better still — come across a British ship on patrol. Whereas going through the surf, they could lose the boat, perhaps their lives. But to stay in the boat called for an iron will John did not possess. A man hardened and tempered by life, a Brooke or a Murray might have done it, but not a boy. He swung the tiller over and headed the boat, bow first, towards the shore. He did not notice Lyapo strapping the cutlass around his waist.

Slowly the boat was drawn into the surf. As it drew near it slewed sidewards, like a balky horse driven to a jump. John strained at the tiller to bring her head round. The white comb of the waters burst overhead, there was a gigantic, thundering noise, as if no other noise had ever been since creation, as if it was the sound of chaos before creation.

'Come on, boat,' John screamed. 'Come on!' and took the boat into the surf.

A Krooman might have done it, or a coast fisherman, but not in a jolly-boat. Even they would have needed their torpedo-like canoes to ride the tumult. As it was, and with a boy's hand on the tiller, the surf lifted the boat, shook it sideways, turned it upside down as casually as a man playing dice, and dashed it to pieces.

24

John was being kicked in the face. The kicking was slow and deliberate, as if the kicker was enjoying his work and wanted to prolong it.

'Stop it,' John mumbled. He opened his good eye and was kicked. He dragged himself on to his elbow and was kicked again. He thought that he saw something move in the palm-trees that lined the beach, a dark, uncertain shape, and felt a spasm of fear. A swarm of little flies rose from the sand and settled on his face. He waved them away and fell back. The sun glared redly through his eyelids and his face throbbed with pain.

He lay there for a while, neither sleeping nor waking; then, with a huge effort, he scrambled to his feet. He reeled in a dizzy, absurd dance, and fell, sprawlng face down. For a moment he rested until with another vast, enormous effort he dragged himself on to his hands and knees. He was very thirsty. His mouth felt like a dry cave with a tiny lizard creeping about inside it.

I must drink, he thought. I must get water. He raised his head and squinted painfully along the beach. The white sand glinted in the sunlight, stretching for miles, but empty, deserted, not even a bird moving, and the only sound the tremendous booming of the surf.

The sun was frighteningly hot but the palms looked cool, dappling the sand with blue shadow. John began to crawl towards them, swinging his head like a dog. He had gone a few feet when a man came from the shelter of the trees. He was carrying a sword in one hand and in the other a round, brown object which he was swinging by its matted hair.

John moaned with fear and tried to creep away, but a hand caught him by the leg. He rolled over and stared into Lyapo's bloodshot eyes and savage, scarred face. 'No,' he moaned. 'No, don't. Don't.'

Lyapo looked down, amazed. He stooped over John but the boy wriggled away, waving his hands in a futile, defensive gesture. 'It is the sun,' Lyapo thought. 'The terrible sun has driven the sense from the boy.' He brushed John's arms aside and lifted his head. 'Here,' he said. 'Drink.'

Coconuts in plenty. The belt of feathery palms bestowed their fruit in abundance. Lyapo chopped them neatly with the cutlass. He and John drank the thin, sweet milk hour after hour until their bellies would take no more. The spectre of death by thirst evaporated.

In the afternoon Lyapo built a shelter of palm-leaves. It looked a rough, crude affair, but when they sheltered in it from the evening rain John was surprised at how watertight it was. And Lyapo had another trick. He made a fire with two sticks and a pinch of grass, spinning one stick between his fingers with the other stick clamped under his foot. John watched as Lyapo bent over the sticks, the big man's face set in concentration. The stick spun, and a little puff of smoke eddied from the grass packed in the hollow of the other stick. Lyapo bent and blew gently on the grass. There was a tiny red glow. Lyapo put more grass on and blew again. The red glow brightened and a little flame appeared. Lyapo looked up at John and grinned. 'Ina,' he said. Fire.

They slept well that night. The rain pattered on the thatch but they stayed dry, and the smoke from the fire kept the worst of the insects away. But before he closed his eyes John took a long look at Lyapo. In the glow of the fire the man's face looked heavy, morose and threatening, the very picture of a savage, the type and image of what, for John, had been represented as a subhumanity bordering on bestiality; a lower order of being only to be redeemed, if redeemed at all, by white men, by himself. And yet within a day of crashing on the beach, with only a cutlass between them, Lyapo had found food and drink, built a perfectly good shelter, and — miracle of miracles — had made a fire. John was pondering on that as he went to sleep.

Lyapo, too, was thinking. Where were they? Had they returned to the land he had left, or were they in some other land? He had no way of knowing, although he suspected they had returned; perhaps, then, he could find his way back to his own country. Would it be possible? It would be a long journey. Perhaps if he found the great river he had been brought down, he could make his way up it. . . .

John moaned a little in his sleep. Lyapo turned. The movement hurt him. Something had smashed into his side as he rolled through the surf, and there was a nagging pain in his ribs. He looked at John's thin, beaky face. How fragile and ugly it seemed with its long, bird-like nose and thin lips. Not for the first time Lyapo wondered where the boy had come from, and how he lived. Certainly he knew little about how to live on land. He had

139

stood by helplessly as Lyapo had made the shelter, and Lyapo had not missed the look of surprise in his eyes when the flame had appeared. Yet the boy was confident on the water, and on the ship grown men had deferred to him. Lyapo had never seen that before. In his village, youth deferred to age.

He felt thirsty and reached for a coconut, moving cautiously so as not to disturb John. He drank and leaned back, the pain in his chest jabbing at him. What a pity, he thought, that he and the boy could not speak to each other. Perhaps tomorrow he would start teaching him Yoruba. He was tired and the ground seemed to be moving slightly, rocking as the boat had done. It was not unpleasant — soothing, rather. His eyelids drooped, closed, soon he was asleep.

When Lyapo awoke, John was already up. He was gathering driftwood and building a beacon. In an elaborate mime and with much drawing on the sand he explained what he was doing. Lyapo frowned. He understood very well that John wanted to signal ships at sea, but smoke could be seen by malevolent eyes as well as friendly ones. Who knew what villains might be lurking on the coast; men ready and willing to clamp fetters on them both. Lyapo had decided on one thing: he would never wear iron again — not if it cost him his life.

In his turn he tried to explain this to John, but it was too difficult. In the end he simply kicked the beacon down, patting the hurt and resentful John on his shoulder.

John stared sullenly at the debris of the beacon, as Lyapo made a rough and ready breakfast of coconut and cleaned his teeth on a strip of bark. He had thought the beacon an excellent — a brilliant idea and had expected Lyapo to applaud it. Instead, after an incomprehensible harangue, which had sounded extremely threatening, the big man had merely brushed him aside as if . . . as if he were a child.

His sullenness became indignation. This was not the way Man Friday had behaved to Robinson Crusoe. It was quite wrong. Although of course possessing souls like anyone else and (as he hazily remembered Murray saying) being neither Jew nor Greek, surely black men were, if not absolutely inferior, then — what was the word? Uncle Hector had used it . . . yes . . . children Children of Nature. Simpletons, everyone knew that. As Potts had said, that was why they were slaves. After all, nobody heard of black men making white men slaves, did they?

Yes, they were children of Nature, whatever that meant, and

that being so it was galling to be treated as a child by one of them. And it was even more galling when Lyapo walked over, a friendly smile on his face, and offered John a coconut. Especially since John needed the nut. He had spent some time that morning trying to open them, and all he had succeeded in doing was smashing them so that the liquid they contained ran into the ground. But drink he must, and so he took the coconut and, sulky though he was he said as he took it, 'Thank you.'

Lyapo's smile broadened. He dipped his head in a courtly gesture. 'Dara,' he said. 'Dara.' Good, good. He straightened and stretched his fine shoulders, clapped his hand on the cutlass strapped around his waist, and made a broad gesture. Come, he said, and strode off through the palms.

John watched him go with alarm. There was something purposeful about the way Lyapo was striding that suggested to John that he was not going to return, and he was taking the cutlass. John jumped to his feet, ran after Lyapo, and caught him by the arm. Another tedious mime, much waving of arms, pointing to the sea, to the sky, claims on the cutlass, indignation mixed with fear on the part of John, patience on the part of Lyapo. John close to tears, Lyapo close to laughter since, although he knew that John thought he was making off with the cutlass, he was in fact going foraging; knowing, as John did not, that a man could not live for very long on the coarse white fibre of the coconuts. Already he was feeling the griping pains that led to the deadly diarrhoea which could drain a man's life away. Finally, after lying down in the hut, closing his eyes, and snoring, he persuaded the boy that he was not leaving for good. With John, still suspicious, at his heels he struck inland through the palm belt.

The palms stretched for a quarter of a mile. There was rain, slashing through the fronds, but it was not as heavy as the day before, or the day before that. John wondered if the rainy season was passing and felt a qualm at the thought of what would have happened to them in the boat if the rains had not come.

The last palm slanted over their heads and they came on to a plain covered with low, grey scrub, already shimmering in the heat. They plunged into it, Lyapo scything a way with the cutlass. The scrub was vibrant with life. Insects swarmed, flying, jumping, crawling. Great dragonflies, a poisonous red and green, hovered menacingly, snakes rustled in the grass, and once a heavy creature bounded away from them, the grass waving as it marked the beast's passage.

Undeterred, and apparently unperturbed, Lyapo chopped on until, at about mid-mornning, he suddenly stopped and gave a grunt of satisfaction. And even John's unskilled eye could make out a path, half overgrown but clearly recognizable.

Lyapo waited for several minutes before starting down the path, and then he walked as delicately as a deer, every sense alert, the cutlass poised: a formidable figure, reminding John, in an odd way, of Captain Murray. After half a mile or so a clump of trees loomed above the scrub. Lyapo halted again, listening, but the only sound was the whine of insects and the cawing of crows in the distance. A little time passed, a hawk floated overhead; John fidgeted from foot to foot but Lyapo did not move, and when he did it was with the utmost caution, step by step through the trees, and into a village.

A strange village, though. A dozen huts, their roofs collapsing, plants poking their fingers through the thatch, a few broken pots scattered across the village square, bones, a skull grinning at them ironically from a doorway, scorpions, spiders, bats. In the centre of the village there was a curious mound made of clay, rather like a termite hill, about ten feet high. Zig-zag patterns were scratched around it and little pieces of tattered cloth were skewered to it.

That would be the village fetish, Lyapo thought. The village ghosts would live there. In his village it had been a tree with a hole in it. The hole was useful because the ghosts could look through and keep guard on the outside world. Much good the ghosts had done their village.

There was a noise in one of the huts. Lyapo turned sharply and saw John coming out with a short stabbing spear and an iron pot. It was curious, the boy was so helpless and yet so bold. Lyapo would not have gone in one of the huts for anything the world could possibly have offered him and yet the youth wandered in and out as casually as if he were at home, quite indifferent to demons and spirits. Perhaps he was right, perhaps the ghosts were mere passive spectators of this earth, and maybe the spirits were no more than children, helpless to influence events; perhaps even the gods, Olorun, Shango, Eshu, and Ifa, merely dawdled in the sky, intent only on their own pleasures and troubles, like men on earth. Did the boy have a fetish, and did his people have gods? He seemed not to, and he and his people were clever, with their great ships and cannon. And there was no doubt about it, the spear and the pot would be useful.

But outside the village Lyapo found what *he* was looking for. Entwined in a tangle of weed and coarse grass were long, delicate tendrils bearing a fragile blue flower. He chopped away the weeds and, using the spear, dug into the ground. Eventually he stood up, holding a large brown tuber, and smiled brilliantly.

Yams, solid and nutritious, and enough to keep them alive for months. Cassava too, and paw-paws, the fruit not yet ripe but nearly so. Lyapo and John ate well that night, secure in their shelter as the surf thundered and crashed on the shore.

During the next few days they explored the plain. It was some ten miles long and three wide. A muddy river flowed through it, eastwards, parallel to the coast, and lost itself in swamps. To the north and west the plain was bounded by dense rain-forest, already encroaching on the land which generations had cleared.

They found three more villages in the scrub. All ruined, all with their clay shrines, all littered with cracked bones left by the hyenas. It was as if some natural disaster, some plague, had swept the plain clean, leaving behind only the dull, grey scrub, insects and birds, and small mammals. But in one village John found a rusting pair of iron fetters. Lyapo nodded his understanding. Yes, the plague had been a human one. The slavers had been here, mercilessly cropping the human harvest.

Once, when they went to the old village for yams, Lyapo carried on, splashing across the river until he came to the forest. If there had ever been a path there it was engulfed now by new growths. But Lyapo hacked his way into the gloom and the bedlam of whoops and screams before retreating, covered with leeches.

Behind, the scrub and the impenetrable forest, before them the sea and the impassable surf. On each hand, of course, the beach, like a white highway stretching east and west as far as the eye could see. Twice they tramped the sand but to the east was the swamp and to the west low cliffs crowded against the sea, covered with heavy forest. Then, and only then, did Lyapo let John build his beacon.

They saw ships, white sails glinting on the blue sea and, more poignantly, lights glowing in the dusk as a vessel went on its steady way. Each time, John fired the beacon, frantically throwing on driftwood and palm-fronds, the fire throwing a column of smoke a hundred feet in the air. But if it was ever seen the seers passed on by, uninterested. No merchantman was going to break her voyage for a cloud of smoke, no slaver was interested in a coast picked bare to the bones, no naval craft in a stretch long since swept clean, and so the smoke built its intangible column in vain.

The days turned into weeks, the weeks into a month. The little shelter turned into a substantial hut; rats appeared, squeaking among the yams, a sure sign that man had appeared, and was staying. Lyapo began to think of clearing scrubland nearer the beach and laying out a plantation. Both of them discarded their clothes, and soon John was as dark as Lyapo.

They began to teach each other words and expressed amazement that the other could understand such astonishing concepts as land, water, fire, and sky. But they did better than that as the days slipped by. Verbs edged in among the nouns, and tenses hovered tantalizingly on the edges of their conversation. And, maddeningly for John, Lyapo was quicker to learn English than he was to learn Yoruba.

But John had one advantage over Lyapo — he knew some geography. One day he paced out a mile on the beach, marked it with two sticks, then knelt and in the wet sand drew a map of the world. And next to it he drew a large map of Africa.

Lyapo squatted next to John and frowned at the maps, running his finger along the corrugations. 'What, John?' he asked. 'What is this?'

John smiled. 'The world. It is the world, Lyapo.'

That day was a revelation to Lyapo. It gave him, for the first time in his life, a coherent picture of where he was, and where he had come from, and that gave him a sense of meaning to his travels. John was no longer a figure from some bizarre dreamland but a person from some perfectly understandable country. Different in many ways from his own, no doubt, but merely a country. And the slavers, too . . . Lyapo looked at the huge lands across the Atlantic and nodded. It was quite comprehensible that men should steal other men and taken them there to work on the land. Cruel but comprehensible.

Lyapo spent a lot of time looking at the map, and at the large map of Africa. Where did he come from, he wondered, where? But even John could not help him there.

Then Lyapo had an idea. He collected seeds, large, heavy pods, scooped little holes in the sand, and taught John the game of *ayo*.

It seemed a simple little game and yet it was surprisingly difficult. The seeds had to go around the holes in a certain sequence, and to get that sequence right called for an alert mind. Lyapo won game after game, keeping the tally on a piece of driftwood. At the end of a week there were dozens of marks on Lyapo's side and none on John's. Then John had an idea.

He cut some little circles of wood and drew a square in the sand. 'Draughts, Lyapo,' he said. 'An English game.'

Lyapo was intensely curious. He crouched over the sand, watching as John played a game against himself. After two or three demonstrations he snapped his fingers. 'Yes,' he said. 'I know.'

They began to play. It was night and the only light was from the fire. The firelight flickered across Lyapo's face as he crouched over the board, his chin cupped in his hand. He looked heavy and morose as he concentrated, his forehead creased and his eyes rolling as they flicked to and fro, studying the pieces on the sand. A month ago that face would have frightened John, *had* frightened him. Now it seemed as friendly as that of Potts or poor old Cawley, and much friendlier than Brooke's sharp features.

Lyapo moved, and John raised a warning finger. 'No. That's cheating.'

Lyapo pulled his finger back. 'Cheating,' he muttered. 'Cheating, cheating, cheating.' He put his finger to the corner of his mouth and then laughed, a deep, delighted baritone. John leaned back and laughed too, looking at the stars.

What am I doing here? John wondered. Three months ago I was a schoolboy in Northamptonshire learning Latin and algebra. Now I am on a beach in Africa, teaching a savage how to play draughts. He laughed again, roaring with laughter. 'Mr Midshipman Spencer,' he roared, 'of the Queen's Navy, ha, ha, ha.'

Lyapo was laughing too, delighted that John should be happy. 'Good, John,' he cried. 'Good, good.'

'Yes,' John laughed back. 'Dara. Dara-dara, very good.'

'Wrong.' Lyapo's deep voice came from the darkness. 'That's wrong, John. It's da*ra*, not *da*ra.'

'Oh.' John stopped laughing. Without warning his eyes filled with tears. He felt a wave of longing for *Sentinel.* He wanted to hear Potts's boisterous voice and Dawlish's Devon drawl, the tinging of the ship's bell and the creaking of timbers. Knowing it was senseless, he ran to the beacon and kicked it into life, sending a trail of sparks to join the stars. Then he dried his eyes and went back to Lyapo and played draughts.

After that night draughts became an obsession. They played hundreds of games, keeping the score on a new piece of driftwood.

At first there were dozens of white marks on John's side of the wood, but as the days passed Lyapo's score slowly crept up to John's. And as they did so the tension mounted. To John it seemed desperately important that he should defeat Lyapo, and continue doing so. Ever since they had landed he had been, in a sense, at the mercy of the Yoruba. Now this game, which he had taught Lyapo, was the last remaining area where he could show his superiority.

Lyapo knew very well how John felt, although he was somewhat puzzled by it. He liked winning too, but it seemed natural to him that a man should beat a boy. Indeed he rather thought that John should be flattered that a man would play with him. That would have been unthinkable in his village, where boys were seen and not heard.

Then the day came when there was only one game's difference between them, and the scene was set for a titanic battle. And a titanic battle it was. It started soon after dawn and by noon it was only half-way through, each player brooding interminably over his moves, each afraid to give the slightest advantage away. They broke for their noon meal but neither moved from the board, staring at the pieces as though they contained the secret of the universe.

After they had eaten, the battle was resumed. John made a bad move and Lyapo took a piece, laughing loudly. Then John took a piece and *he* laughed loudly. Piece after piece was swept from the board, and then Lyapo made a vainglorious move and John gained a crown. From then on Lyapo was doomed. He was levered out of his position until eventually he had only one piece left to John's three and, inexorably, John drove that into a corner. Lyapo had only one move left. Sportingly he made the move and John took the piece.

'I've won,' John cried. 'I've won!'

But Lyapo was not listening. He was on his feet, pointing at the sea. Swooping into shore was a cutter with a triangular sail and a red ensign at the mast.

The sail belonged to the longboat of *Magpie*, brig. It carried eight men under the command of a lively midshipman and was running down to the Isle of São Tomé with mail for *Dauntless*. A bosun's mate on board her had spotted the smoke of the beacon, and the mid — Randall by name — was young enough, and lively enough, and bored enough, to decide to take a closer look.

He trained his telescope on the beach and whistled. 'What do you make of it, Hammet?' he asked, passing on the glass.

'Looks like two blacks, sir,' Hammet said. 'A father and his lad, I shouldn't wonder. They're certainly capering.'

Randall took another look. The two figures on the beach were definitely signalling. 'Wonder what they want?' he said.

'Couldn't say, sir,' Hammet said. 'But if I might say so, we're running in a bit too close to the shore.'

'Yes.' The boat was edging in to the dangerous surf. 'Bring her head round — now, what the devil?'

The boy on the beach had dashed into a hut and come out waving something, and then putting it on himself. It was hard to keep the boy in view from the rolling boat, but the blue coat with its winking buttons was unmistakable.

'Lord!' Hammet said. 'That boy has got a mid's jacket on!'

The bosun grunted. 'They gets all sorts of things along the coast. I've seen 'em wearing top hats. The traders bring them in.'

'I suppose so,' Hammet said doubtfully. 'We can't get in anyway.'

'That we can't,' the bosun was firm. 'That surf would have us upside down in no time.'

'Right.' Hammond dropped from the bows. 'Well, let's away.'

And away they went, dropping down the coast, running fast before the wind. In an hour they were out of sight, even from the tallest tree.

John and Lyapo stood in silence for a moment, then John trudged away up the beach, his head bowed. He did not bother to mark his win at draughts.

25

With the passing of the longboat the great draughts mania died down. Lyapo and John fell into a morose silence, both bitterly resigned to spending the rest of their lives on the beach.

John, perhaps, suffered the worse. The boat had come in so near and he was sure that they had been seen, and to be seen and so casually disregarded had something personal about it. He felt as a man might who has been snubbed by a friend, feeling a sense of personal rejection the more cutting because he could not understand why it had happened. They could have made a signal, he muttered to himself, they could have fired a gun.

He fell into a morose silence. There were no more lessons in geography or English or Yoruba. And he stopped saying his prayers.

Lyapo noticed that. So, he thought, John had abandoned his god. Well, it was no more than he had done himself, and why not? Life was only chance. He no longer believed that the parrot and the spider had anything to do with men's lives. If he had not gone hunting that morning so long ago he would not have been captured by the Dahomeys, and that was all there was to it. He had been there and they had been there, and if there was a reason then it was hidden from him. Life was a riddle, and he no longer believed that any man knew the answer.

And as for John, well, he would come around eventually. When he found that there were no yams for him, or cassava or paw-paws, then they would start talking again and playing draughts. And thinking that, he set to work clearing an acre of scrub.

Lyapo was quite right. John had stopped believing in God. In fact he no longer believed in anything. They were doomed to stay on the coast for ever and ever and ever, with only the pillar of smoke, as insubstantial as a dream, to remind a forgetful world, one day, that they were on the beach, quite forgotten.

And forgotten they were. In London and Paris and New York men went to bed and got up, ate their breakfasts and their dinners, worked, idled, did good, did evil, kept their words and broke them, attacked slavery, defended it, exulted and mourned, as if John Spencer had never existed. And in Africa, in their own way, men did much the same not caring whether Lyapo, or ten thousand Lyapos, or a hundred thousand Lyapos, vanished from the face of the earth. Of course Lyapo's wife cared but, under the guard of an Arab escort, she was shuffling across the Sahara Desert to be sold in the slave markets of Algiers; and Lyapo's brothers would have cared, but they were lying in a slaver off the Carolina coast, waiting to be smuggled ashore. Lyapo's parents and children no longer cared for anything, as they had died of yellow fever in a barracoon in Bonny.

And Miss Honoria Spencer would have cared about John, had she known where he was, and so would Hector Radley of Wapping, and his family, but they believed him to be doing rather well in the Royal Navy — at the Lord's work on the Slave Coast, as Mr Radley told his fellow worshippers at the Church of St Mark, Southwark, where twice a month the vicar sent up a prayer for John's safety.

And above all the Navy would have cared. Had it known where John was it would, if necessary, have sent a whole fleet to rescue him. But it didn't know either. Or, rather, it thought it did for, in Freetown, aboard HMS *Hawke*, a neat hand had already written against John's name the initials, *D.D.* Discharged dead.

That piece of news was in the dispatch which Randall handed over to Ward, Captain of *Dauntless*, as she lay in her mooring in São Tomé. Ward read the dispatch and his face set like iron. 'Do you know about this?' he asked.

'Sir?' Randall raised his eyebrows.

'This business with *Phantom*.'

'Yes, sir. Appalling.'

'That it is,' Ward said grimly. He turned to Havelock, his First Lieutenant. 'Do you remember *Phantom*?'

'Yes, sir. Captain Murray had trouble with her some weeks ago. Had a scrap, lost her, then picked her up again in some lagoon. We had a dispatch from Captain Murray about it.'

'Yes,' Ward nodded. 'Captain Murray sent her in to Freetown with a prize crew. Well, she was picked up by *Firefly* a month ago.'

'Picked up, sir?' Havelock was surprised. 'What was she, dismasted?'

Ward shook his head.

'Sickness, sir? Among the crew?'

'There was no crew,' Ward said flatly.

'Sir?' Havelock was incredulous. 'But. . . .'

'It seems,' Ward's voice quivered with rage, 'it seems that *Firefly* ran into her and she claimed to be American. *Firefly* wasn't having that, and went aboard. Philips, her Master, spotted bloodstains on the deck. *Phantom*'s Skipper came out with a yarn about being attacked by pirates, but a mid was poking around and found a book. It was *Pickwick Papers*, and on the fly-leaf it had *John Spencer, Gentleman Volunteer, HMS Sentinel*, and an inscription from someone or other. *Phantom*'s Master came up with a cock-and-bull story about entertaining British officers on board, but Philips started questioning the crew. In the end the cook broke down and told the story.'

Ward broke off. 'I think I will have a drink. Will you join me?'

Drinks came and Ward continued. 'It seems that *Sentinel*'s crew was involved in some sort of action. The cook couldn't tell just what because he was battened down below. Anyway, Kimber, *Phantom*'s master, broke out with his men and retook the ship. The cook said that they killed most of the Sentinels.'

'Most of them, sir?' Havelock asked. 'What happened to the rest?'

'They were thrown overboard,' Ward said.

Havelock went white. 'My God,' he said. 'My God.'

'Yes.' Ward's voice was thick, as if his tongue was swollen. 'Well, the devils are on their way to England now for trial for murder. We must let *Sentinel* know and announce it to the crew.'

Shock and rage on *Dauntless* and on little *Hornet*, chosen to take the news to *Sentinel* cruising somewhere on the coast. Rutherford of *Hornet*, invited to dinner on *Dauntless*, saying that he was not looking forward to breaking the news to Murray.

'No,' Havelock said, 'it ain't the nicest job a man can have. We came down with *Sentinel*, you know, almost hand in hand. Her Owner's a fine seaman, even if he is a bit . . . you know —' He pointed significantly to the ceiling.

But even rage and shock wore off a little as the wine went around and the talk shifted, little by little, to other topics. Young Randall piped up about the curious incident of the smoke signal.

'That's odd,' Rutherford said. 'I stopped a French brig a couple of weeks ago, just south of Brass, full of iron bars and brandy she was. She saw smoke on the coast. What was your position?'

Randall gave it in a hazy, midshipman's way. Rutherford, who knew the coast like the back of his hand, frowned. 'I know that stretch, there ain't nothing there. It got picked clean long ago.'

Randall, emboldened by too much wine, and rather fancying

that he knew the coast, too, informed Rutherford that he was well aware of that; but *not only* had he seen the smoke with his own glims, *but* not being a lubberly Frog sailing so far out to sea that he could hardly see the land, he had run in and actually seen a man and a boy. The boy — savouring the sensation — the boy wearing a mid's jacket!

Sensation of sensations! Randall lingered over it a little. Ward demanded to know if he was sure.

'Absolutely, sir,' Randall said. 'Brass buttons and all, as plain as the nose on your face.'

'And you did not go in?' Ward's face was crimson. 'A British seaman cast away and you have chosen not even to report it?'

'Ah, sir,' Randall paused, savouring his little anecdote. 'He was wearing a mid's jacket, sir, but he was black. Black as your hat.'

A frozen silence. Ward's eyes bulged and the other officer looked tactfully away. Randall began to feel that his little joke wasn't such a good idea after all.

'Are you making a mock of me, sir?' Ward thundered. 'Are you amusing yourself at my expense? Leave the cabin, sir. Leave at once. Report to the officer of the watch every two hours in full dress and report to me at dawn!'

'Beg pardon, sir,' Randall stammered, leaving the cabin, wishing heartily that he was somewhere else. The middle of the Pacific, perhaps.

Dinner over, the officers scattered to their ships and, as dawn broke, *Hornet* weighed anchor and slipped away on the tide, in search of *Sentinel*.

26

No *Sentinel* off the Oil Rivers. *Hornet* poking her nose into Brass and Bonny. Being challenged off a muddy and desolate creek by a cutter from HMS *Eglantine*, brig. Eight men aboard, one dying with fever, six dead drunk, and the eighth, a lieutenant, twenty-three years old and not up to his job, wringing his hands with despair but telling Rutherford that *Sentinel* was off Whydah in the Bight of Benin. Rutherford chucking the smuggled rum overboard and, quite unlawfully, giving seven drunken sailors two dozen each; his bosun, six feet two and with an arm of iron, laying it on with a vengeance.

The usual gut-grinding slog across the Bight of Benin. Three sail sighted and challenged: one, to the intense disgust of the Hornets, being a perfectly innocent Liverpool merchantman going about her lawful affairs; the second a beautiful clipper with *slaver* written all over her, and which could give *Hornet* a twenty-mile start any day, taking to her heels and running south; but the third, a cranky tub with enough irons on board for half the slaves in Africa, tamely surrendering and hardly bothering to deny her mission, so being taken as a prize. The Hornets then being not too discontented as they beat up the coast.

A slow stretch. To the north a muddy, nondescript coastline which had not yet made up its mind whether it was swamp or beach, and then the ambiguity was resolved and they saw the familiar flicker of white surf on honest-to-goodness sand. And a memory stirred in Rutherford's mind.

'Mr Stokes,' he called.

A gangly, spotty mid regretfully left a fascinating conversation about the mysteries of girls and presented himself.

'Take my best glass,' Rutherford said, 'and go to the masthead. Keep a sharp look out. Anything unusual report at once.'

'Aye aye, sir.' Dolefully.

'And don't fall asleep.'

'No, sir.' Indignantly.

Stokes climbed to his airy perch a hundred feet above the deck, consoling himself with the thought that he might, he just might, see girls disporting themselves, unclothed, along the beach. No girls but, after an hour, he saw something which oddly enough he found almost as interesting.

'Deck,' he hailed. 'Deck there. Smoke. Six points off the starboard bow.'

'Ah ha!' Rutherford clapped his hands with satisfaction. 'Bring her round a little,' he ordered the helmsman. 'Just a trifle, handsomely now.'

Hornet edged into the shore. Not too close, of course, keeping well away from that horror of horrors, a lee shore. Rutherford went into the rigging, reclaimed his telescope, and looked carefully at the beach. The smoke was there, an enigmatic and hazy column, but there was no sign of life. Rutherford whistled a little tune between his teeth.

'Is it worth five shillings?' he wondered. 'Is it?' He paused, then clapped his telescope to. 'No,' he said firmly. 'It ain't.' He opened his mouth to call to the helmsman to take the ship out again, and as he did so a curious thing happened. The column of smoke was caught by a breath of wind, eddied, billowed, and by a freakish little trick, curved into a perfect questionmark.

'Well I'll be damned,' Rutherford said. 'I've never seen the like of that before. Damn my eyes, it is worth five bob.'

A minute or two later the bow chaser cracked out five shillings' worth of gunpowder and flannel wadding. The report echoed back from the palms and John, sleeping among them, was wakened by the bang.

Every man on board *Hornet* saw the small figure dash from the trees, and every man with a telescope saw it run into a hut and come out waving a jacket, and even the worst duffer could see the buttons winking in the sun.

'What do you make of that?' Rutherford asked his First.

The First shrugged. 'Lord knows. Hello, what's he up to now? Do you see it, sir?'

Rutherford nodded. 'I do. Back the topsails, bring the Kroomen up, and get their canoe ready for launching. That boy is praying.'

An explosion of joy. The Kroomen bursting through the surf in their canoe. Stokes shouting above the thunder of the water. John stammering an answer, then talking, and talking in a flood, a torrent, a cataract of words. Spilling them over Stokes, submerging him in an ocean of tearful thanks — yes, tears pouring down John's cheeks until Stokes feared the lad would dissolve before his very eyes. And Lyapo standing back a little, a smile on his lips but a trace of anxiety in his eyes and a touch of sadness on his face as John and Stokes talked, so rapidly that he could not catch one word in a hundred. But John pulled him forward to be patted on the back by Stokes in the manner one might pat a horse.

The fire was kicked out, the column of smoke collapsing behind them as the Kroomen, cheerfully sharing in the joy, charged the surf again. One heart-stopping moment as the white water towered above them, then *Hornet* drew near, every man on board cheering himself silly.

But even then the sensations continued as John reported to Rutherford, remembering the correct form: not saluting, because he had no hat on, but standing very straight and saying, 'Spencer, sir. Midshipman. HMS *Sentinel.*'

'*Sentinel? SENTINEL!*' Rutherford actually dropped, and ruined, his telescope. 'Did you say *Sentinel*?'

'Yes, sir,' John said and, being the upright lad he was, he leaned forward and whispered into Rutherford's red and blistered ear. 'I have to report, sir, that I lost my ship.'

Rutherford beamed. 'You mean your ship lost you, I think.'

'No, sir,' John looked around, desperately conscious of twenty pairs of wagging ears. 'I mean I lost my command, sir. I was in command of a prize, sir, and I lost her.'

'A prize?' Rutherford looked somewhat dubious. 'You were in command?'

'Yes, sir.' John's voice quivered alarmingly.

'Captain Murray put you —' I wonder if the lad is off his rocker, Rutherford wondered. 'Well, bless me. And what was the name of the prize?'

'Please, sir,' John said. 'It was *Phantom.*'

Rutherford, quite literally, could not believe his ears. He turned to his First. 'Did I hear something?' he murmured, but the First could not believe *his* ears, either.

'I thought . . . I thought . . . did he say *Phantom*?'

Rutherford took a deep breath. 'Mr Spencer, I think you had better come below and explain.'

Explanations in Rutherford's cabin, with the hum and buzz of an excited crew coming through the skylight. John stammering gabbling, sobbing, and Rutherford looking gravely at his shoes, not interrupting but making his own sense of the story.

'And they broke out?' he asked. '*Phantom*'s crew?'

'Yes, sir.'

Silence. Rutherford looked up and caught sight of Stokes' face

154

peering through the skylight. Disappearance of Stokes.

'And then you rowed to land?'

'Yes, sir. For nearly two days.'

Rutherford waved his hand, casually brushing that aside. 'And you were on the beach since then?'

'Yes, sir.'

'Just you and that big black?'

'Yes, sir. Lyapo.'

'Oh, that's his name, is it?'

'Yes, sir.'

'It's quite a story.' Rutherford shook his head. 'You and whatsisname —' Lyapo dismissed, his solid black frame vanishing before the phrase. 'I daresay that there will be an inquiry —' Rutherford held out an arm, stifling John's nervous cry — 'don't worry. It's standard procedure and no one is going to take a bad view of you; just the opposite, I shouldn't wonder. All right. We'll fix you up with a berth and you should be back with your ship in a few days. See my First.'

John stood up. 'Thank you, sir. And sir. . . .'

'Yes?'

'About Lyapo, sir.'

'Who? Oh, your big black. Don't worry, he can bed down with the Kroomen. He'll be all right. And relax, Mr Spencer. You've got quite a tale to tell, and that's always useful in the navy. Lord, I wonder what the Sentinels will make of it all.'

27

Sentinel knew already of the butchery on *Phantom*. *Magpie*, following her cutter down the coast, had met *Sentinel* hovering off Lagos and Eagleton, lieutenant, had broken the news.

Incredulity on *Sentinel*, shock and dismay and a brooding ferocity — losing men in battle, in a fair fight, being one thing, but cold-blooded murder another. Thomas having been regarded as a fair-minded man and one who, when flogging, had the knack of making the cat's whine sound worse that its bite; Old Cobber, respected for his gunnery and long service, besides which not every man could say he had fired his gun at Trafalgar; the other seamen growing in skill, valour, generosity, and virtue now that they could not appear to shatter those fond illusions. And as for that young Mr Spencer . . . only fifteen, lads, but always with a smile, quick to learn, as brave as a lion — wounded in action tackling a hell-bound Yankee slaver, six feet six tall, with his bare hands — Rafferty there saving his life that day when that son of a sea-cow, Brooke, made him swing on the mainmast; and an orphan, too. John's lack of parents making his early death a matter of particular solicitude to the sentimental, sincere hearts of the Sentinels, each and every one of whom was thirsting to put all the slavers on the coast to the sword with no quarter asked or taken, and who had regarded Murray's address to them, with his announcement that '*Vengeance is mine, saith the Lord*', as a ludicrous parsonical whimsy no doubt forced on the Owner by a lunatic Admiralty regulation, and not to be taken seriously for one moment by anyone with an ounce of sense or true feeling. Even the Blue-lighters concurred.

'Which it stands to reason, lads,' as Carlin had put it. 'Vengeance is the Lord's right enough, and I don't deny it, but in these parts we're the Lord's strong right arm, so it's only right and proper that we should do a bit of venging for him. And which,' he added, with perfect honesty, 'I'm going to do anyway.'

General agreement, and a row of hard faces raised to the quarterdeck where Murray, Brooke, and Eagleton were standing, their heads bowed in discussion, not of the death of the Sentinels on *Phantom*, but, as the work of the Navy had to carry on, of an interesting sight Eagleton had seen in the Whydah roads.

'Five sail, you say?' Murray was asking. 'And almost at the mouth of the Mono river?'

'Yes, sir,' Eagleton said.

'If they are moored in the estuary it means that they are loaded with slaves and ready to go,' Brooke observed.

'I believe so,' said Eagleton, new to the coast and diffident about offering his opinion. 'One of our ships is off the bar, a large brig, *Esk*. She told me you were going down here, sir, and issued a warm invitation to join her. Er, plenty for everyone she said, sir.'

'Excellent.' Murray was uncharacteristically open in his emotion. But the prospect of a smart action was exactly what *Sentinel* needed. It would stop the men from brooding and a broody ship, as he well knew, could turn into a morose and sullen ship, a bad ship. Action and prizes and a little blood-letting would stop that, and Whydah was a mere hundred miles away. He turned to Keverne.

'Be good enough to lay a course for Whydah. I should like to arrive a few miles off the coast.'

Eagleton and *Magpie* leaving, bound for São Tomé. Furious activity on *Sentinel* as she prepared for the long beat against the current of the wind. One, two, perhaps even three days of heavy labour ahead, but the Sentinels glad to do it; anything was better than the endless to and froing off Lagos, and the prospect of paying back their bloody score enticed them on; and certainly, if perhaps ignobly, the thought of a whacking great chunk of prize money muddied the purity of their fine intention to hack the Whydah slavers into several thousand individual pieces.

Two days, in the event, and a little of the Sentinels' fine frenzy sweated out of them by the time they arrived off Whydah. Smith catching the first sight of the topgallants of *Esk*, a four-gun brig, twenty-five men, seven sick; a black-haired, pock-marked Lieutenant Donnelly in command, his Dublin accent announcing as he climbed on *Sentinel* why he was at the top of *his* promotion ladder. But philosophical and, belying his visage, good-humoured too. A handsome, gap-toothed smile lit his face as he shook hands with Murray.

'I'm glad to see you, sir,' he said. 'I have a feeling that the slavers are trying to make up their minds to come out — make a little dash for it, you know.'

'Are they, indeed.' Murray cast a glance at tiny *Esk* and her pop-guns, wondering what *Phantom* would have made of her. Reading his thoughts, Donnelly laughed.

'They can only come out one at a time, sir.'

'That's the spirit.' Murray warmed to Donnelly. 'And you think that they're laden?'

'Nothing so certain, sir. They are as nervous as a lot of old hens, forever setting their sails then furling them. Sure, they don't know whether they should come out or whether I'm going in.'

'But you haven't gone in?' Murray sounded casual.

'No, sir.' Donnelly smiled again. 'But I do have a reason for that.'

'A good one, I have no doubt,' Murray said.

'Thank you, sir.' Donnelly leaned forward. 'I have a little idea, as you might say.'

For a few moments he spoke softly and fluently. When he had finished Murray looked thoughtfully at the ceiling. Finally he nodded.

'Yes, yes. A good idea, Mr Donnelly, and well worth trying. But first I think I shall take a look into the river myself.'

'Yes, sir.' Donnelly hesitated. 'If I might make a suggestion. Perhaps if you transferred to *Esk*? If the slavers see *Sentinel* coming up, a ship of real force, they might panic and —'

'Might run back to Whydah and get rid of their slaves. You are quite correct.'

Murray took Donnelly back on deck. 'I am going over to *Esk*, Mr Brooke,' he said. 'Keep your position here. I shall be back as soon as may be.'

A mild sensation on *Sentinel* as Murray climbed into *Esk*'s cutter. The crew nudging each other in the ribs, Potts and Bower raising eyebrows; below deck Purvis, edging into the breadroom and looking meaningfully at Taplow, who was working on his accounts and trying to make his vast profits on the voyage so far appear a slight loss.

'What's up, then?' Taplow asked.

Purvis shrugged. 'Search me. The Owner's gone over the side, transferred to *Esk*.'

'Aye?' Taplow stared gloomily at his enormous profit on cheese. 'Another hare-brained scheme, is it?'

'I shouldn't think so, Henry,' Purvis said easily. 'He's just gone to look into Whydah, that's all.'

'Whydah.' Taplow jabbed at his ledger. 'Ain't that where *Lancaster* ran aground a few years ago and the whole crew had to spend five months rotting on the shore with that Da Souza?'

'The very same place, Henry.'

'Well, if it happened to them it'll happen to us. Nothing so certain.'

Purvis grinned. 'Now then, we'll be all right. The Owner's got a good head on his shoulders and Keverne's a prime navigator, give him that.'

'Keverne!' Taplow made the name sound like a curse. 'He couldn't find his way out of his bunk if the light wasn't on.' He paused and sucked his pen. Then slowly, and with sepulchral deliberation, he said: 'There's a Jonah on this ship, Ted.'

Purvis took a step backwards. 'Go easy now,' he muttered.

'I'm telling you,' Taplow said. 'It's a bad luck ship. Look what's happened to us. Ten men dead on that bloody *Phantom*, and we lost four fighting her, didn't we? And look at that prize we took what young Fearnley went on. Him and that Smith is as blind as bats now, ain't they? And how many men is that? Sixteen out of eighty. I'll tell you, we lose any more men and we won't have enough to sail home.'

Purvis, solid and sensible though he was, looked unnerved. 'Now then, we ain't done too bad. We ain't lost one man with the fever, have we?'

'We've got nine in the sick-bay, though, ain't we?' Taplow said. 'And half the crew's got God-rotting ulcers and sores. How many of them'll get back to Pompey? Tell me that. And you just wait till we get the Yellow Jack on board. You just wait.'

Wait they had to as *Sentinel*, under shortened sail, kept her station while *Esk* crept into the mouth of the Mono River.

A dismal place; mud banks sprouting half-hearted palms and screw-pines, the masts of ships showing above them, and a great bar blocking half the estuary with waves beating on it.

'You can see how it goes, sir,' Donnelly said. 'The river runs inland for a bit, then bears to the right. Inside there is a big lagoon where Da Souza keeps his slaves. The Dahomeys live inland and they bring most of their slaves down to Whydah.'

'And to Da Souza,' Murray said grimly.

'Yes, sir. He has miles of barracoons on the lagoon.'

'One day,' Murray said. 'One day. . . . What is the river like?'

Donnelly shrugged. 'It is a difficult channel, sir. For a ship of any size you need a pilot, and Da Souza won't let any of the natives come out for a naval vessel. But it is easier for a ship to come out on the tide than for a vessel to get in.'

'I see.' Murray looked through his telescope. 'And they are slavers, those masts we see?'

'Oh yes, sir.' Donnelly smiled. 'If Da Souza saw a lawful merchantman in the lagoon he would think he was having nightmares.'

'Right.' Murray was convinced. Eighteen armed Eskers climbed in the cutter, a Lieutenant Box following them, then Murray. The cutter raced back to *Sentinel* over the turquoise sea.

Rush. Murray barked out orders before the bosun's whistle had stopped its piercing salute. All hands on deck and every sail set. The boat watered, victualled — rations for twenty-four hours only — the agreeable clash of side arms. *Sentinel* ran down the coast but, as even the dimmest sailor aboard could tell, west, away from Whydah.

An hour, two, three, the shadows on deck lengthening, the helmsman tipping his hat over his eyes to cut out the glare of the sun. Rounding a long, low headland, Murray took the ship into a creek, backed his topsails, and ran out his anchor. Then he took his officers into his confidence.

'This is Grand Popo,' he said. 'I dare say you wonder why we are here and not at Whydah.'

A polite murmur of agreement. Murray leaned back in his chair.

'Very well. Now Mr Donnelly believes that the ships in the Whydah roads are slavers and that they are laden with slaves. I agree with him. He also believes that if we go in with the ship's boat the slavers would simply run into Whydah and off-load the slaves before we could stop them. I think that he is right. No doubt we could have claimed the ships, but that would not have helped the slaves. Da Souza would merely have put them back in his barracoons — and as you know, we are not allowed to raid them. I am sure that you don't need reminding that freeing slaves is why we are here.'

He paused. Potts had a faraway look on his face.

'Is that not so, Mr Potts?'

Potts, who had been calculating the prize money on five slavers crammed with slaves, and who had reached the unlikely sum of nine million pounds, started. 'Oh, yes, sir. Er, rounding up . . . yes, sir.'

'I'm glad to see that you are still awake,' Murray said dryly. 'Now, gentlemen. Mr Donnelly suggested a different plan to me. Down this creek is a stream. The stream leads into a channel — a long lagoon — which runs all the way along the coast back to Whydah. Now, Mr Donnelly's plan is this: if the ship's boats go along the channel they will emerge in the Mono river, behind the slave-ships. They won't be able to run for the sea because *Esk* will be there, and I shall take *Sentinel* back during the night. I am sending as many men as I can spare, and all the Eskers. Mr Brooke will be in command. And you will be accompanied by Lieutenant Box, who knows the channel. That is so, is it not?'

Box, a red-faced man with huge teeth, nodded vigorously. 'Sir.'

'Very well. You have all night to make ten miles, but I do not want you to arrive at Whydah before dawn. When you do arrive you will fire a blue rocket and attack. Let me emphasize that surprise is everything. Dash at them. *Dash.*'

A thoughtful silence as the officers considered dashing anywhere after a ten-mile slog through the dark. But Murray had not finished.

'One more thing. There is a great deal of feeling about the murder of our men on *Phantom*. But I will not allow the killing of our men to be an excuse for a massacre when we take the slavers. I am sure that you all understand.'

Unenthusiastic understanding. 'Dismiss,' said Murray.

Rush again. The boats over the side, light cannon mounted, men swarming over the side. A pleasant surprise downstream, a neat brig with forty slaves on board; its crew clapped in irons and four Sentinels put on board. And then a broad, sluggish inlet. Box swung the longboat into it and the crew settled down for a long haul through the insect-infested night.

Out to sea, *Sentinel* gliding easily back to Whydah. *Esk* lurking off the river mouth, all lights showing. A mist over Whydah, red and blue lights glowing in the darkness. The waters of the lagoon turning from brass to steel and then, as the sun dropped, all was gone as the African night drew her sable fingers across the sky.

28

Brooke was having trouble in the channel. The inlet was choked with fallen branches, which had to be hacked at and dragged away by men leaning awkwardly over the side of the boat. And the depth of the channel was never constant. Now and again there was deep water where the men could lean on their oars and gain a few yards, then, maddeningly, the water would shoal and the boats run into muddy banks which held them in a slimy but unyielding grip. Mosquitoes by the million rose from the waters and gathered in blinding clusters on the men's faces — and the stench was appalling.

After an hour they had made less than a mile, and that was in the light. When night fell it was worse. In the darkness the journey turned into a nightmare in which exhausted men heaved and pulled, cursed and blasphemed, fell sprawling on their backs and dragged themselves, bruised and bleeding, back to their oars. Brooke tried shining his lantern, but a heavy mist coiled from the water and the light was reflected from an opaque curtain of fog.

They came to a series of pools connected by muddy gullies, and had to climb out and drag the boats through the ooze. It took courage to climb out of the boats, sinking deeper and deeper into the slime, and then, knee-deep, thigh-deep in mud, to drag the dead weight of the boats into the next pool.

Bower and Potts encouraged their men; the breath rasping in their throats they urged them on in jolly, confident tones — 'Come on, boys, one more heave, it's better than paddling at Brighton — and all free. No crocodiles here, and if there are they can have first bite at me, that'll poison 'em.'

Brooke would have none of that. As he obeyed his orders so he expected his men to obey theirs, and what matter if the orders were to stand up to the red glow of the cannon, or to wade through a stinking swamp to free a few hundred niggers who would be better off as slaves than they had ever been in their miserable villages. But although he could have stayed in his boat he too led from the front, going over the side with his men, and going over first.

After the second hour they had covered another half-mile and had eight and a half to go. Then the creek broadened into a narrow lake and the moon came out. Brooke called a halt. The men slumped at their oars; Yetts and Parkin, Kemp and Rose, men of iron strength and determination but drained of both, even Dawlish, even the mighty Rafferty. Brooke felt the first flicker of doubt as to whether they would reach the Mono river before dawn, if at all, and what state they would be in when they got there.

In Bower's cutter, O'Brian, his chest heaving, swallowed a mouthful of water. 'Mother of God,' he sighed, 'Cromwell himself couldn't have thought up a worse caper than this one.'

'Stow your gob,' Bower snapped.

'I thought it was against all orders for us to lie up on land after night,' O'Brian muttered back.

'I said *stow* it,' Bower cried. 'Anyway —' with a game effort at humour — 'We're not on land, we're on water, ain't we?'

Amazingly there was a ripple of laughter. Reluctant laughter, but laughter nonetheless.

'That's it, Mr Bower,' Rafferty cried. 'Sure, in these swamps it's all one and the same anyway.'

More laughter. Brooke lay against the tiller of the longboat, and the flicker of doubt died away. If men could laugh then they could row. He pulled himself upright. 'At your oars, row.'

Off again. The green lake luminous in the fog, swirling silver in the moonlight. A full mile gained by the dripping oars, Brooke marking the course by his compass. Spirits rose, even the mosquitoes were less troublesome. And then the end of the lake.

Mud and mosquitoes again. An infuriating search for the channel. Box completely lost. Brooke finding the channel, *a* channel, but the channel an horrific tangle of roots and branches, and the men spent more time out of their boats than in them. An hour of dreadful, shattering labour, and then an end. A barrier of mangroves, thick as a mainmast, dense as prison bars. Impenetrable. The end.

Brooke could not bring himself to believe it. His hand shook on the tiller and there was a terrible pounding in his temples.

'Mr Box,' he said.

Box's huge face loomed by his shoulder. Box's giant teeth gleamed in the moonlight.

'Mr Box.' Brooke could hardly put what he wanted to say in words. 'Mr Box, this is the end of the channel.'

'Yes, sir. It seems so.'

Rage choked Brooke. For a moment he was dumb and blind with rage. With an enormous effort he controlled himself. 'Have you been down this channel before?'

'Yes, sir.'

'This channel? All the way?'

'Well. . . .' Box sounded doubtful.

Should I throw him out of the boat? Brooke wondered. Should I run him through with my sword and then leave him for the crocodiles? 'Did you or didn't you?' he asked.

'Almost. We could see into Whydah.'

'And was the channel choked like this? With mangroves?'

'Er, no, sir.' Box sounded nervous. 'But these channels do change, these mangroves grow terribly quickly. . . .'

'Shut up!' Brooke said. He took a deep breath. 'What was your channel like?'

'Oh, clear, sir. Quite a good row, actually.'

'Then we're in the wrong channel.' Brooke looked at his compass again. They were heading the right way, due east, which was something. 'Give me some water,' he said. Dawlish handed over a pannikin and Brooke drank, thinking hard. Channels did change, alter their courses, but not like this. There must be another channel, but where was it, to the left or to the right?

'Mr Box,' he said, speaking softly, patiently, 'when you went down this channel before did you notice anything? Think now, think carefully. Is there anything that might help us?'

'Help us, sir?'

Brooke raised his hand. He actualy raised it to strike Box. Slowly he lowered it. 'Mr Box. We are in the wrong channel. Somewhere there is the right one. Now perhaps you can think of something that might help us to find it. When you went down the channel did anything strike you as unusual? Did you see anything — or hear anything?'

Box's face was a pale, vacant blur in the darkness. Brooke willed himself not to strike it.

'There was one thing,' Box said slowly. 'Yes. We could hear the sea. I mean, not the sea exactly, but surf. I mean, it sounded awfully close. It was on our right. To the south.'

Brooke snapped his fingers. 'Mr Bower!'

A muffled voice called from the darkness and Bower splashed to Brooke.

'Mr Bower,' Brooke said. 'We are in the wrong channel. I think that the correct one is to our right. I must ask you to try and find it.'

'Yes, sir.' No enthusiasm at all in Bower's voice as he thought of blundering through the mangroves.

'I want you to take two men and, if you find the channel, see if it will be possible for us to haul the boats into it.'

A pause. A longish pause. 'Do you hear me?' Brooke said.

'Yes, sir. I shall ask for volunteers —'

'No volunteers,' Brooke snapped. 'Take Dawlish and Rafferty. And Mr Box can go too,' he added viciously.

Thrashings and oaths in the dark, bumps and bangs, blasphemies, squelching, sucking noises, then silence. Brooke looked at his watch. Two a.m. Four hours to dawn, eight miles to go. Even if Bower found the main channel they had to get the boats into it, reach the Mono river, and then, what was it Murray had said — 'Dash at the slave-ships.' Brooke smiled without humour. Creep on them, he thought. Crawl on them, paddle up to them and ask for a tow.

A quarter past two, half past; in the boats the men snored, oblivious even to the mosquitoes. Things plopped and gurgled in the swamp, thousands of frogs croaked. Ten to three. Even if they got into the channel they would be too late for a dawn attack. The slavers would see them coming and run into Whydah. . . . Brooke's eyes were closing when a hoarse whisper from Potts woke him.

'Sir, sir. I think they are coming back.'

Back they were. Bower, plastered with mud from head to foot, his voice trembling with exhaustion but a broad, a beatific smile splitting his face.

'We found it, sir. It's not five hundred yards away. Sorry we've been a long time, but we went poking around, and, sir, there's a stream connects the two channels, it's not more than a few hundred yards back, we can row the boats through!'

Nothing to it. A little hacking scramble back downstream, a terrible alarm over a crocodile which turned out to be a floating log, and then they found the stream. The boats floated through into the main, the real channel, long strokes on the oars — like rowing on the Thames, mates; time for half an hour's real rest, food even, the nightmare over, and, as the first flush of red tinted the eastern sky, Brooke fired his blue rocket — and the Sentinels *dashed*.

29

Brooke's rocket scrawled its blue signature in the dawn sky, and before its last spark had faded Murray was over the side of *Esk* and into the gig where four Eskers, desperadoes to a man, were waiting at their oars.

Murray seized the tiller. 'Bend your backs, now,' he roared. 'Lay into it.'

Well clear of the roar and tumult of the surf beating on the bar, the gig skimmed into the estuary. Inside the bar it was strangely silent, as if they had suddenly gone deaf. The quiet was broken by a feeble *bang*! Musket-shot, Murray noted automatically. A wisp of smoke eddied away from the bank. More musketry, men running among the screw-pines, the Eskers glancing across their shoulders but never slackening their stroke. Further downstream the slavers' guard boat was moored, but as the gig bore down on it there were signs of panic; men standing, waving their arms, a hasty thrashing of oars until, in an unwieldy, crab-like way, it scuttled off.

'Run if you like,' Murray said to himself, 'but you're too late. Too late,' he repeated as the gig swung round the curve where the tide met the river, and came upon the first of the slave-ships; an elegant, speedy schooner in a neat, green trim, *Dolphin* by name.

Behind the schooner the other slavers lay haphazardly across the river. One, in a desperate attempt to get ashore and unload her slaves, had run aground and lay canted at an angle. But apart from that, the scene was undramatic. The other ships lay at their moorings and the naval boats, zig-zagging among them, might have been carrying on the humdrum routine of any harbour on any normal working day.

Murray was delighted. The plan had worked perfectly, and peacefully. Not a gun shot except the ineffective musketry. Brooke with his habitual cold efficiency had done wonders; the situation was obviously in control. A splendid stroke most deftly carried out. He must certainly give Brooke all praise in his dispatch. He steered the gig towards the *Dolphin* and as it bumped unhandily against the ship's side — the Eskers not being a match for his Sentinels when it came to seamanship — he stood up, ready to accept the formality of surrender. And as he did so, a man appeared at the gangway with a pistol. There was a spurt of flame, a sharp *bang*! and Murray fell backwards into the gig.

Another pistol shot, a volley of muskets, the balls whistling over the heads of the Eskers, who swung away and raced downstream towards Brooke.

Brooke, although very tired, was feeling excessively pleased. Three handsome slavers captured as easily as taking pennies from a blind man. One half-hearted scuffle on *Trinidad*, with the only casualty the loquacious Box, hit on the head with a large wooden hammer by Sergeant Pocock, no doubt unintentionally. The entire crew of the *Bella Dora* had taken to the rigging at one sight of Rafferty, cutlass in one hand and boarding-axe in the other; *Anna Maria* ran herself aground in flight from Bower. And the fourth, *Aphrodite* — a rather old-fashioned vessel, enormous by modern standards, probably built for bulk carrying of slaves in the old days — although well armed and with a huge crew and a sullen and vindictive Master, was clearly not going to fight. Her Captain's melodramatic gestures were designed merely to save his pride.

'None of that rubbish,' Brooke was saying, waving aside the Captain's threat to fight to the last man rather than allow one British seaman on board. 'Stow it. We're coming aboard.' And then the gig reached him.

Brooke stared incredulously at Murray's shattered figure. 'What —' he cried. 'What?'

'That bugger,' cried an Esker. 'That green bugger. Shot him dead without warning, so he did. Plain bloody murder.'

Brooke stumbled into the gig. Murray's face was a mask of blood welling from a great hole in his head. 'Jesus,' Brooke whispered. 'Jesus Christ!'

A voice hailed him. Bower coming up from *Anna Maria* in the cutter, his crew rowing as if they were in the fleet regatta.

'It's the Captain,' Brooke bellowed. 'Shot by that —' He raised his head to point at *Dolphin*, and his jaw dropped. *Dolphin* was under way, her topsails set to catch the land breeze and her anchors slipped, gathering speed as she floated down with the turning tide.

'Is he mad?' Brooke cried. 'Is the fellow out of his senses? Mr Bower, take possession of this vessel and don't stand any bloody nonsense. Take the Captain on board and see if they have a surgeon until we can bring Mr Jessup down. I'll take that lunatic.'

The longboat slid away from *Aphrodite*, burning anger in

Brooke's heart, rage in the Sentinels at the oars. Explosions of rage, literally seeing red; their mates on *Phantom* murdered, young Mister Spencer, and now the Captain — staring eyes, and mouths working — streams of curses, bubbling, vile oaths, blasphemies, and Brooke not silencing them.

Brooke had spoken truer than he knew. The Master of *Dolphin* was mad, but he was mad with fear; for he bore the name Harker, and he and half his crew were renegade Englishmen who, if taken, faced the stone-cold certainty of twelve years in gaol minimum — and, since the shooting of Murray, the gallows.

But mad with anxiety though he was, Harker was a master of his craft. He spread extra sail and, even without a pilot, brought his ship round the bend of the river and into the estuary as easily as though she were a cutter; his stern chaser, a handy twelve-pounder cannon, blasting away at Brooke, forcing him to dodge and twist and lose his distance. But *Dolphin* was in deep trouble, and if she did not realize it as she showed the longboat a pair of heels she did when she saw, waiting for her beyond the bar, *Esk* and *Sentinel*.

Dolphin's mate, a one-eyed Liverpudlian, gave a shrug of despair. 'What now?'

Harker spat. 'We'll run for it,' he said. 'We've got the wind and tide with us.'

'Run?' the mate scowled. 'We'll be blown out of the water.'

'Would you sooner dance at the end of a rope?' Harker said brutally. 'It's our only chance. Lighten the ship.'

The mate gaped. 'What?'

'You heard. Lighten the ship. Everything except the water and you know what to start with first.'

On *Esk*, Donnelly, with three invalids to handle the ship, had the light of battle in his eyes. 'Coming out, are you?' he gloated. 'Couldn't ask for anything better.' He put his telescope up. 'Hello,' he said to no one in particular, 'what's up — Mother of God, oh Mother of God.'

And on *Sentinel* — manned by Taplow, Jessup, Hayes, Purvis, and the ship's cats — Keverne, in command, said something not dissimilar. 'Take a look at that, Mr Taplow,' he said, handing over his telescope. 'Take a good look. You can have a good laugh about it over your dinner.'

Low in the water, and with *Dolphin* partly shielded by trees,

Brooke could not see what was happening, but as he rounded the bend he, too, saw.

Dolphin was throwing her slaves over the side. Dragged from their homes, dragged from the barracoons, now they were dragged from the choking filth of the slave-deck, hammered by musket butts, slashed by cutlasses, and hurled into the sea by men whose faces were not human, if they had ever been. Shackled in pairs, men and women — who, had they met otherwise, might have been friends, or if not friends at least neighbours, ready enough to pass the time of day with each other as, bearing a basket of yams or a pitcher of water, they met by the village well, now, bound together with iron, they pulled each other into an ocean they had never heard of or even conceived existed. In a terrible mockery of affection, clutching each other, gasping, choking, drowning, they sank into the clear waters where, among trailing strands of weed, they could be seen quite clearly, their mouths opening and closing and their limbs still thrashing.

And as they thrashed they made turbulent currents. Beyond the bar dark shapes quivered as they sensed the disturbance, dark fins cut through the waves, mouths like enormous grabs gaped and snapped shut and the froth of the waves turned red.

On little *Esk*, Donnelly snapped his telescope shut. 'I've had enough of this,' he said. He elbowed the steersman off the wheel, took it himself, brought *Esk* round in a tight arc, and, against the wind and tide, tacked in diagonally across the mouth of the estuary.

His steersman grasped his arm. 'You'll wreck the ship,' he cried, horror-struck at the Navy's worst heresy.

'Damn the ship,' Donnelly said and, as *Dolphin*, trailing her bloody skirt, came to the mouth of the estuary with an open sea before her, *Esk* smashed her amidships; the bowsprit, like a knight's lance, carrying away *Dolphin*'s forward rigging and driving the slave-ship squarely on to the bar.

The shock of the collision threw the crew of both ships down like nine-pins. Timbers screamed and groaned, cracked, splintered. *Dolphin*'s top-masts collapsed and crashed down in a vast, billowing chaos of canvas and rope, and before the crew could recover their senses the longboat was snapping at their heels and the Sentinels were over the side.

Over went Dawlish and Rafferty, howling like dogs. Brooke followed them, to find Rafferty swinging his boarding-axe two-handed into the neck of Harker, and Dawlish splitting the mate with his cutlass. Carlin, a horrible growling coming from his throat, elbowed Brooke aside and chopped a man to death as he slid down *Dolphin*'s sloping deck. More Sentinels rushed on board, the Dolphins throwing down their weapons but being hacked to death on the spot. Blood flowing, *gouting*, men bolting below deck like rabbits and the Sentinels pursuing them as mercilessly as stoats. The fo'c's'le a scene from hell, men being beaten to death in the hold, plucked screaming from the rigging and thrown down to join the slaves and the sharks. Hard cases and Blue-lighters, would-be saints and actual sinners now all demons together, men without mercy.

Brooke tried to stop them, but he might as well have attempted to stop the tide. He was brushed aside by men who could see only a red haze. And then it was over. The ship a slaughter-house and the Sentinels butchers, blood-soaked, *saturated*, red from head to foot, and the ship stinking of blood and vomit, excrement and entrails. A slow dawning of what had happened, the Sentinels afraid to catch each other's eye, looking away like guilty dogs. A clank here and there as men threw their cutlasses down, as if they could dissociate themselves from the slaughter. Brooke stood by the mainmast, his chest heaving. Blood was running past his feet, actually running. He had heard of it — the scuppers running with blood — but he had never seen it, had always thought it was a ridiculous exaggeration, but it was true. Presumably this was what it was like in the old days, when ships fought it out the live-long day, yard-arm to yard-arm, and losses of half the crew were not unknown.

He looked round the ship, at the bodies and the Sentinels. He had lost them, he thought. He had lost control of them. He stared stupidly at the bloody deck. 'What disgrace,' he whispered, 'What utter disgrace.'

Someone took his elbow. Bower was standing next to him, a curious expression on his face. 'Sir,' he said. 'Sir?'

Brooke shook himself like a man struggling to free himself from a nightmare. 'Yes?' he said.

'The Captain, sir.'

Brooke's head jerked up. 'Dead?'

'No, sir. He's still alive. He's on that slaver, *Aphrodite*. They've got a surgeon on board, but I've sent the cutter for Mr Jessup.'

'Good.' Brooke nodded vaguely, but Bower had not finished.

'Yes, sir. And Mr Donnelly is here. May he have some men to

work on his ship? He thinks there may be a chance of saving her. And it seems that there are still slaves below deck. . . .'

A rush of responsibility. Men waiting on Brooke's orders. Work to be done *now.* And, as if to give emphasis to the urgency, *Dolphin* gave a shudder and slipped a little, her decks tilted just that much more. Brooke brushed his eyes as if wiping away a fog of doubt and hesitancy. 'Right,' he said. 'Let's get to work.'

A stream of orders. Sentinels rushed downstream to aid Potts. The talkative Box, who now had a large lump on his head, ordered to warp *Anna Maria* off the mudbank. The dead on *Dolphin* heaved overboard and a hundred terrified slaves brought on deck, soothed, pacified, transferred by exhausted men to *Aphrodite.* Another group of men chopping *Esk*'s bows free from where she had gouged into *Dolphin*, more men bowsing out great coils of hawser to tow *Esk* off. The morning passed away, the sun blazing down but the weather changing. Ominous purple clouds piling up over the land, the wind was higher and the sea rising, pounding on the bar, gobs of spray flying across the two ships.

Noon. Suffocating heat and humidity. Four Sentinels and an Esker were found dead drunk in *Dolphin*'s spirit room, men barely able to totter about their work. But all the slavers were now out at sea, their crews securely in irons, for Potts had found a pilot on *Trinidad* who was ready to take the ships out once a pistol had been clapped to his head. Purvis slid down from *Esk* and reported that *Esk*'s bows, stoved in when she crashed, were patched as good as they could be, and if ever she was towed off and out to sea she *might* make Freetown.

Brooke clambered up to *Esk*, slipping on a rivulet of blood, treading on a fragment of human being, reached up to *Esk*'s rail and swung up and over. Donnelly was below deck, crouched for'ard, in the very bows of the ship, a lantern gleaming on newly cut timber. It was hotter there than on deck.

As he heard Brooke, Donnelly screwed his neck round. 'She looks all right,' he said.

Brooke ran his hand over the timbers. 'Yes.'

'Right as rain,' Donnelly said.

'As you say.' It was like a furnace in the tiny peak. Brooke mopped his neck. 'Did you do it on purpose? Ram *Dolphin*?'

Donnelly met Brooke's eyes. 'I did.'

'I hope their Lordships at the Admiralty see your point of view,' Brooke said.

'So do I.' Donnelly gave a little, nervous laugh.

A pause. Brooke licked his lips. 'Have you any water?'

'Here.' Donnelly passed a bottle and Brooke drank.

'There is a certain amount of hostility outside.' Brooke said. 'It seems the inhabitants aren't very friendly. And the weather is breaking.'

'Oh.' Donnelly's face set in a bitter expression. 'I see.' And he did see. *Esk* could not be pulled off until the next high tide, if then. It would be a difficult task, the night rushing in, the bar perilously close, hostile natives possibly. It would be easy for Brooke to condemn the ship, burn her and *Dolphin*, and get safely away. No one would question his judgement and he could sail away to the warmest commendation for a brilliant little action, with promotion to captaincy a certainty. Whereas Donnelly himself . . . well, he knew the charge as well as anyone: 'Whereas you did wilfully and recklessly endanger your ship and its company, thereby causing its loss. . . .' No defence against that, and no lordly uncles to speak for him, no friends in Exeter Hall either, and many a one glad to see the back of a Catholic. Broken from the service and lucky if he picked up a mate's post on a rotting merchantman.

'I would do it again if I had to,' he said.

'You would?' A touch of wonder in Brooke's voice. He remembered Murray after the fight with *Phantom*. How easy it would have been then for Murray to have damned him utterly, and how handsomely he have behaved. He hesitated. If he could bring *Esk* off, something might be saved from the disastrous day and Donnelly would get the commendation he deserved. He sighed, and as if in answer *Esk* struck a deep, reverberating chord.

Things squeaked and scampered over Brooke's legs. 'The rats are deserting,' he said.

'Yes,' Donnelly answered. 'Leaving the sinking ship, sagacious creatures that they are.'

Brooke smiled, a rare, wry, self-mocking smile. He opened his mouth as if to speak, but if he had intended to his words were lost for ever, because a large, shaggy head thrust itself into the peak and a hoarse voice, quivering with excitement, roared: 'Sir, *Sentinel* signals a strange sail in sight, and sir — the Captain is on board!'

Amazement. More staggering astonishment than if Lazarus himself had climbed on board, casting his grave-clothes aside.

172

But there the Captain was, a vast turban of a bandage wrapped around his head, but with nothing worse than a six-inch furrow across his scalp. And sensation piled on sensation. The strange sail being *Hornet*, her longboat coming across, Rutherford heaving himself aboard *Dolphin* and, to the astonishment, the *utter* astonishment of all, Mister Spencer himself climbing over the rail. A *double* resurrection. Nothing like it in the history of the squadron, nothing like it in the history of the Royal Navy, nothing — in a spectacular burst of pride — nothing like it in the history of the world. Even Brooke was taken by surprise, just like a normal human being, and the Owner and all the crew were grinning like so many Cheshire cats.

But even a midshipman plucked from death by pirates, a watery grave, and the beach, took second place to the Navy's business and John was unceremoniously thrust aside as Murray, Brooke, Donnelly, and Rutherford gathered on the wreck of *Esk*'s quarterdeck and Donnelly reported to the grim Murray.

Donnelly finished his tale and, with a clear emphasis, added: 'I must stress, sir, that no other officer was involved. It was entirely my responsibility.'

Murray was abrupt. 'Of course it was. You were in command. Is your ship cleared?'

'Everything moveable, sir.'

'Good.' Murray turned on his heel and looked at the sky with its menacing canopy of cloud. 'No sense in wasting time. Burn them both.'

'Burn —' Brooke could not believe his ears. He strode after Murray. 'Sir,' he said in a low voice. 'I was thinking *Esk* could be towed off.'

'Towed off?' Incredulity in Murray's voice.

'Yes, sir.'

'Bless my soul,' Murray said. 'I can't believe that you are serious. Risk a sloop-of-war and the lives of eighty men to bring off a four-gun brig that is shattered to the core? Really, Mr Brooke. I am surprised that a sound, seamanlike officer like you should even think of such a thing. No, no. We must get off this shore at once. Burn them.'

And burned they were, from truck to waterline, their masts glaring skeletons, crackling with fire, as *Sentinel* and *Hornet* drove the prizes out into the Bight of Benin.

30

A fresh and wholesome gale. The wind so steady and unchanging that hardly a sail needed trimming the whole day. Rest for the Captain and rest for his crew after a week of struggling from the baleful Bight of Benin, groping for the south where the merry easterlies blew fair. A week of staggering labour as the Sentinels, stretched across five ships, had worked until men dropped asleep at the ropes. But the wind found at last; a glowing sun and a sparkling sea shimmering turquoise and gold, dolphins and flying-fish, the ship sailing itself, and tired men allowed to take their ease — six solid hours of blessed slumber, and the Owner turning a blind eye to any dawdling on deck.

In the bows a handful of Sentinels looking with fond eyes at their argosy; two miles ahead, *Aphrodite* with Brooke on board sailing like a haystack and setting the pace for the convoy. Behind her *Trinidad*, a silent, melancholy Donnelly on her poop, then *Anna Maria*, Keverne aboard, two loaded pistols in his belt, in her wake *Bella Dora*, Potts lounging in her Master's best armchair, which had been dragged on deck, and reflecting on the pleasures of a captain's life; and, last of all, *Sentinel*, like a dog driving a flock of sheep which might, after all, turn out to be wolves in woolly disguise.

The glittering, crystalline waves curled and sparkled, and the jolly dolphins grinned and chattered as they rode before the ship. Rafferty, a tattered shirt over his knees, his calloused fingers threading a needle with surprising delicacy, raised his vast, red Irish head and, with a leprechaun grin, addressed Dawlish:

'And what do you reckon they are worth, then?' with a comprehensive wave at the convoy.

Dawlish, trailing a fishing-line over the side, grinned sideways out of the corner of his mouth.

'Which I've told you ten times already.'

'Ah.' Rafferty gurgled. 'Sure I know you have — but tell us again.'

'Well.' Dawlish leaned on the rail, not unwilling to pull himself from the hopes of catching a fish to the reality of the prize money sailing before his very eyes. 'Well, four vessels, so that's at least — *at least* — fifteen hundred, and they're carrying a thousand slaves, so that's five thousand quid, so put the two together and it's . .

wait a minute . . . six thousand and five hundred pounds, and divide that by sixty-nine and it's . . . well, near enough a hundred quid each. Easy, maybe more.'

Yetts, refusing to eat fish on the grounds that they ate dead seamen, and having no shirts to mend, spat over the side. 'A hundred quid. Two years' pay. Two years' pay. . . .'

His voice died away, carried on the wind past the cold-eyed seagull perched on the bowsprit which grinned its long grin, blinked its orange eye, spread its snowy wings, and flew away.

The gull's shadow, and its cynical cry, which told of seamen long since dead and gone into the deep waters of the ocean, disturbed Taplow, who was falling asleep over stolen rum in the gun-room.

'Wha'?' he cried, 'Wha'?', staring at a shadow in the doorway.

The shadow shook, quivered, and solidified into the bulky shape of Purvis, a long-jack plane dangling from his meaty fist.

'We're doing all right.' Purvis said. 'I just heard Dawlish there, hundred quid each — and that's the ratings. That Jonah of yours must have gone overboard.'

'Jonah?' Taplow blinked. 'Has he? Has he? Well, tell me this. Tell me why them as wasn't in the action gets full shares with them as was? Tell me that. Why should them buggers what is lying snug in a hospital in Freetown or wherever they is get the same as you and me what took them slavers there at the risk of our lives?' He sprawled forward, knocking over six penn'orth of Her Majesty's prime Jamaican rum.

'I don't know what you mean, Henry.' Purvis was embarrassed, uneasy.

'You know what I mean,' Taplow cried. 'That prize crew what is all supposed to have gone blind. Same shares as us, they're getting. And what about them layabouts on *Phantom*? Lost us a prize cruiser and two hundred niggers, and what's happening there? All their bloody dependants is getting equal shares — a hundred quid each, and what did they do? Tell me that?'

'Now then, Henry.' Purvis was disturbed. 'That's just fair dos.'

'Is it? Is it?' Taplow groped for his glass. 'And is it fair dos that them blackies, them Kroomen, should be getting ten quid each?'

Purvis shrugged. 'Well, the ship's company voted that, Henry. Out of their own pockets. And what's eighty quid when all's said and done? It wouldn't come to much more than a quid each if it was split between us.'

'Aye? Well, it's a quid out of my pocket.' Taplow groped for his rum. 'Wonderful, ain't it? Ship's company voting, *voting*! Scrubs what don't know port from starboard deciding matters. . . .' He stared into his pannikin. 'Want a drink?'

'Well,' Purvis looked thoughtfully at Taplow. 'I don't think I will, Henry.'

'No, you. . . .' Taplow's voice died away in a sour mumble. A long silence broken by a hail from the deck.

'Wha's that?' Taplow demanded.

'The cutter coming back with Jessup,' Purvis said.

'More bad news.' Taplow lurched to his feet, his narrow face a mask of discontent. 'Jessup. If he's a doctor I'm the Admiral of the Fleet. Come on, let's see how much we've lost today.'

Staggering as he went Taplow went on deck with Purvis at his heels. The cutter with John at the helm had come alongside and Jessup's red face was appearing over the side of the ship like the rising sun. Jessup mopped his face and waddled up to Murray.

'A little better today, sir,' he said. He fished a piece of paper out of his pocket. 'None lost on *Bella Dora*, the fever seems to be dying down there. Three dead on *Santa Maria*. Seven on *Trinidad* and, I regret to say, thirteen dead on *Aphrodite*.'

Long faces among the listening Sentinels. Dawlish mouthing '*twenty-three*', and a whisper running the length of the deck: twenty-three slaves dead since last night, lads. Fifty-seven pounds ten into the briny.

Murray frowned at Jessup. 'I am disturbed by these figures, Mr Jessup. So far two hundred of these poor souls have died. Is there nothing we can do?'

Jessup made a small, helpless gesture. 'These tropical diseases, sir. Señor Figuerras, the surgeon on *Aphrodite*, thinks that there is little that we can do. I must confess his experience of *malaria* is more comprehensive than mine. He suggests Peruvian bark.'

Murray waved the suggestion aside. 'What bark we have we must keep for our own men.'

Jessup coughed. 'Sir, the, er . . . the señor strongly advises dancing the slaves, as he puts it. He is quite convinced that it shakes the fever from them.'

'Well, we may try it,' Murray said, 'but I must confess I do not like to see it. And how are our men?'

Jessup peered at his list. 'All things considered, sir, not too unsatisfactory. Twenty-three cases of mild fever, and another fourteen quite unfit for their duties. *Aphrodite* is badly hit.'

'Not shamming?' Murray asked sharply.

'No, indeed not, sir. Parkin, for instance has ulcers under both arms, the ulcers exuding a greenish pus —'

'Thank you,' Murray said. 'I leave the details to you.' He leaned over the side. 'Mr Spencer, I am coming aboard you.'

Five men told off for duty on *Aphrodite*, shuffling forward with their kit and sitting reluctantly in the cutter as, under its huge sail, it sped forward along the convoy.

Murray sat in the bows and watched John approvingly as he held the tiller. The lad was a born seaman, handling the cutter as if born to the sea. And made for command. Once reassured that he would not be hanged for the loss of *Phantom*, he had begun to behave like an officer. All the old nervous diffidence had gone. Now he gave orders as if he expected them to be obeyed. A remarkable young man who had survived a remarkable experience.

The cutter swooped down on *Aphrodite* and Murray climbed on board.

'Good morning, Mr Brooke,' he called. 'I have brought you some replacements, good men all of them.'

Brooke punctiliously saluted. 'Thank you, sir.'

Murray pursed his lips. He was well used to Brooke's formal manner but, on this bright morning, he found it somewhat disappointing. 'Is there anything more I can do for you?' he asked.

'There are one or two things,' Brooke replied. 'I have a list.'

'Perhaps we could discuss it in your cabin,' Murray said.

'As you wish, sir.' Brooke led the way below. 'Do you wish some refreshment?'

'Perhaps some coffee.'

Deakin, an Esker who claimed once to have been a cook in a coaching inn, shambled into the cabin with a pot full of brown, warmish liquid, grinned sheepishly at Murray, and shambled out again.

Murray sipped his coffee. 'Deakin does not improve. I remember him in the old *Warrior*. Foster, the first, swore he would have him flogged if he did not learn to make better coffee.'

He put down his cup. 'Mr Brooke, we have been so busy this past week or so that we have not had time to talk properly. But now I must say something. Coming out we had our disagreements, but after the fight with *Phantom* I found a new warmth between us — yes, a warmth — which was most congenial. Now we seem to be at loggerheads again. Why is that?'

'Do you need to ask?' Brooke said.

'Indeed I do.' Murray leaned forward. 'I ask you as man to man, forget rank.'

Brooke turned his face away impatiently. 'I cannot believe that you are so . . . obtuse.'

'Perhaps I am, though,' Murray said. 'I am only a rough seaman making no claims to cleverness. But tell me, is it because I have not disciplined the men who went berserk on *Dolphin*? Is that it?'

Brooke turned back. 'That episode was a disgrace to the Royal Navy. An utter disgrace. I cannot understand how you take it so calmly. Did you not say that you would not have any revenge? And have you not, the whole voyage through, preached at the crew about love and forgiveness? And now, when there has been bloody murder, you lean back as if there was nothing to it.'

'Well, now.' Murray clapped his broad hands on his knees. 'What would you have me do? Men will lose their heads in a fight. Do you wish me to flog them? On what possible charge? Should I put them into the civil courts? That is not possible, since they were under naval law. Come now, I have spoken to the men and they are thoroughly ashamed of themselves. I am convinced of it. A fight is a dirty business and it may be that now and again it is no bad thing that we see how dirty it is. The incident is best forgotten, believe me.' He paused but Brooke was silent, unyielding. 'Or is it because of *Esk*? Is it because I burned the ship?'

He paused again, and this time Brooke did speak. 'We could have towed her off,' he said.

'Well now,' Murray smiled. 'You think we could, I thought that we could not. That is a mere professional disagreement. There is no need for us to fall out because of it.'

Brooke flushed a little. 'I was about to give my word to Donnelly,' he said.

The shadow of a frown crossed Murray's face. 'About to? Are you not being too sensitive about this?'

'Perhaps,' Brooke said. 'You should ask Donnelly about that.'

'Why should I?' Murray cried. 'But let me put this to you. Mr Donnelly was in command of his own ship. He rammed *Dolphin*. Very well, that was his decision and he made it. I admire him for it. But he must take the responsibility for his actions. He cannot expect other officers to risk their ships, and the lives of their men, to save him from the consequences; it would be unreasonable. No. It was a gallant and noble action but Mr Donnelly must stand the responsibility for his actions, as I must bear the responsibility for mine.'

'What of that?' Brooke demanded. 'No court martial could possibly blame you. They would regard your action as prudent. But Donnelly will be broken. His career is over.'

Murray waved his hand. 'He may equally well be commended.'

'No.' Brooke was certain. 'The Humane Society may give him a medal and Exeter Hall will give him a Wedgwood pot, and the Quakers will slobber over him, but he will never find another commission in the Navy. It will be glad to be rid of a nuisance. An Irishman without friends or influence. He is merely filling a berth some admiral's pet could fill. If he had rammed a man-o'-war it would be a different tale, but some tub of a slaver. . . . What will the Admiralty care that a few slaves were saved?'

'And you wished me risk the lives of my men so that Mr Donnelly would keep his position?' Murray asked.

Brooke made an impatient gesture. 'Not that entirely. It would — had we tried to tow *Esk* off — it would have brought some honour into the day, into this disgusting campaign.'

'Is it disgusting?' Murray asked.

Brooke stood up and peered through the cabin window. The slave-ships bobbed along in an untidy line, *Sentinel*'s red ensign at the end like a full stop.

'Yes,' he said. 'I find it disgusting. What are we? A mixture of the spy and the policeman. Smell this ship. It is like a cattle-scow bringing beasts from Dublin to Liverpool. And what is the use of carrying on like this? The Navy has been on patrol now for thirty-five years and the trade is worse than when we started.'

'Then,' Murray looked at his boots, 'then why do it, Mr Brooke?'

'Because I am in the Navy,' Brooke cried, 'and because the Navy sent me here, and because if I left the Navy I would be —' He was about to say, I would be begging for my bread off rich relatives. 'I would be like Donnelly,' he said.

Murray sighed. 'But we have saved a few souls from a lifetime's slavery.'

'I do not deny it,' Brooke said.

'Well. . . .' Murray rose. 'I shall do my best for Donnelly.'

'I do not doubt that, sir,' Brooke said. He paused and turned, his face stiff. 'Sir. I regret it if you feel that I am . . . hostile to you. I assure you that I am not. In fact, sir, I hold you in high esteem.'

'And I you,' Murray said, warmly. 'Well, we will say no more about it. It may be that in a voyage such as ours we must all discover something new about ourselves, and the men we rub shoulders with.'

Days passing. Sun and rain. The fever dying down and the slavers dumping their sombre sailcloth parcels into the sea less frequently. The invalids on *Sentinel* recovering, although Parkin — *Surrender* Parkin as he was now known — had to walk about the ship with his hands held high. A general mood of cheerful optimism as Freetown and its delights drew near.

John the darling of the convoy as he raced up and down in his cutter. Lyapo, rated ordinary seaman, on pay and drawing his rations with the men, well liked for his affability and respected for the strength of his arm; only Dawlish being his equal and only the mighty Rafferty his superior. And he began to get an adequate grasp of the language so that, as Carlin put it, 'He don't speak as good as you or me, mates, but I've heard more from him in three weeks than I did off Old Cobber the voyage through.'

Murray noticed this and, one calm evening, he took John aside.

'Your man, Lyapo,' he said. 'I wonder if he would like to stay on the ship. Give him two or three months more and I will rate him Able. After our tour he could return to England with us — oh yes —' noting John's surprise — 'that isn't so uncommon. A fine, strapping fellow like that will get on all right. See how he feels about it.'

John put the suggestion to Lyapo in a quiet spot on the yard-arm of the mainmast. 'And if you come to England you can stay with my Aunt Honoria,' he added recklessly.

Lyapo swung his legs. 'I don't know,' he sighed. 'I don't know.'

'Well,' John leaned back against the mast. 'What would you like to do?'

Lyapo shook his head. It was a difficult question. What was there for him in the world? Time and tide and tears had washed away his home, and what remained? The ship was some kind of home but the work was hard, the food was poor, and the routine, with its endless tolling of bells, was trying to a man used to making his own division of the day. And then there was the mysterious Freetown to which they were sailing. What happened there? He had been given hazy hints of freedom and land, but what did that mean? He was free already, or so he was told, and as for land . . . what sort of land would it be? And how would he farm it? A man could not grow food on his own; he needed a wife, children, brothers, a whole village. And the people in Freetown, would they speak Yoruba or English? He was baffled by the choice. How could he decide, he who knew so little?

He looked sideways at John. On board *Sentinel* he had little chance to talk to him. They had their different duties to perform, and John was an officer. Sometimes Lyapo pined for the days on the beach when he had been the master, caring for the boy, feeding him, showing him plants, playing draughts by the fire. Now it was he who was like a child.

The ship's bell rang. 'My watch,' Lyapo said. 'I tell you in Freetown, I wait till then.'

John reported back to Murray expecting the Captain to be annoyed, but got a nod of approval. 'Very sensible. Very sensible. He is a most valuable, sensible man. Carry on, Mr Spencer.'

Carry on John did, and all the Sentinels, until one morning Murray brought the ships north. The day following they came upon the lush and verdant coast; hills wreathed in mist, clearings yellow with yams, smoke curling from village fires, people walking, unafraid, on the beach, fishing boats out at sea. Red cliffs, white houses, one with a flag-pole, chapel roofs, the Middle Ground, St George's Bay, *Sentinel*'s anchor roaring through the hawse-hole and securing her firmly to the bottom of Freetown harbour.

31

Monday, four bells in the forenoon watch: ten a.m. A pleasant smell of fresh paint and vinegar on *Sentinel*. The ship stripped, cleaned, watered and victualled. Brass gleaming, mahogany glowing, and the deck scrubbed as white as a lily. The hard labour finished and time for a little repose. The Owner in his cabin, immersed — submerged — in paperwork; Scott, John, and Potts listening drowsily to Keverne expounding the mysteries of the astronomical tables; Taplow, Hayes, Purvis, and Jessup playing whist in the gunroom; Tiger and Ginger blinking at each other on the roof of the galley.

Half the ship's company ashore on liberty. The Blue-lighters of the port watch having tea with the ladies and gentlemen of the New Zion Chapel under the unwilling guidance of Brooke. The non-elect having rum with other ladies and gentlemen in the Hallelujah Bar.

In the bows of *Sentinel*, paint-brushes in hand, leaning companionably over the rail, Dawlish, Rafferty, Pike and Lyapo.

'Which it is the same old stink-hole,' said Dawlish, without malice.

'Now I wouldn't go all the way with you there, Zeb,' Rafferty said. 'It ain't all that bad.' A wave of a vast hand at the tropical magnificence of mountain and bay. 'When it rains it puts me in mind of Galway,' he added, improbably.

'Galway!' Pike, who had never been within two hundred miles of the place, screwed up his face in disgust. 'That ain't even as civilized as what this dump is.' He turned to Lyapo. 'What do you make of it?' he asked, speaking very slowly. 'This like your place, in Africa?'

'Which this is Africa, you silly old fool,' Dawlish grunted. 'But what about it, Lyapo? Is it like your home?'

Lyapo shook his head. It was not like his home at all. He had never imagined a town of such size, with such huge houses and so much bustle. 'No,' he said. 'This. . . .' He wanted to say that the town made him feel small, insignificant, like an ant, and yet somehow bigger and more important. That it was a place where, instead of being a big fish in a small pool, he was a small fish in a large pool, and only one of many at that. But still, having larger waters in which to swim, having more space, more possibilities, more danger — but more excitement, too. Yes, a place where a man would need to have his wits about him, but where those wits would be sharpened, like a knife on a grindstone. But he could not express those thoughts in English and so he remained silent.

Kindly Rafferty, mistaking his silence, and knowing himself what it was like to leave his birthplace for ever, clapped Lyapo awkwardly on the back. 'Don't you go fretting there, me old fellow. Sure, it will all come right in the end. He's a good lad, you know,' he said to the others. 'He's not a bad lad at all.'

No dissent. Lyapo a hard worker, ready to learn, and would give you a hand any time. His difference in language and colour not worrying men who had learned to rub along with half the nations of the earth.

Silence, self-contented smiles. The sun not yet too hot and a faint breeze fanning the harbour, bringing with it a distant, mildly discordant echo of music.

'Hear that?' Pike cried. 'Listen — it's a hymn. It's them Blue-lighters at that chapel!'

A rich burst of laughter. The very idea of men voluntarily spending their liberty sitting in a chapel, singing hymns, seeming ludicrous.

Dawlish looked over Pike's head and winked at Rafferty. 'Which it ain't an hymn, though. That's an anthem.'

'Which it ain't,' Pike yelped.

'Which it is.'

'It ain't,' Pike in a passion. 'Do you think I don't know a bloody hymn when I hears one?'

'You wouldn't know your own father — if you've got one,' Dawlish said to another burst of laughter.

Murray, as Brooke had done on a less pleasant occasion, heard the laughter through his sky-light and smiled fondly. A happy ship, he thought — rightly — and how it had pulled together after the fight at Whydah. No unhealthy brooding on the past; a proper sense of sin, of course, but not unwholesome; and work, prayer, and a little relaxation were bringing out the best in the men. With a lighter heart, he turned to a vast form which required him to enumerate the numbers of slaves taken by his ship, when, where, how, number reaching Freetown, their sex, probable age. . . .

A bang on his door, and Potts sticking his genial head round it. 'Two gentlemen come aboard, sir. Want to see you. Should I bring them down?'

'No.' Murray was glad to get away from his forms. 'I will come on deck.'

A ripple of activity as the captain appeared. Earnest attention to Keverne from the mids, Dawlish and company making vague, mystical passes with their paint-brushes, even the cats raising their sleepy heads and opening their eyes wide.

Two men were waiting in the waist. A small, black man, and a languid Englishman whose yellow skin said that he had been too long on the Coast.

The Englishman raised his hat. 'Captain Murray? My name is Stour, sir, from the governor's office, and this is Mr Azoka. Sorry to bother you but I understand that you have a freed slave on board, a Yoruba.'

'I have,' Murray said. 'And what is that to you?'

'May we speak to him?' Stour asked.

'What about?' Murray said.

'Well, sir,' Stour was tentative, 'it is to make sure, sir, that, that he is not being kept on board . . . er . . . against his will.'

Murray's face went red. 'Did I hear you aright?'

Stour raised his hand. 'Please don't misunderstand me, sir. It is a mere formality. No one would dream of suggesting that you . . . but there have been cases . . . merchantmen and so on. It is the law. Mr Azoka speaks Yoruba. If he might have a word?'

Murray rubbed his chin. 'I suppose so,' he said. 'You had better come below. Mr Potts, send Lyapo to me.'

The four men crowded into Murray's cabin. A ripple of Yoruba from Mr Azoka.

Lyapo's eyes widened and a delighted smile crossed his face. 'He speaks my language, sir,' he said. 'That's Yoruba!'

A long conversation. Lyapo deep in thought, concentrating, finally nodding emphatically and giving a little grunt.

Azoka turned to Murray. In excellent English he said, 'Sir, this man says that he is happy on this ship and that everyone has been kind to him. I have told him that he may stay on this ship or go to the King's Yard.'

'And what have you told him about that?' Murray asked.

'Sir, I have told him what is true,' Azoka said, with dignity. 'I have told him that it is a compound where the freed slaves are held until they are resettled. I have said that there are other Oyo men there. And I have told him that if he wishes to stay in Sierra Leone he will be a free man and that he will be given some land.'

184

'I see.' Murray tapped on his desk. 'Lyapo, what do you want to do?'

'Sir,' Lyapo leaned forward. 'I think I go to King's Yard. I —' He broke off and spoke rapidly to Azoka.

'Yes,' Azoka cleared his throat. 'He says that he wants to see what the King's Yard is like. He would like to talk to the Oyo men there and to other freed slaves. But he asks you, if he does not like it there can he come back to the ship?'

'A very sensible answer,' Murray said. 'Of course he must go, and he may return at any time. He is a most valuable man.'

A few hasty farewells, and Stour's boat departed. The watch on board, reassured by Murray that Lyapo was merely going ashore for a spell, bawling friendly, lewd advice after him. Then silence, peace, dinner.

Tuesday. The port watch ashore. Leave for the mids. John and Potts begging the use of the gig and paddling contentedly around the harbour. John paddling, that is, Potts leaning back with a lordly air and smoking a cigar not quite as long as a yard-arm.

'Just row a little faster,' he commanded. 'I like to feel a bit of breeze on my face when I'm on the water.'

John obediently bending his back over the oars, bottles of beer chinking in the keel.

'I say, Potts,' he grunted. 'Let's go to the King's Yard and see Lyapo.'

Potts emitted a vast cloud of smoke worthy of Vesuvius. 'All right. But you row back.'

John rowed to the ramshackle jetty and tied up, and the two mids strolled past the courthouse and down to King's Yard.

The yard was a huge, walled enclosure. At the main gate a neat African listened to their request and obligingly darted into the compound to find Lyapo. John and Potts peered into the yard.

Inside the vast compound there were stalls and lean-tos selling food and cloth. Here and there craftsmen were making small articles from scraps of wood and metal, groups of people strolled about, and a fair-sized crowd was gathered around a band of musicians.

'Make themselves at home, don't they?' Potts said, and indeed he was correct. With the vast resilience of the human race the slaves, quite naturally and spontaneously, had recreated their lives and, under the shadow of Europe, were keeping the fires of

Africa burning. And from out of that typical African scene came Lyapo.

'John,' he cried, 'and Mr Potts.'

'Lyapo!' John shook Lyapo's hand. 'We just called to see you. How are you? Are you well?'

'Oh yes,' Lyapo smiled entrancingly. 'There are Oyo men here, in the yard. We have talked and talked and talked. That is nice for me, to speak my language again.'

'And what do they say?' John asked.

Lyapo looked serious. 'They say I can have a farm here. Stay here, in S'a Leone. Maybe get married again.'

'That's it, cock,' Potts said. 'That's the idea.'

'What will you do?' John asked.

Lyapo shrugged. 'I don't know yet. I wait. I think. Then I see Captain Murray.'

'That's the right thing to do,' John said. 'Take your time. Don't rush it.'

'Yes, I think about it.' Lyapo suddenly grinned. 'I tell you one thing, John. I teach them draughts in there.'

John laughed delightedly. 'And I bet you win all the time. You had plenty of practice. Well . . . we must go, Lyapo. We — I will come again.'

They shook hands and parted. Suddenly John turned.

'Lyapo! Have you any . . . I mean, do you need any money?'

Lyapo smiled. 'Oh no, John. Captain Murray gave me two pound when I leave ship and Mr Brooke come this morning and give me a pound.'

'Well now, who would have thought that,' Potts said as they walked back to the gig. 'Old Brooke. I tell you one thing, my lad. I don't know what's been happening to the man but he's becoming almost human. Perhaps he got a bang on the head at Whydah.'

They rowed back to *Sentinel* feeling pleasantly virtuous, Potts drinking beer and watching the sloop *Messenger* warping into the harbour.

'I'll tell you another thing,' he said. 'There is something *up*.'

John raised a red face from the oars. 'Meaning what?'

'Meaning this,' Potts said significantly. 'There's *Messenger* coming in, and *Waterwitch* came in last night. That's five men-o'-war tied up here, not counting our own tub. And there's been a lot of coming and going. And you take a look about you — I've hardly seen an officer or a rating of any of them ships. Well, when you've been in the Navy as long as I have you'll know what that means.'

John leaned on his oars and took the beer-bottle from Potts. 'Well, what does it mean?'

'It means action, sonny. That's what it means. And something big.'

'What action?'

'Which not being a fortune-teller, and not having had a chat with Captain Denman just recently, I can't rightly tell. But there's something in the wind, my lad, there's something in the wind. Now you just get a move on or we'll be late for our dinner.'

Wednesday. The day of wrath. Rain, sticky heat, and ALL LEAVE STOPPED. Murray in a rage, a fury, a thunder-cloud of temper visible over his head as, from the quarterdeck, he faced the *whole* of the utterly, totally disgraced starboard watch.

'British seamen,' he thundered. 'British seamen! Sentinels! I'll rig the grating and *flog* some sense into you.'

'Which we only did it for a joke, sir,' Dawlish said.

'A joke!'

'Well, sir, we had a whip-round — begging your pardon and no humour intended there, sir — and got a few quid off the lads and took it down to old Lyapo, thinking he might need a few bob, sir.'

'Yes.' Murray raised his eyes to the heavens. 'Highly commendable. And did you, and Rafferty, and all the rest of you, did you take off all your clothes, rub mud all over yourselves, and run about the King's Yard? Did you?'

A muffled snort from Kemp.

'Are you laughing, Kemp?' Murray bellowed. 'Are you?'

'No, sir,' Kemp cried. 'Something in my throat, sir.'

'I'll put something *round* your throat,' Murray cried. 'Now, Dawlish?'

'Well, sir,' Dawlish said. 'Old Lyapo there, he's got some mates and we had a bit of a do, like. There was some musicians, and Lyapo gave us a lot of palm-wine. It didn't taste like much, sir, no more than water, but it wasn't — like water, I mean — and we got a bit lively, like.'

'Lively.' Murray folded his arms. 'You were drunk. Drunk, the whole lot of you. Rafferty.'

Rafferty stepped forward.

'Rafferty, did you pick up a horse — *a horse* — and *carry* it down Water Street?'

187

Rafferty rubbed his face. "Twas only for the crack, sir. The lads bet me. Sure it was no bigger than a pig, sir, and I didn't hurt the wee beast.'

'And the beast's owner, Rafferty? Did you hurt him?'

Strange gargling noises in Rafferty's chest.

'Speak up, man.'

'He run after me, sir.'

'Yes?'

'Well, he threw stones at me, sir, so I gave him a little push, like.'

'And why did he throw stones at you?'

'Well, sir.' Rafferty ducked his head sheepishly. 'He couldn't catch up with me, sir.'

Two distinct sniggers from behind Murray. Without turning his head he snapped: 'Mr Spencer, Mr Scott. Go to the mast-head immediately and stay there until night without any dinner. Pike!'

Pike shuffled forward.

'How old are you, Pike?'

'About forty, sir.'

Murray took a deep breath. 'Pike, you *joined* the navy fifty-four years ago. Did you yesterday approach a lady called —' Murray consulted a piece of paper — 'called Mrs Ozumba, a respectable member of the Wesleyan Chapel, and did you propose marriage to her, claiming to be Master and Commander of the ship and telling her . . . telling her that I was your father and, when her husband objected, did you hit him in the eye?'

'Can't rightly remember, sir,' said Pike, wise in the ways of naval inquiries.

'All right,' Murray snapped. 'All right. Until further notice, all leave stopped, all rum, all pay, and watch and watch about until further notice.'

'I really don't know what came over them,' Murray said later to Brooke. 'Behaving like madmen. And Pike — are you smiling, Mr Brooke?'

'No, sir,' Brooke said hastily. 'I suppose they were letting off steam. It has been a trying cruise.'

'Trying,' Murray snorted. 'A couple of months at sea and a couple of minor actions. No, they are unmitigated ruffians, past all redemption.'

'If I might say something,' Brooke said. 'Thank you, sir. I noticed that the defaulters were the men who went amok on *Dolphin.*'

'Exactly,' Murray snapped. 'Exactly my point.'

'Yes, sir. But it occurred to me that the men . . . perhaps they were trying to wipe out that memory in a wild spree, sir.'

'Spree! Running naked through the streets? Scandalizing every respectable woman in the town? Knocking down innocent men?'

'I agree, sir,' Brooke said. 'But no one was seriously hurt. If Rafferty had meant it he could have knocked that trader over Lion Mountain, but all he did was give him a clip on the jaw. And it all sprang from a generous gesture.'

'I won't deny that,' Murray said. 'But Mr Brooke, at the start of this voyage you would have been the first to insist on a flogging all round. Are you changing your views?'

Brooke hesitated. 'Perhaps I am, sir. Perhaps.' He shrugged. 'I lost control of my men on *Dolphin*, so perhaps I am a little less inclined to blame men for losing control of themselves.'

'Aye,' Murray nodded. 'Perhaps we all have to find that out. Well, I still say that the men are a crowd of reprobates and I will see that they suffer for it — but perhaps not too severely.'

Thursday. The Sentinels with downcast eyes tiptoeing about the ship, speaking in hoarse whispers. Pike sneaking in and out of the captain's cabin, until an exasperated Murray roared at him to walk like a normal human being.

A slight lifting of the clouds. Near normality by ten o'clock, complete normality by eleven when a smart launch came alongside and an elegant young man delivered a letter inviting the captain and his officers to dinner at Government House; which, since an invitation from the Governor was pronounced *order*, Murray accepted.

Six in the evening and a grinning crew, who bore Murray no ill will at all, watched him leave the ship with Brooke, Potts, John and Scott, all immaculate in their best uniforms.

'And have a very good time, sir,' said Pike at the gangway. 'And if they gives you any of that nasty, wicked palm-wine, don't you drink it.'

The pleasant gardens of the Governor's house. The Governor himself, two commanders, eight lieutenants, dozens, hordes of midshipmen, and five faded officers from the West African Regiment. Drinks, chatter, laughter, grave-faced officers offering condolences to Murray for the loss of his men, envious mids surrounding John. Dinner served. John almost a guest of honour, sitting near the Governor who listened to his story with deep interest and said that he must, he positively must, meet Lyapo when he had the time.

Dinner over, the guests departing. Murray gathered his officers but the Governor laid a hand on his arm.

'If your ship could spare you for an hour, Captain, perhaps you would join Captain Denman and myself.'

Murray dismissed the Sentinels and was led into a pleasant sitting-room with fans whispering in the ceiling. Denman was waiting, his burly figure crammed in a wicker chair. Tea was brought in, cigars lighted, legs stretched.

'A nice boy, your Spencer,' Doherty said. 'And came through a remarkable experience.'

Murray agreed. 'But let us not forget Lyapo. It was largely because of him that the lad survived.'

'Certainly,' Doherty nodded. 'But he is the only white survivor from *Phantom*, is he not?'

'Yes,' Murray said.

Doherty blew on the end of his cigar. 'I'm afraid you're going to lose him.'

'Am I?'

'Yes. He will be needed as a witness against Kimber and his crew.'

'I am sorry,' Murray said.

'Yes.' Doherty glanced at Denman. 'Mr Denman has offered to provide a berth for him. If you are agreeable to the boy going, of course.'

The 'of course' was mere politeness, Doherty being the master of all he surveyed.

'I'll send him home on *Badger*,' Denman said. 'With Donnelly.'

A silence. A beetle six inches long zoomed through the window. A dog barked.

'I have a conscience about that man,' Murray said.

'Don't have,' Denman said. 'I read his dispatch. He did what he thought was right, you did what you thought was right. Let the court martial sort it out.'

He was right, of course, but still Murray sighed. 'I have been thinking,' he said. 'If I sent someone home with him, an officer who saw what was happening —'

'No.' Denman was blunt. 'You may send home any invalids, but nobody else.'

'I see.' Murray clasped his hands. 'There is something up, then.'

'There is.' Denman leaned forward, his blue eyes glittering in his swarthy face. 'You know that a hundred miles or so south-east of here there is the Gallinas river — the Rio Pongas, some call it. Yes? Then you also know that the whole river is infested with slavers and that Carnot, the Frenchman, and Pedro Blanco are kings of the castle. We've been blockading the river for forty years now and it is still a running sore.'

'I understand,' Murray said.

'Good.' Denman nodded. 'Well, we're going in. Every ship we can muster. We're going in and we're going to burn out the barracoons.'

Murray frowned. 'But our orders — we must not interfere with property —'

'Right.' Denman cut off Murray with a flat, emphatic gesture. 'That is so. But this time the slavers have overstepped the mark. They have made a mistake, Captain Murray. A very big mistake. They have delivered themselves into our hands.'

'I am mightily glad to hear it,' Murray said. 'And what is the mistake they have made?'

'Ah,' Doherty smiled. 'Allow me to tell you a story, Captain. Allow me to tell you a story about a washerwoman.'

Friday. Breakfast over, John was called into the Captain's cabin. His cry, 'Leaving, sir!' heard all over the ship.

'I'm sorry,' Murray said. 'But you are needed as a witness. Believe me, I shall miss you — the whole ship's company will miss you.'

'But —' John began.

'There are no buts in the Royal Navy,' Murray said, quietly. 'You are under orders and they are the end of all arguments. I must tell you, though, by going to England and being a witness against those devils from *Phantom* you are serving the Navy just as well as staying on board this ship. And you know, Mr Spencer, the naval life means change, a coming and going, leaving old friends and making new ones. It is a restless life, like the element on which we serve. We all have to learn how to handle change. *Now* is not too soon for you to start learning.'

'Yes, sir.' John stood as straight as it was possible for him to do. 'Sir. Will I be returning to this ship?'

'That I hope,' Murray cried. 'I will write to the Admiralty saying I most particularly want you back. Most particularly.'

'Thank you, sir.' John's voice trembled a little. 'Will I be sailing soon?'

Murray leaned back and smiled a grim little smile. 'I think that I can say we are all going to sail soon.'

'May I ask when, sir?'

'Yes.' Murray smiled again. 'Yes, and I shall tell you. Will you be good enough first to ask all the officers and Mr Keverne to join us? All the officers, mark you. The bosun is to keep the deck.'

The ship aquiver with expectation as Brooke left the deck, Potts tumbled from his hammock, Scott came down from the mainmast, and a solemn Keverne elbowed his way from the breadroom. Much digging in the ribs, jerking of thumbs, raised eyebrows, and the bosun straining his ears to catch the goings-on in the cabin under his feet. Disappointed though as Murray banged the sky-light shut.

'I am sorry for that,' Murray said to his officers. 'It makes us a trifle hot but I prefer to announce any orders myself. I think, however, before we begin, I shall offer you tea. Pike!'

Pike in — out — polite, strangled conversation as the men waited for his reappearance. Tea arriving, served, sipped, and Murray ready to begin.

'Gentlemen,' he said. 'I have two pieces of news for you. First, Mr Spencer is leaving us to go home as a witness against the Phantoms.'

A mutter of regret, sounding genuine, cut short by the Captain. 'Farewells later, if you please. The second point is this. We are going to sail with Captain Denman to the Gallinas river and give the slavers there a pounding. I am glad to say that we shall be going in and burning them and their property out.'

Amazement, glee, doubt, Murray raising his hand.

'I know, I know: what about our orders? Well, I am about to tell you a story the Governor told me last night. A story about a washerwoman.' Fire in Murray's eyes and a smile on his lips. 'There is a woman called Mrs Norman, a washerwoman. A Mr Lewis owed her money but a few weeks ago he cleared off to the Gallinas river to try and get a boat to the West Indies. Mrs Norman, who is poor in everything but courage, put her baby on her back and went after him. While she was up there she was seen by a man called Manna, who is the son of King Siaka, who is another rogue. Manna had seen Mrs Norman in Freetown and knew that she worked for a well-to-do woman called Mrs Grey. Manna says that Mrs Grey owes *him* money, and he wrote to her

192

saying that if she didn't pay him that he would sell Mrs Norman and her baby into the barracoons. Mrs Norman also wrote to Mrs Grey, and she took the letters to the Governor. The Governor has ordered Captain Denman to take all his force to the Gallinas and to teach the villains a lesson they won't forget.'

Murray slapped his knee. 'It is a God-given opportunity. God given. Yes, Mr Potts?'

'Excuse me, sir.' Potts's voice was puzzled. 'I thought that our orders. . . ?'

'Yes.' Murray nodded. 'Our orders. I wonder if Mr Brooke can explain.'

'I can guess, sir,' Brooke said. 'This Mrs Norman. Is she a British subject?'

'She is!' Murray was triumphant. 'She is. She is as black as your hat, Mr Potts, but she is British — and no British subject is going to be held in slavery. We sail on tomorrow's morning tide. And, Mr Spencer, you sail on *Badger* on the same tide.'

Saturday. The tide turning, a land breeze filling the sails of decrepit *Badger* with its crew of invalids; Donnelly silent on the quarterdeck and John standing silent next to him. Behind *Badger*, forming into a steady line, *Messenger*, *Waterwitch*, *Firefly*, and, bringing up the rear, *Sentinel*.

Memories flooding John's mind; unexpected severities, and unexpected kindnesses, vivid images of battle and death, of the long row and the weeks on the beach, and of Lyapo, John's last memory of Freetown his farewell to his saviour Lyapo, who had stood at the gate of the King's Yard shaking his head sadly. 'I am staying here,' he had said. 'My people, John. Mine. My people and my country.' The big man putting his hand on John's shoulder and saying, 'Don't cry, John. You should be happy. We are alive. We should be dead but we are alive. And you are going home.'

Sadness and unmanly tears, but all the salt tears in the weary world were not able to wash away orders, or the movement of history; which Lyapo knew, and John was learning to know.

A little rain falling. Heavy cloud hiding Lion Mountain, grey waves fretting on the middle ground. *Badger* heading a little north of west, groaning and creaking like the old tub she was as the rollers from the ocean struck her battered sides. *Messenger*, *Waterwitch*, *Firefly*, and *Sentinel* coming out of Kroo Bay. A familiar flat thud and a puff of smoke from *Messenger* and the little squadron swung away south, all wheeling with the precision of sentries.

And that *is* what they are like, John thought. They are like sentries, guardians. All the ships and all the men on them; the good, the bad, the indifferent, the heroes and the villains, there for whatever motives; greed, glory, three meals a day and a damp hammock, yet all fulfilling their role under the red ensign their lords and masters in England have sent to fly along the hot and fever-stricken coasts of Africa.

Yes, he thought as he turned away to his duties. They are all sentinels.

Epilogue

A bitter wind blowing off the Solent. Portsmouth shivering in February. A little snow dusting the ships in the harbour and powdering the blue and green train which puffed into the new station. Falling, too, on John Spencer's broad shoulders as he left the train and made his way down the Royal Naval Dockyard.

Half-way along Queen Street, by a frozen preacher who was proclaiming that if God had wanted men to travel by steam he would have given them boilers, he heard a rush of feet behind him. He turned sharply, swung up his fists, and almost planted a right hook into the face of Dawlish.

'Which I give in, sir!' Dawlish beamed. 'It is Mr Spencer, ain't it.?'

'It is so,' John cried, grasping Dawlish's hand.

'I thought it must be.' Dawlish stepped back a pace. 'My Lord, though, I wasn't too sure. You must be a foot taller than the last time I saw you.'

'Still not as big as you.' John eyed Dawlish's civilian dress. 'You're out of the Navy?'

'I am that.' Dawlish slapped his thigh. 'I've got a pub! Yes, sir, the Liberty Arms!'

'Well, and I'm glad to hear it,' John said. 'I've been in Canadian waters for the past three years so I'm out of touch with my old shipmates.'

'Aye?' Dawlish shuffled a little and looked at John a trifle shyly. 'I wonder if you might step in for minute or two? It's just down the lane here. The missus would be glad to meet you, and there's someone else there.'

'A child?'

Dawlish laughed. 'No, no. Mind, I've got plenty of them. But if you would step along I'd be mighty pleased.'

'But certainly.' John fell in step with Dawlish who ambled down an alleyway, turned left, turned right, and came to a halt by a long whitewashed cottage with a vast sign hanging from it.

Dawlish pointed a large thumb at the sign. On it was a jolly sailor with a bottle in his hand, and a negro breaking his chains.

'Liberty, Mr Spencer. I thought that it was only right and proper to put the black on, seeing as how they helped us to pay for the place.'

He led John into a taproom. "Tain't big. More like your brig than a ship of the line, but it's snug and dry so it's better than the old *Sentinel*. Speaking of which, you'll remember this old shipmate, I'm sure.' With an airy flourish he opened the door of a small parlour.

'Well, I'm damned,' John said. 'It's old Smith!'

Smith it was, sitting by the fire, a cat on his lap, and drinking porter. Rising and holding out his hand, saying that he couldn't say as how he was glad to *see* John, and meaning it since the milky orbs of his eyes could see light and shade but little else.

'Which it was that God-rotting disease on *Nuestra Señora* which gnawed at his eyeballs,' Dawlish said. 'Mr Fearnley got his looking back, but Jack here . . . well.'

Brandy and water brought in, and various little Dawlishes ushered by their mother, anxious for them to meet the officer who had been a castaway among the savage cannibals. The fire made up, legs stretched out, Smith explained.

'I could have gone into the naval hospital at Greenwich, right enough. Captain Murray made sure I got my rightful place. But old Zeb, he said, let's put our prize money together and start this pub, and being as how we were old shipmates we dropped anchor together. And very snug we is.'

'And doing well,' Dawlish said. 'Plenty of old Sentinels dropping in. Rafferty was here only a matter of weeks ago. Full bosun he is now, in the *Phoenix*, somewhere in the Med. Pike comes in, too. He helps behind the bar when we're busy. Old Taplow is dead, left thousands of pounds he did. And Mr Purvis has slipped his anchor, too. Just a year ago.'

'Don't forget Mr Potts,' Smith cried. 'He was in last year. Stayed here he did. He made lieutenant. Just off to China, he was, Second in the *Larkspur*. But what about you? Did you get made lieutenant yet?'

'No,' John grinned. 'But I ain't been at sea six years, so I can't get my step. But I go up for it next year, and Mr Brooke has promised me a berth.'

'Ah!' Dawlish kicked the fire. 'We saw how he got his step. In the *Naval Gazette* it was. Captain Brooke now, and very nice for him, too.'

'That it is,' Smith cried from his corner. 'But that's politics, that is. Being as how the Tories are in power now they sticks their own men in, don't they? Politics. I'm telling you.'

Dawlish grinned easily at John. 'Jack's got interested in the political line. The missus reads him the paper so he knows what's going on. Speaking of which, guess who we had here in Pompey?'

'Well,' John said. 'I could guess till Doomsday about that. Must be half the world comes through here.'

'You're right there,' Dawlish said. 'Well it was Mr Donnelly — that young lieutenant what rammed the slaver off Whydah.' He leaned forward and poured huge quantities of brandy in John's glass. 'He was here as large as life, speaking at a public meeting! He was court-martialled, as I dare say you know, and dismissed the service. But he turned into a regular hero! All the papers was full of him and now he goes about speaking for the Anti-Slavery League. We went to hear him. Ain't that a turn-up for the book?'

'My word it is,' John said. 'Still, I'm glad to hear he got something out of it all.'

'Me too,' Dawlish said. 'He deserved better than he got off the Admiralty. Not that I'm saying Captain Murray was wrong when he burned them ships. He was a seamanlike officer, right enough, and knew his duty when he saw it.'

'But he ain't got no ship, neither,' Smith yelped. 'On the beach he is, too. Being as how he's a Whig, see. Politics, it is. And he ain't likely to get no ship neither, is he?'

'No.' John sipped his brandy. The wheel had turned full circle. Murray was on the shore and likely to stay there. The nominal reason was that he failed in judgement by sending *Phantom* as a prize with a mere mid in command. It was an excuse, nothing more, but enough to deny Murray command.

More brandy, less water, the fire made up. Mrs Dawlish calling her husband into the bar. A muffled oath, a scuffle, a bang, reappearance of an unruffled Dawlish.

'A drunken sailor,' he said. 'Not that he meant any harm. But about Captain Murray. Do you ever run into him, Mr Spencer?'

John looked over his glass at Dawlish. 'As a matter of fact I saw him yesterday. In London. You know what I'm talking about.'

'Damn me!' Dawlish slammed his glass down. 'It was that —'

'Yes. The Court of Appeal met.'

'Just a minute, sir.' Dawlish jumped to the door and called his wife in. 'Just listen,' he told her. 'Mr Spencer's got something to say.'

'Well.' John stared at the fire. 'You remember I left *Sentinel* at Freetown?'

'That's right,' Dawlish said. 'You had to come for to be witness against Kimber and his gang.'

'Yes, and they were found guilty of murder and sentenced to death.'

'To be hanged at Execution Dock,' Mrs Dawlish said, 'and serve the murdering heathen right.'

'And to be left hanging in irons for three tides as a warning to others,' Smith whispered. 'Which is right and proper.'

'Ah!' Dawlish took a mighty swig of brandy. 'But they appealed. They appealed to the House of Lords.'

'That's right,' John said. 'And that's why I'm in England. I was brought back for the appeal. The Lords gave their judgement this morning.'

'Good,' Dawlish said. 'And when are they going to swing? I asks because I'll go up to London to watch the bloody murderers get what's coming to them.'

'They're not,' John said. 'They've been let off.'

Mrs Dawlish sat down with a bump. Smith lifted his blind head. Dawlish thrust his chin forward like the bows of a three-decker.

'I don't believe you,' he said, flatly.

'But it's true,' John said.

True it was. That morning the judge in his scarlet and ermine had leaned across the bench and in a cracked, old voice had read out the judgement of the Law Lords; that *Phantom* had not been condemned by the Court of Mixed Commission in Freetown and was, therefore, the lawful property of its Owners and, that being the case, Kimber's action in retaking it, and in using force so to do, was no more than they had a right to do, and therefore no charge against could stand and, therefore, they could not be guilty of murder and were to be freed forthwith.

Astonishment, rage, bitter, furious resentment. The seamen in the bar adding their curses. The news spreading into the street, all Portsmouth damning the Law Lords to hell and back, and back again, but that not altering the facts of the matter.

Dusk. John had to report to his new ship. Farewells, promises to meet again, whenever that might be. Dawlish walked John down to the harbour and found him a wherry for half-price, standing at the top of a weed-grown flight of steps. The lights of a score of ships glinted on the dark waters.

'Just one last thing,' Dawlish said. 'The children will want to know. That big black you was cast away with — what happened to him?'

'Lyapo?' John smiled. 'I saw him four years ago in Freetown.

He's married. Had two children then. He runs a shop and he's a preacher at the Methodist chapel. He's called Mr Spencer, now.'

'Is he now?' Dawlish wagged his head. 'I always did say he'd got brains. Well, some good came out of it all in the end, then.'

A last shake of hands. John slithered down the steps and into the wherry. From the darkness came a last cry.

'Good luck, sir. And there's always a berth for you at the Liberty Arms.'

The tide was on the turn and the wherry slipped easily down the solemn line of ships. John lit a cigar and leaned back on the thwart. Five years since he had first sailed these waters and climbed aboard *Sentinel*. Since then, as Murray had promised him, the Navy had shown him the wonders of the world and the marvels of the deep. And since then *Sentinel* herself had gone, shipwrecked off Java Head, and the Sentinels themselves had gone; some promoted, some downgraded, some dead, some snug in their own homes, and the rest . . . scattered across the face of the earth, moving restlessly on that restless element on which they earned their daily bread. Most of them knowing little, and most of that little wrong, but knowing their duty; stubborn, unyielding, and taking with them the seeds of a change that would shake and convulse the earth more than the mightiest king or emperor had ever done.

'And after all,' John thought as the wherry came alongside the mighty *Defiance*—sixty-four guns and three hundred men—and a gruff sentry hailed them from the dark, 'some good did come from it in the end.'

He threw his cigar into the water and climbed aboard.

NO HERO FOR THE KAISER

Rudolf Frank   ISBN 0 86267 200 7

The world closed in on Jan Kubitzky on September 1914 — his fourteenth birthday. Russian soldiers, armed with guns and cannon were in the fields and similarly armed German soldiers were in the wood. Between them lay the small Polish hamlet of Kopchovka, which had been Jan's home until the day when everything in it was destroyed. When the firing stopped, only he and Flox, Vladimir the shepherd's dog, were left alive.

'*NO HERO FOR THE KAISER* is a work so remarkable that you have to wonder why it has taken so long to reach us here. The German-born author served in the 1914 war, and wrote the book from that experience. It was banned and publicly burned by Hitler in 1933. Its acclaim, we learn continues . . . Graphic, memorable . . . it's clear to see why this book was put to the flames.'

Naomi Lewis *The Observer* 1986